SILENT SUSPECT

JESSICA DANIEL BOOK 13

KERRY WILKINSON

ALSO BY KERRY WILKINSON

ONE

NOW

Bosh-bosh-bosh-bosh.

Detective Inspector Jessica Daniel rolled over with a groan, top lip lapping at the crusted drool that coated her chin. Her mind strained and flailed in an attempt to figure out exactly what was going on. She had one clear, concise and entirely accurate thought: some bastard was being noisy. *Really* noisy. And they were nearby, his or her thumping hand disturbing the peaceful utopia of whatever it was she had been dreaming about. Actually, it was definitely a 'him' – only blokes biffed and banged around that loudly.

There was a pause, allowing Jessica to open her eyes and slowly survey her surroundings.

Grotty, she thought, the word swirling into her mind from the final embers of sleep. Greying light flooded through the gaping raggedy curtains, as a gust of wind shook the single-pane windows, the frames of which were cracked and peeling with years-old scabs of paint that had once been magnolia. Jessica wondered why the drapes were open – they must have been left like that all night.

Then she remembered precisely why she was in this hotel room.

She clung to the threadbare pillow, even though its cushioning properties were somewhere in the region of a deflated balloon.

Bosh-bosh-bosh-bosh.

The pounding rattled once more, louder this time. As Jessica shuffled in a failed attempt to get comfortable on the squished mattress, the additional throbbing in her head left her wondering how much of it was real and how much was alcohol-induced.

'Ms Daniel?' A man's voice sounded from beyond the door. 'If you're in there, can you open the door, please?'

It took Jessica a few moments to realise that she was the 'Ms Daniel' to which the mystery voice was referring. She kicked her legs free of the bedcovers, surprised to find herself wearing the same pair of jeans and top from the previous day. Then she tried to sit up.

The room spun.

The spattered black and brown mould spots from the ceiling darted at her, blending with the faded, flowery grimness of the carpet. Jessica clamped her eyes closed, swallowing, trying to get some sort of lubrication to the back of her parched throat.

'Ms Daniel?'

'Um... yeah... hang on.' Jessica's mouth was dry, the words cracking and sticking as she tried to speak. When she opened her eyes again, they spiralled in on the battered alarm clock on the nightstand next to the bed, green digits telling her it was a few minutes after nine as the colon in between the numbers blinked hypnotically. She grabbed the glass of water that sat next to it, downing the contents in one, allowing her to finally feel as if she was something close to human.

She stood and approached the door, pausing mid-stride with her hand outstretched. 'Who is it?' she called.

'It's the police.'

That was strange. Jessica squinted towards the door, wrestling with a creeping sense that the universe had somehow become muddled. *She* was police. Shouldn't she be on the other side, knocking and trying to wake someone up?

Jessica straightened her clothes as best she could, turning sideways to face the full-length mirror that was covered in a thin film of... something translucent. She didn't step any closer to find out what it was. Jessica untied her hair and then scrunched it back together, clumping it into a greasy ponytail. For now, it was the best she could manage.

A blink and then the groaning creak of the door to reveal a man in the hallway. His dark hair was waxed to a point at the front, with a chin speckled by day-old stubble. He was early forties, hands in his Marks and Spencer trouser pockets, elbows jutting in front of the long brown raincoat that hung to his ankles. His red and white tie was loosely knotted and slightly askew, top button undone, jacket collar turned up.

He offered a watered-down, non-committal CID smile. It was the type of facial expression at which Jessica was an expert: not too friendly, not too stand-offish. It said everything, yet it said nothing.

'Ms Daniel?' he said.

'Hi.'

'DCI Ashley Fordham,' he thrust his warrant card towards her, adding: 'I understand you're an inspector...?'

'Yeah...'

Jessica glanced at his ID, not taking it in before he tucked it away again. They shook hands and then Fordham bobbed awkwardly in the hallway, peering over her shoulder into the room.

'Oh, er, come in,' Jessica added, stepping out of his way.

He ambled inside, hands back in pockets as he peered around. 'Greater Manchester?' he said.

Jessica closed the door, fighting gallantly against a yawn, the cloud of confusion still winning a battle with her sensible thoughts. 'Isn't this Blackpool?'

'I mean you work for Greater Manchester Police...?'

'Oh, right, yeah. Metropolitan division, in the centre.'

'That must be fun.'

'You could say that.'

Fordham's gaze swept across the scattering of mini vodka and whisky bottles close to the bin next to the bed before he focused back on Jessica. She leaned against the wall, still grappling with the urge to yawn, embarrassed at the leftover remnants of the previous night.

For a moment, he said nothing, allowing the gentle hum of traffic to filter through the window. There was a distant beep of a car horn, but it was quiet compared to Manchester. Still, it was early. It had been a different story the previous evening.

'Do you know the name Peter Salisbury?' Fordham finally asked.

Jessica nodded.

'And did you spend time with Mr Salisbury last night?'

Her eyes gawked past him towards the ruffled bedcovers, reading his thoughts. 'Well... yes, but not like that. Not how you're thinking.'

His smile crept slightly wider, head angling fractionally towards the bed. 'What was I thinking?'

'Just that...' Jessica huffed in annoyance. She should have simply said 'yes'. 'I saw him yesterday. It was the first time we'd met.'

'You didn't know him before?'

'No.'

'He's not an old friend, or anything like that?'

'No.'

Fordham nodded knowingly, as if that was something of which he was already aware. 'So... how did you come to meet one another?'

Jessica could no longer hold his stare. This was all wrong. *She* was police. *She* asked the questions. *She* made others squirm.

'It's complicated,' she coughed, trying to keep her voice level. 'I was... looking for a friend.' She could feel Fordham eyeing her, wanting her to meet his gaze. She knew that game. 'What's going on?' she added.

He ignored her question: 'You were looking *for* Peter?'

'No, I told you, I only met him yesterday. I sort of... stumbled across him.' Jessica realised her arms were crossed, protecting her midriff from who knew what. It was bad body language – defensive, as if she had something to hide. She dropped them to her sides and then stared at a spot on the carpet next to Fordham's feet. 'It's hard to explain,' she added. 'Look, you're going to think it's a bit odd. I would if I were you.'

'Okay...'

'I've been looking for a missing person... a missing friend.' Jessica nodded towards the rattling windows. 'She called me from the phone box across the road.'

Fordham turned to face the outside, removing a hand from his pocket to scratch his chin and then replacing it. 'There's a phone box over there?'

Jessica shrugged. 'It's this sort of kiosk thing. On the seafront.'

'I didn't know anyone still used them nowadays.'

'Me either.'

He spun back. 'So how did you come to meet Peter?'

Jessica sighed, quickly scanning the hotel room as she knew Fordham already had. Crumpled bedcovers; inhabitant still asleep at nine in the morning; empty alcohol bottles. That was before he got to her breath, which likely smelt like a sailor's on leave – it certainly tasted like it.

It all felt wrong.

That wasn't because hotels weren't a haven for residents with hangovers at this time of the morning; it was because of *her*. She was a detective inspector in a grungy, cheaper-than-chips, hellhole of a room, still wearing the same clothes as the night before. *She* was what was wrong in this scenario.

'I can tell you what you want to know,' Jessica said, 'but I know how it's going to sound. If I were you, looking at me, I'd be thinking it was a bit weird, too. Perhaps if you could tell me what the problem is...?'

She met his stare, seeing the imperceptible signs that something bad had happened. Deep down, she'd known the moment the banging had woken her up. Things had felt strange the night before when she'd met Peter. It had been too convenient.

Fordham was chewing on his bottom lip, nodding slightly. 'Have you been here all night?'

Jessica nodded at the pile of empty bottles. 'I had a one-woman party.'

'Is there anyone who can vouch for that?'

She shrugged. 'Only one woman.'

He was still nodding but puffed out a large breath. 'Peter Salisbury was found on the beach a few hours ago with his throat slit. As far as anyone can tell, you're the last person to see him alive.'

TWO

Jessica cupped her hands around the lower part of her face and blew hard. She'd never been to the Arctic or Antarctic, but it was hard to believe either would be colder than Blackpool seafront. She'd long thought Manchester had the worst weather in Britain, but it had nothing on this place. Even though she was sitting inside her car and wearing gloves, the glacial blast still howled, making her teeth chatter, her fingers tremble.

It was a few minutes after four in the afternoon and already close to dark. Those government bastards were always arseing around with the clocks, sending them forward or back whenever they saw fit. Assuming it was the government. If not them, then who? MI5? MI6? The BBC? Some member of the Royal family? Someone, somewhere was having a laugh. It would have been grim in any case, but with the clocks recently having gone back – or forward – it was far darker than seemed normal. Winter was well and truly on its way.

Jessica stared across the empty road towards the small booth attached to the railing of the sea wall. She wasn't sure what she'd expected – not flashing lights and a big 'LOOK HERE' banner – but it felt too small, too insignificant.

She reached into the well on the side of the door for a bobble hat, zipped up her coat and then climbed out of the car. She'd barely closed the door when the chill bit at her face, clawing and scraping as she tried to bury her mouth under the collar of the coat. Jessica tugged the hat down further, looked both ways and then crossed the still deserted road, stopping in front of the phone kiosk. The receiver was black plastic but surprisingly heavy, attached via a metal cord to an aluminium facia, into which someone had carved the word 'BENDER'.

Jessica held the phone to her ear, listening to the low, unbroken dial tone, before replacing it on the cradle. It was a wonder to find a working public telephone in the twenty-first century. Many of them had been removed as the gadget plague of mobile phones had spread across the nation; those that remained – at least most of the ones she knew of – had been smashed up by kids, drunks or druggies. Whoever it was things got blamed on nowadays.

She stepped away, forgetting the cold as she stared at the telephone. Two days previously, this phone had been used to call her a few minutes before midnight. The young woman had said only one word – 'Jessica' – and that was that. There had been silence and then nothing. The voice was her friend, Bex – Rebecca – and Jessica had spent the ensuing hours trying to read as much as she could into the three syllables. Had Bex sounded scared? Worried? Was it an assuring tone to say she was fine? A pleading tone to be picked up? In truth, Jessica couldn't remember. Bex had spoken for less than a second and then it had been over.

Then there was the other voice in her head, the one that asserted it hadn't been Bex at all. The one that whispered and conspired, insisting that Jessica had twisted the tone to make it that of her missing friend. There was no recording, no number to call back and check.

Bex had been a troubled teenager living on the streets on Manchester when Jessica had offered her a room to stay. They'd shared a house for the best part of a year in a relationship that was hard to define, but which worked for them. It wasn't mother–daughter, nor sister–sister, but it wasn't exactly friends, either. It was simply them, living together and being there for one another. Bex had plans to go to college, to make something of herself. She had friends, a life, she'd just had her birthday... and then she disappeared. Since then, Jessica had heard nothing from the girl – until the phone call.

It had taken her two days to find out the origin of the call. During that time, she'd had to travel to Wales for something heartbreakingly important, and then she'd jumped through hoops and greased palms in order to find out where the call had come from.

Here.

Fifty miles up Britain's motorway network from her Manchester home, on the west coast of the country. This was the spot from which Bex had called and whispered Jessica's name.

Jessica knew that coming here wouldn't lead to anything spectacular. The word 'Unknown' had shown up on Jessica's phone, so Bex had gone out of her way to pre-dial 141, hoping to mask her location. With that, the teenager was hardly going to be waiting on the nearby bench, legs crossed in anticipation of being picked up. Yet everything was so... *normal*... that it felt crushingly underwhelming. Bex might have been here, but she certainly wasn't now.

After picking up the receiver a second time and listening to the steady tone, Jessica replaced it again and stood staring beyond the sea wall.

The dark waves of the Irish Sea lapped in the distance,

washing silt, seaweed, used condoms and the odd shopping trolley onto shore. She remembered coming here as a kid with her parents, being told by her dad that – on a clear day – she'd be able to see Ireland. It sounded fishy and distinctly made up at the time – and she sure as hell couldn't see it now. It was so cloudy, she could barely see the moon.

Despite the fading light, a couple were on the beach below, apparently oblivious to the onset of night and the freezing temperature. A twenty-something man was striding in white trainers, tracksuit bottoms and an England football polo shirt, dragging his protesting other half behind him. She was swigging from a can of foreign lager, calling him a string of garbled, barely literate obscenities. He continued stomping across the sodden dark sand until she yanked her hand away and started to stumble in the direction from which they'd come. The man yelled at her, finger jabbing wildly at her retreating back, until he gave up and disappeared after her, still pointing and gesticulating.

Young love. It wasn't quite the picture painted by the holiday brochures.

Jessica turned away from the beach, peering along the street towards the centre of the town. One long road stretched from Lytham St Annes at the south of the resort, hugging the coastline for fifteen miles until it hit Fleetwood to the north. Jessica was on Blackpool's southern promenade, close to the Pleasure Beach and within walking distance of the attractions. In the distance, Blackpool Tower was lit up, a golden beacon beaming into the dimming sky. Underneath, the long road was lined with rows of blinking neon lights, the illuminations carving themselves into the approaching night. They were another thing Jessica remembered from her childhood visit: tens of thousands of winking, shimmering bulbs lining the entire seafront from the end of summer until the first or second week of November. She'd been told that visitors would come from miles around to see Blackpool Illuminations. Thirty or so years ago, they probably did. Now, people were a YouTube clip away from seeing it for free.

The first row of illuminations was a few hundred metres away, a dancing set of cowboys that ran up a set of lamp-posts on either side of the road and then jinked across a tightrope of wires high above. On the cowboys' hats were the unmistakable golden arches advertising McDonald's, with glimmering arrows close to the road pointing drivers in the right direction.

It was all a bit... tacky.

Were there competing Burger King cowboy illuminations on the north shore? A boogieing cavalcade of lights in the shape of a sandwich somewhere close to the tower underneath a Subway logo?

Jessica doubted she'd missed much by not returning since she was a child.

She turned in a circle, taking in the dilapidated hotels across the road, before spotting the CCTV camera high on a pole close to the phone kiosk. She stared up at the monitoring device as it peered down at her and wondered if someone was watching. If the cameras in Manchester were anything to go by, the answer was no. Hundreds were plonked around the city in a display of Orwellian power but very few actually worked. Of the ones that did, the picture quality generally left it hard to tell if the subject being filmed was human, let alone male or female.

Across the road, the lights in the café built into one of the hotels flickered off. Aside from a silhouette shuffling out of the door and locking it behind him, there was no one anywhere near her. Jessica couldn't even hear the beach couple arguing their way into the distance any longer.

What should she do?

Jessica had never seriously expected to find Bex next to the phone booth, but she'd expected... something. A clue to her whereabouts, a note, an explanation. In so many ways, that was the one thing Jessica had craved since the moment she'd arrived home three months previously to find Bex gone. She desperately wanted an answer to the question of 'why?'. If Bex had left because of something Jessica had done or said, then perhaps she could begin to move on. It was the not knowing that was eating at her.

She was about to return to her car when Jessica noticed the poster glued to the side of the metal shelter that surrounded the phone. It was an A4 sheet of paper covered with splurges of grainy black and grey ink, as if someone had used a cheap photocopier with a dodgy toner cartridge. The top corners had started to rub away with the dew or frost from the previous night, leaving a gloopy residue on the metal.

MISSING

The capitalised word spewed from the poster, atop a speckled monochrome photograph of a young woman. When it came to pictures of missing people, so many of the images showed individuals striking similar expressions: passive, almost dispassionate smiles as they stared somewhere close to whomever was snapping the photo. Jessica's mouth started to open – it was an image of Bex.

… Except that it wasn't. She was seeing what she wanted to.

The girl was in her late-teens or early twenties, with long dark hair and large hooped earrings. The rest of her features were difficult to make out through the fog of the poor print quality. Underneath her picture were the words: 'THIS IS KATY. CALL IF SEEN', followed by a phone number.

Jessica stared at Katy's image for a few moments, taking her in. People went missing all over the country: young, old, male, female, single, married. Many were found, some weren't, but each left behind a story of confusion over where they had gone and why.

Even though she had her mobile, Jessica delved into her pockets and emerged with a pound coin. It felt apt, somehow. She pushed it into the payphone socket and dialled the number from the poster. There was a clicking, silence, and then it started to ring.

Jessica held her breath. One ring. Two.

A man's voice: 'Hello.'

'Oh, um... hi. My name's Jessica and I saw a poster with a missing girl.'

'Have you seen her?'

He sounded excited as Jessica realised she was offering false hope. 'Sorry, that's not why I'm calling. It's a bit, er, complicated...'

'Complicated how?'

'Can I ask who Katy is?'

There was a pregnant pause, the awkwardness booming through the silence. Eventually, the voice stammered a reply: 'She's my sister. She's been missing for three months. Are you saying you've seen her?'

'I wish I had,' Jessica replied. 'It's just that I've lost some-one, too. They look similar and my friend has been gone for three months. I saw your poster and... I'm not really sure what came over me. I shouldn't have called.'

There was another pause, longer than the previous one. Jessica could picture the man on the other end of the phone, shrugging his shoulders, wondering why some nutjob had bothered to call. Perhaps he got this all the time: lunatics calling the number on the poster and then gabbling on about something or other.

'Sorry,' Jessica added.

'No, it's okay. Where are you? I put up posters all over.'

'I'm in Blackpool on the South Shore, calling from a phone box overlooking the ocean.'

'Near the Pleasure Beach?'

'Sort of.' Jessica spun around, looking for a closer point of reference. 'There's a hotel opposite – the Prince, plus a row of others and a café.'

'Do you want to talk?'

It was Jessica's turn to sigh and pause. She'd driven up the motorway hoping for... something. She could go door to door on the hotels opposite with a photo of Bex, asking if anyone had seen her, but that was a long shot to say the least. There was the CCTV camera next to the phone, but she'd have to find out who operated it and then get onto them about whether they stored footage. That would take time, however. Beyond that, she wasn't sure what to do. There was her empty home awaiting her back in Manchester, or...

'Where are you?' she asked.

'I can be with you in twenty minutes or so if you stay put.'

Jessica gazed through the blur of the early evening towards the dancing cowboys and then peered back to her car. 'Okay,' she replied. 'I'll be here.' She was about to return the phone to its cradle when a thought fell into her mind. 'Oh, sorry, I should have asked. What's your name?'

For a moment, she thought he'd gone, but the man's voice was cool and clear. 'I'm Peter,' he said. 'I'll see you soon.'

THREE

Jessica and Peter passed underneath the wibbling lit-up cowboys on their way towards the town centre. The long line of illuminations continued as far as she could see, stretching over the road in a variety of different shapes. After the cowboys, there was a rainbow of crabs batting their claws towards the passing drivers. Beyond that were fluorescent amphibians playing frogger across the top of the street. Like Vegas but a bit rubbish. A bit *British*.

At first they walked in silence, but as the hum of traffic and visitors increased, they started to talk. Peter was a few years younger than Jessica, stubbly with short dark hair, but otherwise sporting nothing too identifiable, especially as he too was bundled up under a large jacket. He sounded local, northern at the very least. To the untrained eye, they were a couple having an evening stroll along the prom.

Jessica glanced sideways towards him and then back the way she was heading. 'You said Katy was your sister...?'

'Right – she's only nineteen.'

'What happened to her?'

Peter waved an arm ahead, in the vague direction of the

centre. 'We live a mile or two away on the other side of town. She left the house one morning saying she was going out with her friends and that was the last I saw of her. The police said they'd been trying to find her but... y'know, this place is notorious for people going missing. Couples get pissed up and argue with each other; groups of lads end up getting lost when they're on the lash. There's something in the paper every week. Most of them turn up somewhere or another, so you can't really blame the police.'

At least he wasn't one of *those* people who blamed the police for everything that had ever gone wrong. Jessica wasn't sure if she should let on that she was an inspector. Some people reacted badly, clamming up and forgetting a police officer was still a normal person. Well, comparatively. Jessica knew a few officers whom she'd struggle to class as 'normal'.

'Have they told you anything officially?' she asked.

They continued for a few paces before he replied: 'Not really, only that there's no sign of her. They went around her friends and checked through her stuff at our house. There's no sign of anything weird. No note, no dodgy emails or texts. Nobody has a clue. One morning, she was there; the next, she was gone.'

He spoke matter-of-factly, relating a series of events as opposed to cracking with emotion. Jessica wondered if that's how she sounded when talking about Bex. Sometimes the only way to push away the grief was to pretend it wasn't there.

'What about you?' Peter asked, his pace slowing ever so slightly.

Jessica took a gulp of the crisp air. Now she was out of the car and walking around, it didn't feel so cold. 'Similar. She was my housemate... my friend. One morning she was there, the next she'd gone.'

'What was her name?'

'Rebecca. Everyone called her Bex.'

Jessica slowed to a stop and delved into the pockets of the coat, taking out her phone and flipping through the images until she found one of the teenager. She held up the device for Peter to see. In the first picture, Bex was smiling and giving a thumbs-up and a weary smile for the camera. Her skin was pale, appearing even more ethereal because of the blackness of her hair and swish of thick eyeliner. A small silver ring piercing her nose glinted in the light. In the next photo, Bex was in a sleeveless top and sunglasses, enjoying the sunshine in Jessica's back yard. It was the day of her eighteenth birthday and she'd had friends over for a celebration. After the upbringing she'd had, it had been her first-ever birthday party. There had been that usual blend of bad – well, modern – music, finger food, laughs and fun. Undeniable fun – something that Jessica had rarely had in recent times. In the image, Bex's skin had a slight tan, the spider's web tattoo on her inner arm angled towards the picture-taker, with a doffed bottled beer in her other hand.

Peter eyed the two photographs, nodding slowly as they set off walking again. 'She's pretty,' he said.

Jessica opened her mouth to reply, but the only thing that came out was a spiralling wisp of breath. Bex *was* pretty... yet it sounded weird coming from a stranger. Jessica shivered slightly, unsure if it was from the chill of the evening or the edge of creepiness that had laced Peter's remark. She wondered why he'd said it. Perhaps he was one of those social misfits who didn't realise that praising someone's appearance wasn't automatically a compliment. It was about context – and talking about a missing girl's looks as a first point of reference was unnerving.

They continued walking in silence for a little while, passing the Central Pier along with its assortment of dinging arcade machines. Jessica turned to see a woman in a mobility scooter rhythmically feeding two-pence pieces into one of the penny pushers. She delved into a large plastic cup without looking and hovered over the drop slot, pausing, waiting for the in-and-out mechanism to draw back before letting the coin go. Without waiting for it to land, she was already back in her cup, hunting for another coin: pausing, pushing, pausing, pushing.

Nearby, two young girls, only ten or eleven, were leaping around one of the dance machines in perfect unison, matching ponytails bouncing behind them, the moves imprinted onto their brains. Next to them, a teenage couple had plastic rifles pressed into their shoulders and were blasting away at a screen filled with zombies. Or vampires. Or possibly werewolves. Jessica wasn't entirely sure. Either way, they were doing a lot of shooting.

They were well and truly on The Golden Mile.

'What happened to her?'

It took Jessica a moment to realise that Peter was talking to her. His voice had almost been lost among the tinkling assortment of sound seeping from the arcade.

'Bex?'

'Right – your friend.'

'I pretty much told you. I went to work one morning, leaving her at home. When I got back in the evening, she was gone. She'd left all of her stuff, including her phone and shoes. The front door was unlocked and the stove was on. As far as I could tell, the only thing gone was her and the clothes she was wearing.'

'No note or anything?'

'Nothing.'

Jessica continued walking but could sense Peter peering sideways at her. He'd slowed, forcing her to move at his pace, and he kept edging closer to her, brushing his arm against hers and forcing her to move further towards the inside of the pavement to get away. Before long, she'd be against the rail separating the promenade from the beach.

'Did the police talk to all her friends?' he asked.

'I... *they* spoke to everyone.'

'With Katy, I think the police thought she'd gone to stay with one of her mates, that she'd had an argument with me or Dad and would turn up eventually.'

'Did she live with your dad?'

'We both do,' he gulped. 'Well, *did*. I still do.'

Peter took another half-sidestep, the thick padding of his jacket grazing against the material of Jessica's, while the back of his hand nudged her skin as if he was trying to persuade her to hold hands. Jessica didn't break stride and tried not to show her discomfort, instead taking a forcible step towards him until their shoulders collided. She had the momentum of movement, but Peter hadn't expected it and stumbled, taking a moment to regain his balance.

'Oops, sorry,' Jessica said.

Peter appeared to take the hint, moving slightly further away. She could still feel him watching her and he continued speaking as if nothing had happened. 'The police kept asking if she'd run away before. Was it like that with Rebecca?'

'Sort of.'

'Had she run away before?'

'It's complicated.' Jessica didn't want to say that Bex had been homeless precisely because she'd run away from her mother. Suddenly, the conversation felt wrong.

'Katy hadn't,' Peter added. 'This was a first. They kept asking about familiar places she might have gone to stay. Clubs she was a member of, whether she had a favourite pub, that sort of thing. Did they go through all of that with you about Rebecca?'

'They asked all of that.'

'But there was no sign of her anywhere...?'

Jessica stopped, turning to face Peter and then gazing past him and upwards, realising they were level with Blackpool

Tower. It soared high above on the other side of the road, a sparkling arrangement of golden bulbs winking on and off in time to a silent song. Considering the time of year and the temperature, there were a lot of people out. Hundreds of tourists and locals streamed back and forth along the prom on one side, with more bustling past the shops and attractions on the other.

She could feel Peter staring at her but Jessica kept her gaze on the tower, a little over his shoulder. There was something about him that gave her the creeps. She bit her lip and then nodded in the direction from which they'd come.

'I should be getting back,' she said.

'Oh, right...'

Jessica took a business card from her pocket – one of the blank ones that didn't identify her as a police officer – and handed it over. She knew she probably shouldn't, but then thoughts of Bex got the better of her. 'Just in case you ever stumble across Bex while you're looking for Katy,' she said.

Peter eyed the card and then pocketed it. He stood with his arms open slightly, as if inviting a hug. Jessica wasn't sure. She might have read him wrong and definitely wasn't feeling herself. So she put her head down, offered a 'see ya then', and set off back towards South Shore.

She kept walking until she felt sure Peter wouldn't still be watching and then crossed the road, finding a spot on a wall outside a pub and turning back to watch the Central Pier. On the area at the front, a woman had hitched her skirt up and mounted a low-rent bucking bronco machine. As the plastic-looking bull threw itself upwards, the woman grasped its horns, her neck jolting backwards in a whiplash claim waiting to happen. Her friends were nearby, whooping and cheering for the entire six seconds until she was thrown clear, landing with a padded thump on the matting.

Jessica hadn't been in the town for long but it was already

beginning to get to her. The noise... the lights. She lived in a quiet, generally secluded area of Manchester where the only thing she had to keep an eye on was the odd bout of curtain-twitching from the neighbours. There would be areas of Blackpool like that, too – but not here. She thought of Bex. The girl Jessica knew wouldn't have been happy here with the relentless chatter and over-the-top feast of twinkling bulbs. Would she really have come here to get away from Jessica?

After a few more minutes, Jessica stood and continued walking in the direction of her car. She wasn't sure what it was about Peter that had got under her skin – for the most part, his questions had been reasonable – so perhaps it was her that was the problem. His sister had disappeared and she was the one who'd called him. The fact he was a little awkward was neither here nor there. Loads of people were. When Jessica had first started seeing Adam, he could barely string a sentence together if he was talking to a female. By the end, he was Mr Confident.

Adam.

Another person no longer with her.

Before Jessica knew it, she was back at her car. She scrabbled into her inner pocket and took out the key, unlocking the door, ready to leave. She knew it was time but couldn't force herself to get into the vehicle, instead staring across the road towards the phone box. There were two missing girls – both a similar age, both gone for the same period of time, both with some sort of connection to that phone kiosk.

It really was quite the coincidence.

FOUR

Jessica continued to stare at the phone booth from across the street. A friend of Bex's natural mother had told her that he might have seen Bex in Blackpool. He was a drug dealer and hazy about his own whereabouts, so hardly a reliable witness – but that and the phone call left a double link to this place. Peter said that Blackpool was a hotbed for people disappearing, something Jessica loosely remembered from the vagaries of police training days. Lots of people who didn't want to be found ended up at the resort because of the apparent ease in getting cash-in-hand jobs and the ability to evaporate among the throng of tourists. Many seaside towns were like that and Blackpool was bigger than most.

With all the time in lieu she was owed from work, Jessica had planned to visit the area, have a poke around and then return home. Ideally that would have been *with* Bex, but that now seemed unlikely, if it had ever been anything else. Now, Jessica wondered if she should stay for a day and ask some questions. Go door to door a street or two over if necessary. It was better than sitting in her empty house by herself.

The five hotels across the road from the phone box each

displayed varying degrees of grunge. The one on the far end – Saint Andrew's – was boarded up, with big banners pinned over the old vacancies board, telling would-be tourists it was 'out of bounds' and a 'toxic health hazard', which sounded welcoming. Given that, Jessica immediately ruled out the Seaview Pleasance next door, figuring toxic health hazards could probably spread further than the single wall between them.

That left her with the Prince Hotel, the Sunshine Resort, or Excalibur. There was little between them outwardly, each showcasing a typically British sense of outdatedness. Each offered 'colour TV's' – including a dodgy apostrophe; and en-suites – or an 'on-suite' at the Excalibur. The colour TV advertisement was something Jessica had spotted on the outside of guest houses up and down the prom, a particularly bizarre boast in the twenty-first century given that black and white had gone out of fashion before Jessica was born. The trio of hotels had matching sepia awnings with strips of crusted, peeling paint; chipped window frames; faded welcome signs – and a general air that they belonged to another time.

Jessica peered back towards the centre of the resort. There had definitely been nicer B&Bs that way, but there was something about this spot, close to the phone booth. Bex *had* been here, so perhaps she'd been staying in one of these fleapit rooms?

In the end, it was the Prince Hotel's 'full English Breakfast' that swung it for Jessica. The Prince was also connected to the café she'd seen earlier, offering a glimmer of hope – nothing more – that the food would be edible. Gastroenteritis might be the all-new Hollywood diet but she didn't fancy trying it herself.

Jessica moved her car onto the car park at the front of hotel. The five hotels shared the stretch of crumbling tarmac, with room for hundreds of vehicles, though Jessica had fingers to spare when counting the number of parked cars. Admittedly, the train station wasn't far away, but she doubted the hotels were anything close to full.

The Prince's front door was stuck in its frame, but Jessica shouldered it open and stumbled into a musty reception area. The 'WE COME' mat was well-worn, but the strangest thing was the carpet on the lower half of the walls. It matched what was on the floor, creating an illusion whereby Jessica wasn't quite sure where she should be walking.

A sudden movement to her left made her take a half-step backwards. There was a young man behind a counter tugging out his earphones, wide-eyed with surprise that someone had entered.

'Welcome to the Prince,' he said, failing to hide the headphone cord as he tucked it into his top. He was nineteen or twenty, lean, with spiky hair, sporting a weariness that told her he was only doing this until he could get a better job.

Jessica returned the smile. 'Hi, Brandon. How much is it for a night?'

He was momentarily confused until he realised Jessica had read the name from the badge pinned to his lapel. 'It's forty-five – but I can knock a fiver off for cash. There's also a ten-pound deposit for the minibar, but you get that back when you leave.'

Sounded about right.

Jessica peered around the reception area. It wasn't great, but she'd stayed in worse places. Well, she probably had. She couldn't see any immediate sign of bugs or dirt. The brochure would read something like 'quaint', which would code for 'medieval'. She could try the other guesthouses adjoining the car park, but they might end up being worse than this. She slipped out her purse and found a pair of twenty-pound notes plus two fivers, holding them a little out of Brandon's reach.

'Does that include breakfast?' she asked.

He nodded towards the door behind her that she had assumed was a cupboard. 'You can get into the café through there. We share the dining room with Hotel Excalibur next door, plus it's open to the general public. Just give your room number to the person at the counter and they'll tick you off. They open at six.'

She passed him the money. 'I *definitely* won't be up at six.'

He grinned – perhaps winked, or maybe it was an innocent twitch. 'I didn't even know there was a six in the morning,' he replied.

'Not a morning person?'

He snorted as the till under the counter dinged open: 'You could say that.'

Brandon disappeared through a door behind the counter, returning moments later with a key attached to a large fob with '7' etched into the plastic. He took her details, tapping them into the computer on the counter, and then passed across the key.

'You're on floor two,' he said, nodding towards the stairs.

She held it up: 'Room seven?'

'What gave it away?'

'It's not often you get a real key nowadays, it's usually those stupid card things that never work, then you're up and down the lifts trying to get someone at reception to re-scan it.' Jessica weighed it in her hand. It was heavy. 'Good key,' she added. 'Very good key.'

The smile crept back onto his face. 'Thank you, I'll take that as a personal compliment.'

Jessica took a step towards the stairs and then stopped herself. Brandon sounded local and seemed friendly – or bored – enough to talk to her. She turned back to him. 'Does room seven face the ocean?' she asked as if it didn't bother her.

'Is it an ocean?'

Jessica puffed her lips together, thinking. 'I guess so. Isn't it all the same? The water just sort of flows into one big puddle? We do live on an island, after all.'

He nodded. 'Well, ocean, sea or puddle – you can definitely see it from your room.'

She waited for him to reach for his earphones but he didn't, instead continuing to offer a flirty half-smile. He was half her age... but somewhere close to Bex's.

Jessica moved back to the counter, nodding in the general direction of the town centre. 'What's there to do around here?'

He shrugged, pursing his lips, seeming very teenagery. 'Aww... y'know... pubs, clubs. Depends what you're into.'

There was a twinkle in his eye and she was pretty sure he was flirting with her, though there was every chance this was how he was with all women. Jessica thought about playing along but... half her age and all that. Besides, she really wasn't in the mood. She took out her phone and found the photograph of Bex offering the thumbs-up, flipping it around for Brandon to see. 'I'm looking for my friend. She was definitely in the area recently, perhaps only a couple of days ago.'

He squinted as he leaned in and then reached to take the phone. She allowed him, watching as he tilted the device to have a proper look. Some people, perhaps most, would only give a cursory glance before shaking their head, but he was really studying the image.

'What do you mean by "in the area"?' he asked, glancing at Jessica.

'Around Blackpool.'

He peered back to the screen. 'Like out and about in clubs, or specifically around South Shore?'

'I don't know.'

Brandon handed back the phone, pouting his bottom lip. 'There are always pale girls out and about, but I don't think I recognise her. Sorry.'

'Is there any chance she could have been staying around this area?'

'Not that I've seen. I'd have probably remembered her. I've been off for a few days and this is my first shift back. I can ask around if you want?'

Jessica shook her head, wanting to have a snoop around the area herself. If somebody *did* know something, there was no point in allowing them to be tipped off before she got to them.

'I'm new anyway,' Brandon added. 'I've only been working here two and a bit weeks in the afternoons and evenings.'

'Are you from around here?'

'More or less. I spent the summer working on the crazy golf course, but that's only seasonal.' He shrugged. 'Y'know what it's like – it's packed when the sun's out. Not so much at the moment.'

Jessica did her best to appear breezy, not wanting to sound too nosy. 'Who's going to be here in the morning?'

'Probably Luke – he owns this place, the café and the Excalibur. Maybe the other hotels, too. I'm not completely sure. Sometimes his wife's about, then there are cleaners and kitchen staff. They've all gone home by this time of day.' He stifled a yawn, as if it was first thing in the morning. 'Sorry...'

'You by yourself?'

Another shrug – and a definite wink this time: 'I keep busy.'

Jessica wasn't sure exactly what that meant, hoping he was referring to his music. She matched his smile and moved towards the stairs. She didn't have any luggage but couldn't be bothered going to the nearby Tesco Express she'd spotted for essentials. She'd get by this evening and then try to have a chat with the hotel owner in the morning. She had one foot on the bottom step when the cough came from behind her.

Brandon was watching her and, as she turned, he flicked his eyebrows up, letting her know she had his attention.

'Everything all right?' she asked.

'I was, er, wondering if you wanted a drink or something later?' He tugged on his collar.

'I think you're probably a bit young for me.'

'Oh, right... I mean, I don't mind if—'

'Thanks for the offer.'

'Right...'

Before either of them could become embarrassed any further, Jessica padded up the steps, rounding the banisters and continuing until she was on the second floor.

Room seven was more or less as she'd have guessed. There was a big-backed dinosaur of a television on a scratched dresser, no phone, tired-looking wallpaper and furnishings, plus a thin crust of dust on top of the plastic light switch. She turned the lights on and then off again before locking the door, leaving the key in the slot.

The large window at the front of the room overlooked the ocean/sea/puddle. She dragged across an armchair that was far heavier than it appeared and then sat in the dark, watching the phone booth. From her location, Jessica had a perfect view of the seafront – if she'd been here a couple of days before, she'd have seen Bex at the kiosk, making the call underneath the street light and CCTV camera.

It wasn't long before a cacophony of yawns ripped through Jessica, leaving her cheeks brushed with tears, her lids heavy. She closed her eyes, thinking about how comfortable the chair was, especially given the slightly stale smell...

Jessica jumped awake as her head slipped along the curve of the chair's headrest and flopped to the side. She narrowly caught herself before falling from the seat entirely, blinking, yawning, wondering what was going on. The street outside was deserted, the phone booth apparently untouched. The only difference was that the tide had finished coming in and was lapping at the bottom of the sea wall, out of sight from Jessica's viewpoint.

She yawned again, spinning to peer through the dark at the green digits on the alarm clock. It was a few minutes after ten o'clock and a chill was creeping around the edges of the window frame, making her shiver. Jessica fumbled her way around the walls until she found the light switch. The bulb hummed and fizzed before spewing a dim yellow haze. Still yawning, she had a proper look around the room. There was a second chair underneath a table, which had a *Best of Blackpool* hardback on top. Or *Blackpoo*, given the 'l' had been scraped away by a comic genius. Jessica checked the back, noting the 2001 publication date. She wasn't sure too much had changed in the years since.

She sat on the bed, bouncing up and down as the springs squeaked in annoyance. She hated soft mattresses. There was a print pinned on the wall above the bed, showing an unidentified field with a hay bale in the middle. Aside from that, there wasn't much to look at.

Jessica tried the wardrobe – empty; the dressing table drawers – empty; and then a small cupboard next to the bed. Except that it wasn't a cupboard – it was a minibar cunningly disguised as a cupboard. She'd already forgotten about the deposit she'd paid but was at the seaside by herself. What else was there to do? Jessica fished out the micro vodka and whisky bottles, arranging them on the dresser in order of alcoholic percentage.

Best start low and work her way up.

As she relaxed back in front of the window, she unscrewed bottle number one and took a sniff.

'Cheers,' she said to the empty room, raising the plastic bottle and then downing it in one.

FIVE

DCI Fordham picked up the *Best of Blackpoo* book and sat in the chair facing the window. He peered down towards the seafront – and the phone booth – and then twisted to face Jessica, pointing towards the front cover of the book. 'Seen many of the attractions?'

Jessica was standing next to the bed, struggling with the news that Peter was dead. She'd thought he was a bit strange but now wondered what might have happened if she'd continued her evening with him. Maybe he'd be alive?

'I only got here yesterday,' Jessica replied.

'Right... so you said.' Fordham opened the book and flipped randomly to a page, holding it up for her to see. 'Do they really need to tell you to see the tower? You can hardly bloody miss it.'

Jessica wasn't really listening. 'How did Peter die?'

Fordham snapped the cover closed with a dusty snap, dropping it onto his lap. 'I want to make sure there's no confusion here. The last time you saw Peter Salisbury was close to the Central Pier? You'd been talking about your missing friend and his missing sister, and then you came here and checked into a room?'

'Right.'

'And that was about six o'clock?'

'Sometime around then. I wasn't paying attention.'

Jessica knew how vague she was being – this was *exactly* what she hated when she was interviewing a potential witness. It was funny how things sounded when on the other side. She wasn't trying to be obstructive, she simply didn't know.

Fordham's gaze again flickered towards the bin and the discarded alcohol bottles. He was drumming his fingers on the book. 'Peter's body was found on some rocks close to the beach in the early hours of the morning. By the looks of things, he was stabbed repeatedly in the neck. There would have been a significant amount of blood. His wallet, driving licence and your business card were the only things on him.'

It took Jessica a few seconds to take it in. Peter hadn't simply died – there were no natural causes involved, no accidental fall. He'd been murdered.

'I only met him yesterday,' she whispered.

'So you said.'

'That's why he had my card. I'd given it to him in the evening.'

She paused, weighing up Fordham and wondering if she should push her luck. Police officers often had an unspoken bond of knowing how one another felt. Not always, of course. Some were officious bell-ends, driven by ego and power. She wondered if Fordham was like her, willing to give someone a break.

Only one way to find out...

'Who is he?' she asked.

The chief inspector said nothing for a while, the only sound the tapping of his fingers on the hardback. Eventually, he nodded slightly – just a minute dip of the chin, but it was his tell sign. 'Peter Salisbury's a local electrician,' he said. 'He had a couple of his own business cards in his wallet. We're still going through the motions, but he's self-employed by the look of it. His dad is coming down to ID the body at some point this morning.'

Jessica bowed her head a tiny amount to show her thanks for the admission. 'I'm not sure what I can tell you. I said goodbye to him near the pier and that was that.'

Fordham stood, placing the book back onto the table and putting his hands into his pockets. 'You've not got any foreign holidays planned for the next few days, have you?'

'On our wages?'

That got a grin as he nodded towards the door. 'Let's have a look at this phone box poster of yours.'

Jessica hunted under the bed for her shoes and then they headed down the stairs, past the empty reception desk and into the car park. They crossed the road side by side until they were next to the sea wall where Jessica turned to see a big empty space on the side of the kiosk. The poster of Peter's missing sister had gone, leaving small sludgy paper marks in four corners. Jessica turned in a circle, wondering if there were somehow two booths and she'd missed one the previous night, but there was nothing.

'It was right there,' she said, pointing to the metal.

Fordham peered at the gap and then at her. There were posters advertising gigs pinned to the wall, plus more on the lamp-post, but nothing about Katy Salisbury.

'Are you sure?' he asked.

'It's the only phone here.'

He nodded, confirming she wasn't crazy. 'Well it's not there now.'

'But that's how I got Peter's phone number. I wouldn't have known him otherwise.'

Jessica couldn't stop her voice from rising in a mix of

confusion and annoyance. She couldn't quite twist her mind around what was happening.

'Why would someone remove a missing person poster overnight?' Fordham asked, eyeing her.

'I don't know.'

'If it was the council, the other banners would be gone.'

'I know – I can't explain it.' Jessica turned in another circle, wondering if there was a second poster anywhere nearby. If there was, she couldn't see one. She was making herself dizzy. 'Did Peter's body have a phone on it?' she added.

Fordham had his own phone in his hand, nose wrinkled in annoyance as if he'd just got another one of those endless PPI claim texts. 'It wasn't among the listed possessions.'

Jessica took out her phone and scanned through the contacts, thumb hovering over where she'd added Peter's number. 'I called him last night. I'll try his phone again now. Somebody might have found it, or it could be under a rock or something.'

She wasn't quite sure what she was trying to prove but Jessica pressed the button to call, waiting as she felt Fordham watching. She hoped for a ring and at least expected the long single tone to indicate an unobtainable number. Instead there was silence and then a female voice telling her that the call could not be connected.

'It's not even ringing,' Jessica said, putting her phone away. The two of them stared at each other, but Jessica felt small under Fordham's gaze. 'I've told you everything I know,' she added.

'Did anyone see you and Peter separating in the centre last night?'

'I don't know. Maybe. There were people around – there was this woman riding a bucking bronco on the pier and a bunch of lads. Then there were some girls on one of those dancing machines.'

Fordham tapped something into his phone and then put it away, hands returning to his pockets until he emerged with a notepad. 'What was Peter's number?'

Jessica read it out and he scribbled it down, knowing the call history would be checked to corroborate her version. She pointed to the CCTV camera on the pole. 'You can check the footage on that. You'll see me and the poster.'

'Will do.'

They crossed the empty road in silence, moving into the car park. Jessica's red Corsa was in a spot by itself, but there were three other vehicles dotted around.

Fordham nodded at the car. 'That yours?'

'How'd you know?'

'Police wages, remember?'

She laughed gently. 'Right. I should probably get it washed.'

They had almost passed it on the way towards the hotel when Fordham stopped and crouched, pointing to a spot on the rear bumper. 'What would you say this looks like?' he asked.

Jessica stepped around him so that the area was coated by shadow. She gulped, knowing exactly what it was. A person couldn't spend as many years in the force as she had and not recognise a scene such as this. Her throat felt dry, a sinking sense of inevitability setting in.

'It's blood,' she whispered.

SIX

The sticky red liquid was relatively fresh, perhaps a few hours old judging by the way it had glooped together on the bumper of Jessica's car. It was spread in a circle underneath the clasp for the boot, with a speck or two clinging to the mud already on her number plate.

DCI Fordham was still crouched, but shuffled backwards, peering from one end of the back bumper to the other and then stooping lower and looking underneath. When he was done, he stood, walking around the vehicle and stopping every few moments to inspect the various marks of grime and filth. Jessica followed him like a sullen, silent lapdog. She was afraid to say anything stupid, let alone protest her innocence too much. The guilty ones always blabbed about how blameless they were. Fordham soon arrived back at the rear of the car, standing with both hands in his pockets, coat-tails flapping gently behind.

'Why is there blood on your car?' he asked. He didn't sound as if he was accusing her, more that he was staring at a nearly complete puzzle with three spaces and only two remaining pieces.

'I don't know. Roadkill? Maybe I ran over a rat or a squirrel or something on the way here?'

'Do you remember running over a rat on the way here?'

Jessica glanced away and didn't answer. She couldn't. Why would the blood be on the back bumper?

Fordham's features were unmoving. 'You're not making this easy.'

'I don't know what to tell you. It's not... I don't know why there's blood on my car.'

'We both know the drill...'

Jessica didn't know if the uniformed officer had just arrived, or if he'd been hanging around the front of the Prince Hotel the whole time she'd been with Fordham. Either way, after the merest wave of the chief inspector's arm, a fresh-faced too-young officer bounded across the car park, appearing from nowhere.

'When do I get it back?' Jessica asked, staring longingly towards her car.

The uniformed officer must have been telepathic because he held out a hand, silently asking for Jessica's car keys without being asked and then hovered next to the driver's side door. His arms were crossed, stare fixed across the empty road. Christ alone knew what he thought might be about to happen.

'I've got to call in a flatbed to come and pick it up,' Fordham said, removing his phone from his pocket and frowning at the screen again. 'Be right back.'

He ambled across to the furthest side of the car park, either talking into his phone or doing a good job of making it appear that way. Jessica stared at the dried blood and then realised she was being watched. As soon as she glanced up, the uniformed officer's head spun away, pretending he hadn't been looking at her.

'All right?' Jessica asked, trying to sound friendly.

He mumbled something she didn't catch and then took a

couple of quick steps backwards to put himself between her and the car. She tried a warm, welcoming smile, but he was deliberately not looking at her.

Jessica backtracked from the car, thoughts muddy, and found a spot on the low wall that circled the car park. She sat, staring across the road towards the sea, wondering what she'd got herself into. Had she stumbled into a trap that had been laid for her? Everything had happened so quickly that she hadn't had time to take any of it in. One moment she'd been staring at a phone that had called her a couple of days before; the next, there was a dead man and blood on her car.

As Fordham continued to talk on his phone, Jessica closed her eyes, plotting through what she'd be doing if the situation was reversed. First, there would be the forensics from the body, then her car. They'd check phone records and the CCTV if it was working, plus ask for any witnesses in the town centre who may have seen Peter with her the previous evening. She wasn't automatically a suspect, not yet, not until the results came back on the blood on her back bumper. If it turned out to be Peter's then who knew what would happen? Presumably they'd charge her, bail her and start looking to build a case. There was nothing to build – the last time she'd seen him, he had most definitely been alive – but then that was what everyone said. The angry mother with a dead baby daughter *definitely* didn't shake her. The furious drunken man whose fiancée had been beaten into a coma *definitely* hadn't laid a finger on her. The BMW driver *definitely* hadn't driven at the cyclist on purpose. It was always the way – but this time she was on the other side.

The wrong side.

'Jessica...?'

She opened her eyes, realising Fordham had taken a seat on the wall next to her.

'Hi,' she replied.

'They're on the way to remove your car. I don't know when you'll get it back. I guess that depends on what the results say.'

'I've told you everything I know. You can ask the guy on hotel reception – I checked into my room at half six or so, whatever time it was, and then I didn't leave. His name's Brandon – he'll tell you.'

'We've already talked to him.'

Jessica's mouth was open to protest some more when she clocked onto what he'd said. 'You *already* talked to him?'

'I rang him before I knocked on your door. Got his number off the manager.'

'Oh...'

Neither of them spoke for a short while. Slowly, Jessica was beginning to realise how much trouble she might be in.

'I want to have a proper look in your room,' Fordham said.

'You were already in there.'

'I know.'

There was little point in arguing and Jessica had nothing to hide, so they headed back inside, past the still empty reception desk towards the stairs. From the door on the right, there was a clattering of teacups on saucers from the breakfast room as a woman's voice cracked with laughter. The smell of burnt bacon scorched the air, attracting both of their silent attentions.

Jessica half expected her room to already be turned upside down by investigating officers but everything was as she'd left it. Not that there was much to see. The sight of her jacket hanging over the back of a chair made Jessica realise she'd been outside in just a thin top and jeans. She'd not even noticed the cold.

Fordham had said that the stabbing of Peter Salisbury would have produced a lot of blood. Someone would have had to ditch their clothes – exactly in the way it appeared Jessica had, given the bare room. Fordham headed straight for the empty vodka and whisky bottles, using gloved hands to drop them into an evidence bag he'd either magicked from thin air or his pocket when she wasn't looking. He lifted the bedcovers and peered underneath, then opened a couple of drawers.

'Not much of a party, was it?' he said.

'I guess not.'

'Have you got an overnight bag or something?'

'I wasn't planning on staying. I'd only come to check out the phone box and then things just... happened. I didn't have any spare clothes.'

He nodded, pretending he hadn't been asking about that. 'Good job they had a minibar, hey?'

'I guess.'

Fordham peeped inside the empty wardrobe and then stepped towards the door. There wasn't much else he could do. 'Why did you stay here?' he asked.

'Blackpool? On a whim, I suppose. I didn't fancy the drive back to Manchester.'

'I meant here in particular. There are better hotels in Blackpool.'

'Police wage, remember?' He didn't smile, waiting for the real answer. 'It was convenient,' Jessica added. 'Across the road from the phone. I don't really know.'

'Manchester's only an hour and a bit down the road.'

They locked eyes and Jessica suddenly realised what he was implying. 'I've not been down and back,' she said. 'Check the motorway ANPR cameras if you want.'

She knew what he was thinking because it's what would have been on her mind. Drive to Manchester, ditch the clothes she was wearing when she killed Peter, get some clean ones, then nip back. It didn't matter much whether her vehicle showed up on the automatic number plate recognition cameras, because, if this *had* been planned, she'd have a second vehicle anyway – plus the alibi from Brandon on reception.

'Do you live with anyone in Manchester?' he asked.

'No.'

'I really hope we won't need a warrant.'

Jessica continued holding his stare and then, from nowhere, there was a flash of white anger burning within her. A flicker of fury from her younger days, sizzling and raw. '*A warrant?!* Who do you think I am? You won't need a warrant, because you'd never get one. What do you think you'll find in my house?'

Fordham blinked his gaze away, saying nothing and remaining annoyingly calm. In an instant, Jessica's anger had gone and she felt stupid for raising her voice in the first place. He was only doing his job – saying he hoped they wouldn't need a warrant because the blood on her car wouldn't turn out to be Peter's. He *hoped* it was a big misunderstanding. For some stupid reason, she'd thought it was an implied threat.

'I've got to get back,' he eventually said, moving towards the door. 'Don't go far.'

'I can't if you've got my car.'

'You know what I mean.'

'Am I under arrest?'

He stopped in the doorway, turning to face her. He took a deep breath and reached for the handcuffs on his belt loop. For a moment, Jessica thought she'd misread the situation – that she *was* under arrest. He could nick her if he wanted and wouldn't be breaking any rules. At this point, with so little information and no positive ID of Peter's body, all sorts of things were up for grabs. It's why cooperating with the police was always a good idea – at least at first. Investigating officers could play as nicely or harshly as they wanted. Bundle a person into a cell for twenty-four hours without a second thought.

Fordham's fingers brushed the cuffs before they scratched a spot close to his belly button. 'Not yet,' he whispered, before turning and heading for the stairs.

SEVEN

Jessica sat in the armchair in the bay window of the hotel room. In the daylight, she could properly see the car park, the road, the sea wall and browny-grey beach, plus the sea tickling the horizon. No Ireland, though.

She was by herself, watching as a large flatbed truck hoisted her car onto the back. It was beeping for no apparent reason as the uniformed officer half watched, half tapped away on his phone. Three burly garage-type men had fixed the various winches in place and were now standing back gawping as the crane hoisted her vehicle into the air. A smattering of bemused onlookers were standing close to the sea wall, pointing, chattering and taking photographs. They were too far away for Jessica to make any proper judgement, but if they were from overseas, they'd likely think this was some bizarre English ritual.

Detective Chief Inspector Fordham was gone, off to the police station or wherever else he had things to do. Jessica hadn't been able to read him and was unsure if he genuinely suspected her of being involved in Peter's death, or if he accepted that she'd been in the wrong place at the wrong time.

She'd have been suspicious if it was the other way around, leaping on what she knew were small inconsistencies in her own story. The biggest one was why she was in Blackpool at all. The call from Bex had been traced to the phone booth – but there was no particular reason to drive up and see it. She wasn't sure she knew the reason why she'd come, other than the indisputable fact that curiosity was an infrangible part of who she was.

The question was: what now?

She could get a train back to Manchester and wait for Fordham to call with the results. If she'd been formally arrested, there was a chance she'd be suspended – it wasn't automatic – but, as it stood, to all intents, nothing had changed. She hadn't been planning to stay in Blackpool for longer than a night, but there was something going on that she couldn't quite get her head around. Coincidences were a fact of life and happened far more often than a lot of people believed – but there were too many here. Had someone drawn her to this resort to set her up? Was Bex involved, or was it Bex herself? If so, why?

As her car was lowered onto the back of the flatbed, the lorry continued beeping. It took her a few moments to realise what was happening, but Jessica's stomach was gurgling in time to the beeps, a mixture of hunger and protest at her previous night's liquid dinner. It was getting on for eleven in the morning and she'd have to check out of this pit of a hotel.

With few belongings to collect, Jessica reloaded her pockets and locked the room behind her, heading down the stairs towards the reception desk. There was a man standing behind the counter, glancing quickly between a sheaf of papers and a computer. He pressed one or two keys at a time and then shifted his attention back to the papers, muttering under his breath in frustrated annoyance.

''Kin' thieving shites,' he mumbled, before noticing Jessica was standing in front of him. He stared up in surprise.

'Who's a thieving shite?' she asked.

The man's forehead bristled into a crescent of wrinkles. He was in his fifties with a dodgy porn-star moustache. Wiry black hairs sprouted from the top of his shirt and there were beads of sweat coating his bare arms. He'd made an effort to paste his thinning hair across the top of his wilting scalp, but he was fooling no one. Give it a year or two and he'd be completely bald.

'Cash and bastard Carry,' he hissed, motioning towards the papers with a hairy finger. 'Twenty per cent this year – that's how much their prices have gone up. Twenty. Sodding. Per. Cent.' He punctuated his annoyance with a jab of the finger and then stood up squarer. He wasn't very tall, five six or seven, and winced as he straightened, clutching the base of his back. 'Can I help you?' he added.

Jessica waggled the room seven fob towards him.

'Oh,' he said. 'That's *your* car outside. I'm Mr Eckhart – I own this hotel.'

So this was the mysterious 'Luke' that Brandon had mentioned. No wonder he was so bothered about his spread-sheets, considering he owned the adjoining café, the hotel next door – and quite possibly, according to Brandon, the entire rank of hotels, too.

'Yeah, it's mine,' she confirmed, trying to sound as if having a vehicle taken away by police was a normal everyday occurrence.

'The inspector said something about—'

'I'm a witness, that's all. Nothing serious.'

Eckhart's eyes narrowed with suspicion. 'He said it was nothing to do with the hotel... nothing I needed to worry about.'

'Precisely.'

'He, er... didn't say exactly what this was all about...'

'Oh... didn't he...?'

Eckhart's head was nodding slightly, expecting the full story, but Jessica didn't expand, leaving an awkward pause. When the hotel owner realised his fishing expedition wasn't going to get him anywhere, he stretched out a hand for the key. Jessica nudged it slightly out of his reach.

'I was wondering if I could stay another night or two.'

He was so surprised that his heels clicked involuntarily as he bounced onto the balls of his feet. 'Oh... of course. How long were you thinking?'

'I'm not sure.' Jessica opened up her purse, taking out a twenty-pound note and two tens. 'Can I pay day to day? I have cash.'

Eckhart's tongue flickered hungrily across his lips as he eyed the money. 'That's fine. I gather Brandon took your details last night... they must be here somewhere...'

He started bashing the computer keyboard, eyebrows meeting in the middle in annoyance as he tortured the enter key.

'Um... Daniel-something...?'

'That's my last name.'

'Right, of course.' He was a one-finger typist, preferring brute force to any degree of subtlety. 'Got you.' He peered up at her. 'That'll be forty pounds, please. The maids refill the minibar once a day and you pay as you go.'

'I sort of emptied it last night. I paid a deposit when I got here.'

They went back and forth over charges and whether she should pay now or when she left. In the end, Jessica gave him her final fifteen quid to settle it, agreed she'd get her deposit back at some point in the indeterminate future and then got down to the serious business.

'I was told there was breakfast...'

Eckhart's joy at fleecing every last penny she had from her was short-lived as the money disappeared into his pocket. His features scrunched back into the scowl that seemed to suit his face.

'*Technically,*' he said, 'the complimentary breakfast offer finishes at half past ten.'

Jessica tugged at her hair, not wanting to argue, though her stomach was burbling a reminder of its emptiness. 'I would've been down in time, but that chief inspector wanted a word, then they decided to impound my car. Can't you make an exception just this once?'

She offered her sweetest smile, which, by her own admission, wasn't that sweet any longer. Age and her job had been eroding it year by year. Her friend Izzy often said she didn't know whether Jessica was being sarcastic or genuine. Half the time she wasn't sure herself.

Eckhart bored down upon his spreadsheets and then turned to the computer monitor as if trying to work out how much this breakfast might cost him. 'Fine,' he eventually tutted without looking up. 'The café's through that door. Tell them I said it was okay.'

Jessica's stomach was still murmuring, this time in disapproval at the grease-ridden bacon and eggs she had put away. Considering how out-of-date the rest of the area was, the café was in surprisingly decent nick. It wasn't like the swanky café-bars that frequented so many pavements in Manchester, but it was clean and the food decent. The bloke behind the counter had a loose grasp of English, but that was hardly uncommon.

She was back in the hotel room unpacking bags for life after finally making it to the nearby supermarket. She'd got a cheap change of clothes, some wash stuff, a notepad, a pen and a phone charger. For a reason of which she wasn't entirely sure, Jessica had also withdrawn the maximum three hundred pounds from the cashpoint. She didn't like having that much cash on her but had a niggling sense that she'd need it at some point.

The morning was already gone but Jessica still wanted to do some asking around about Bex. The limescale-tainted shower had been bearable and she was ready to head out when her phone started to ring. She rushed across the room, wearing only a scratchy towel, and grabbed her phone from the floor. She had yanked the cord for the lamp from the wall, replacing it with the newly bought charger. Why did hotel rooms never have enough plug sockets?

The number was unknown. 'Hello,' Jessica said.

'DI Daniel?'

'Who is this?'

'DCI Fordham. I'm at the station. Well, our station.'

Jessica could tell from his weary tone that it wasn't good news. 'What's going on?' she asked.

'The father of Peter Salisbury has formally identified his son's body. It was always likely to be him; now we know for sure.'

'Oh...'

'We looked into the phone number you gave us for Peter, too. It was pre-pay, one of those use-and-throw things. A burner. Not under a contract.'

'So there's no proof of who contacted who and the times?'

'We're talking to the phone companies, but...'

Jessica unfortunately knew the issues that came with trying to get phone records. There were warrants to apply for, channels to go through. If Peter had a contracted phone in his name, it was easier. An anonymous number wasn't as straight-forward – and, even if it was, she could have obtained the phone number herself in order to come up with an alibi. There was no proof she'd spoken to Peter in the way she'd described – only that she'd been with him on the night he'd been stabbed.

'What about the CCTV by the phone booth?' she asked.

'We're looking into it. I just thought you should know about Peter's phone number.'

He sounded genuine, so Jessica thanked him and hung up. With a stabbed dead body, blood on her car, her absence of spare clothes, no proof she'd called Peter and a general lack of reasoning for why she was in Blackpool at all, Jessica's explanation for what had happened the previous evening was unravelling in spectacular fashion.

EIGHT

Detective Sergeant Izzy Diamond sounded in a good mood when she answered her phone. She didn't bother with a 'hello', or 'hi', jumping straight in with, 'You'll never guess what Archie's been up to.'

Jessica was ready to spill everything that had happened in the previous few hours, but even that could take a back seat to DC Davey-related gossip.

'What's he done now?' she asked.

'Someone from the Met was on, asking us to check some information for them. Franks dropped it on Arch and he ended up calling them back. Anyway, turns out this London bloke was a Chelsea fan, so Arch was—'

Reality came crushing down on Jessica as she realised life was too short for another incident of Archie taking football far too seriously. He took any slight on Manchester United as if someone had insulted him personally. Probably worse.

'Sorry,' Jessica interrupted. 'I'm in a bit of trouble.'

Izzy went silent and it took Jessica a few minutes to explain the path that had led her to Blackpool and then the series of events that had culminated in her car being carted off to a forensic compound somewhere. She didn't know where that type of thing was done in Manchester, let alone Blackpool.

When she finished speaking, there was a short pause and then Izzy asked if that was everything.

'Isn't that enough?' Jessica replied.

'Yeah, sorry... I didn't mean it like that. It all sounds a bit... weird.'

'You're telling me.'

'What do you need?' Izzy asked.

It was a sad state that Izzy knew instinctively that Jessica was calling for a favour, not simply a friendly catch-up. Jessica wanted information on Peter and Katy Salisbury – whatever was in the police system. Did either of them have criminal records? Where precisely did they live? Was there anything in the file to indicate why Katy might have disappeared? And so on. If she was being accused of killing the bloke, it would be nice to know who he was. Someone had stabbed him to death and it wasn't her.

Jessica started to ask and then stopped herself with a resigned sigh. 'No, I can't. Not at the moment, anyway. You've got a daughter and a life. If it ever comes to it, they'll be able to check my phone records and see that I've called you. If you search for anything on the system, it's you who'll end up in trouble.'

'We both know ways to look things up without *actually* looking them up.'

'I know, but let's leave it for now.' Jessica could hear Izzy breathing at the other end of the line, then added, 'Just keep all of this to yourself for now.'

'Of course,' Izzy replied.

'I'm going – I've got things to sort out.'

'If you need me...'

'Thanks.'

Jessica hung up and spent a few moments staring at the blank screen. She really could have done with the information, but it wasn't fair to involve Izzy, not while she still had a degree of control over her own destiny. She wondered how quickly that might change.

After such a long period as a police officer, Jessica took it for granted that she could discover information on pretty much whomever she wanted whenever she wanted. As well as their own databases, she was able to put in requests to all sorts of companies and agencies that would build a picture of who a person might be. Away from that, and with only her phone's Internet connection to help, she felt a little lost.

Searching for Peter's name threw up very little, although Jessica discovered a partial address from the edited Electoral Register. After a bit more work, she realised the full Electoral Register was viewable – but only in person.

Jessica headed downstairs, to where Eckhart was still working on the computer in the hotel reception. If it was possible, he seemed even more annoyed than he had before. She caught the words 'bastards', 'think I'm a charity' and 'son of a...' before he noticed her.

'Is Talbot Square easy to find?' Jessica asked.

'Whatcha going there for?'

'I heard the town hall was a good-looking building.'

He didn't seem convinced. 'You into architect-stuff and all that?'

'Sort of.'

Eckhart poked a thumb towards the town centre. 'Past the tower, opposite the North Pier. Kinda hard to miss...'

'Thanks.'

'If you're after something to do, people say the zoo's nice. Wouldn't know myself.' The forced smile still wasn't suiting him, but he was at least trying to be nice. Jessica had taken two steps towards the door when he added: 'Is that chief inspector guy coming back?'

Jessica didn't turn as she answered with complete honesty. 'I really hope not.'

Talbot Square was slightly harder to miss than Luke Eckhart had made out, largely because it wasn't a square. Not only was there no *physical* square, there was barely a public clearing. It was more of a junction; full of conflicting signs with a mish-mash of white lines and yellow cross-hatches painted on the road. There were a couple of bars, a bank, buses, cars and an Ibis. It was all a bit dull. Eckhart had been right about one thing, though – it was opposite the North Pier.

The only thing making the area stand out was the rabble of people with banners protesting outside the town hall. If it hadn't been for them, Jessica would have been left walking up and down, oblivious to where the town hall was. It was red-bricked with a clock tower in the centre, but nothing out of the ordinary compared to the rest of the area. There was a small paved area at the front, the focal point of which seemed to be a bin, which was presumably how they rolled in Blackpool. Vegas it wasn't.

Jessica was heading for the town hall steps when one of the protestors touched her arm. She turned defensively, but it was only a rakish young man offering her a leaflet. He was all loose dark curls, beaded bracelets and casual shirt.

'Have you got a minute?' he asked.

Despite her instinct to send him packing, Jessica figured that, if he was local, he might be able to help.

'Sure,' she replied.

He breathed a sigh of relief, having presumably been sworn at, ignored and generally abused through the morning.

'Do you know what percentage of young people are unemployed in Blackpool?' he asked.

Jessica glanced past him towards the array of banners. She realised that everyone was in their late-teens or early twenties. There was a small collection of flasks and mugs on the paving slabs between them as the protestors spread out, trying to get their message across. It was all delightfully British.

One slogan said: 'JOBS, JOBS, JOBS', another: 'FAT CATS, FAT PROFITS'. Off to the side, a girl was thrusting a '1 IN 5 NOT IN EDUCATION OR EMPLOYMENT' sign into the air.

'Twenty per cent?' Jessica said.

'Twenty per— Oh...' The young man stopped himself and stared at her, then nodded towards the town hall. 'You're the first person who's known that. I'm Darren and we're here today trying to make that lot in there realise what a problem the lack of jobs is creating in our community.' Darren pushed one of his leaflets into Jessica's hand. 'Unemployment in Blackpool is among the highest in the whole of the country – especially for young people. All of us are qualified, we've all done exactly what the government told us to do, and yet there's nothing here for us. If we want jobs, we have to move away from our friends and family.'

Jessica glanced at the leaflet, wondering how she could break it to him that she was only heading into the town hall to check the electoral roll, not because she had any connection to the area.

He was already off and away, sounding overly rehearsed: 'In years gone by, there were minimum-wage jobs in hotels and cafés for young people to get themselves onto the jobs ladder, but even those are dying out. Statistics show there were more than a thousand fewer seasonal posts available this last summer. Next year will be even worse.'

'What is it you're hoping to achieve?' Jessica asked.

'Awareness – we want people to know what it's like being young in the area. The papers have been down already and the local TV lot are on their way.'

Jessica didn't want to break it to him that Peter Salisbury's dead body would likely be keeping the protest from anywhere near the top story.

'Well, you've certainly achieved your goal,' she said, trying not to make it sound like the metaphorical pat on the head that it was.

'That's all we're after. We want local business owners and politicians to give us a chance.'

Behind Darren, a group of girls broke into a chorus of 'What do we want?' 'Jobs, jobs, jobs.' 'When do we want them?' 'Now, now, now.'

For all the assumptions that adults made about younger people, it was an impressive show. It was all too true that the moment someone bought a house and started getting up early to go to work, they forgot all about what it was like to be anything other than the height of middle-class respectability.

'This is good,' Jessica said, meaning it.

Darren took a step back, one hand on his chest, beaming with pride. 'Thank you – hopefully it'll do some good.'

Jessica muttered some more compliments and then strode past the town hall, heading towards the town centre. The poster in her hand had given her an idea that she should already have had. She quickly found a print shop, Bluetoothed across the photograph of Bex giving her thumbs-up, and then put together a poster with 'HAVE YOU SEEN?' across the top. She added her mobile number to the bottom and then printed a couple of hundred. It had sort of worked for Peter the previous evening, perhaps it would work for her?

With a roll of tape, Jessica attached a few to the lamp-posts that weren't on the main throughways. There would definitely be by-laws about flyposting and, though she wanted people to see them, Jessica didn't want to go out of her way to incite trouble.

After getting rid of around half the stack, Jessica returned to the town hall, where the protest was still in full swing. It was a little after three in the afternoon, but the clouds were low, darkness already threatening.

Darren clocked Jessica as she neared the steps, walking quickly across to her. He seemed more upbeat than he had been when she'd last seen him.

'Back again?' he asked.

'Still got things to do.'

He wasn't listening: 'The TV cameras have been and gone. They even interviewed one of the councillors. They made him answer questions about funding for training.' He stopped, as if noticing her properly for the first time, and nodded to the papers in her hand. 'Everything all right?'

Jessica held up one of the posters for him to see. 'I don't suppose you've seen my friend in the past couple of months? She's called Rebecca – Bex. She's been missing for a while but I'm sure she's in the area.'

Darren took a poster and stared at the image. 'Don't think so.' He paused for a moment and then added: 'Did you ask at the Help the Homeless place?'

'Where's that?'

He motioned past her. 'Not far that way. There are a couple of signs for it. I've never been in, but they run these fundraising events a couple of times a year and so on.'

Jessica made a mental note of where he'd indicated – it was something to think about later.

'I'll take some of those if you want,' Darren added. 'We've got a youth action meeting later and there'll be loads of young people there. Someone might know her.'

Jessica handed them over, trying to pretend that she hadn't engineered this, though she knew herself too well. 'My number's on the bottom and I'm staying at the Prince Hotel on the southern prom in case you hear anything.'

He nodded, adding the papers to his own as she thanked him again and headed into the town hall.

Jessica was so used to public officials going out of their way to obstruct what she was doing that she was pleasantly surprised by the helpfulness of the woman behind reception. She was escorted to the library room, in which the full electoral roll was kept, and then, within a few minutes, she had the information she wanted.

There were only two Salisburys listed in the Blackpool area. One named Greg, the other Lewis. Assuming Peter's father was registered to vote, then he would be one of the two.

Jessica typed both addresses into her phone's maps application, picked the closest and then went on her way. Who needed a police database?

NINE

Greg Salisbury lived on a street that ran parallel to Blackpool's main promenade. It was a few roads back from the city centre, largely anonymous unless a person was to go looking for it. Long terraces ran along each side of the street, with cars parked nose to tail half on the pavement, leaving a vehicle's width along the centre of the street. Wheelie bins were lined up at the edge of everyone's pathways and a small group of children were congregating on a low wall at the far end, cigarette smoke and youthful chatter drifting into the rapidly chilling air.

Peter's father lived halfway along the road, in between a pair of properties both listed 'To Let'. There was a small, cluttered paved yard at the front, with weeds seeping between the gaps around the edges. It was close to dusk, the final embers of daylight finally swallowed by the clouds and evening. Jessica knocked and took a step back, waiting as the curtain in the living room window wisped back and forth, revealing a man's face. They locked eyes for a moment and then he disappeared. There was a clatter of locks and bolts and then the door opened.

'Are you Greg?' Jessica asked.

The man peered over her shoulder, twisting to look towards the far end of the street. 'You a reporter or something? I told them I wasn't talking.'

Jessica shook her head. 'I'm really sorry but I have to ask if your son is Peter Salisbury.' She almost corrected herself to 'was', but there was no need because his tight lips and mention of reporters confirmed it. She could see the resemblance, too. It wasn't glaring, but he had the same eyes, looked at her the same way that Peter had.

Greg started to close the door, so Jessica spoke quickly: 'I think I was the last person to see Peter alive.'

He stopped closing the door, eyeing her suspiciously. 'You knew Peter?'

'Not exactly. It's complicated.'

'*Complicated...*' He repeated the word, but made no effort to reopen the door fully or invite her in. He was unshaven, with large rough hands that betrayed a lifetime of manual work. His upper arms and chest bulged against his shirt, but it was difficult to tell if it was muscle or middle-aged spread. Perhaps both. Jessica felt guilty for thinking it, but he definitely had a whiff of dodgy plumber about him. 'How is it complicated?' he asked.

'I called a number on a poster about a missing person. Peter was the one who answered.'

'Missing person?' Greg's eyes goggled. 'What missing person?'

For a moment, Jessica wondered if she'd gone to the wrong house. Surely there couldn't be two men named Salisbury with sons named Peter?

'He said it was his sister, Katy.'

'*Who* was his sister?'

'The missing girl.'

They stared at each other, neither apparently knowing

what was going on. 'I think you've got the wrong person,' Greg eventually said, starting to close the door again.

'Didn't you identify your son's body this morning.'

The stare-off continued. 'How do you know that?'

'Because the police visited. They say I was the last person to see Peter.'

'But Peter doesn't have a sister. He's an only child.'

'I...' Jessica had no idea what to say. She'd not expected cream tea and a scone as a welcome but this was just... strange.

Greg's face suddenly contorted into anger. He threw the door wide and took a step towards her. 'What are you trying to do? Why are you lying about a sister? Is that what you told the police?'

Jessica stumbled backwards, surprised at the sudden movement. 'No, I—'

'What did you do to him?'

He was shouting so loudly that the kids at the other end of the street stopped what they were doing. They were each on their feet, pointing towards Jessica, wondering what was going on.

She backed quickly onto the pavement, trying to get away.

'It wasn't like that. I didn't do anything.'

Greg was on the edge of his yard, thankfully barefooted and seemingly unwilling to venture any further. 'I'm calling the Old Bill,' he said. 'Who the hell do you think you are?'

Jessica broke into a jog, heading in the direction from which she'd come, not peering back over her shoulder. She moved into the first alleyway she came to, zigzagging through a series of cut-throughs and following the lights until she found herself in front of an Asian supermarket. Two young men were pushing through the front doors, carrying a drum of cooking oil between them, before loading it onto the back seat of an Audi. Neither said anything to her as they returned inside. She leant on the wall and caught her breath, half expecting to hear Greg Salisbury padding after her.

What on earth was going on?

Her explanation for the previous night was already falling apart – and she had told DCI Fordham that she'd spoken to Peter Salisbury about his missing sister. Now it turned out there was no sibling. Fordham would already be aware, of course. He might have known when he'd spoken to her. There were only two explanations – either the man who'd identified himself to Jessica as Peter was someone completely different; or it *was* Peter and he'd lied for some reason. The only certainty was that he was now dead.

As she was lost in her gloomy thoughts, Jessica felt her phone begin to vibrate. The ID read 'unknown' – but that only meant one thing.

'Hello,' Jessica said.

'DI Daniel?' a man's voice replied.

'Chief Inspector Fordham.'

'Are you still in Blackpool?'

'Why would anyone want to leave a place like this?'

'I was hoping you could come to the station in the morning.'

'Oh… I don't know where it is.'

It was a pathetic piece of reasoning that had slipped out. Fordham sounded stern and didn't soften. 'It's at the back of Madame Tussauds, next to the court. I can send a car for you if you want?'

'No, I'll find it,' Jessica replied. 'Why do you need to see me?'

'It'd be best if we talk here.'

'Right… I can come now if you want?'

He shot straight back. 'Now's not a good time, Inspector. Tomorrow morning – let's say nine o'clock.'

'Right…' Jessica wondered if she should mention the fact

that Katy Salisbury seemingly didn't exist, but figured she'd deal with everything at the same time.

'You still there?' he asked.

'Yes. Nine o'clock – I'll be there.'

'One more thing.'

'What?'

'If you have a solicitor, bring him or her along. If you don't, get one.'

TEN

The interview room of Blackpool Police Station was similar to the ones at the Longsight station where Jessica worked. There was a video camera high in the corner recording everything; an old-fashioned cassette recorder built into the wall; a table bolted to the floor; grim, grey walls; and uncomfortable plastic chairs. There was a thick metal curve screwed to the table, through which handcuffs would be attached if she were considered dangerous or a flight risk. Luckily, she was apparently neither.

It felt strange to be on the other side of the table, claustrophobic with the eyes of whomever was beyond the video camera watching her – not to mention DCI Fordham across the table. He was interviewing her by himself and had done everything as officially as if she was some pleb off the street who was being done for a Saturday night D&D. He read her the usual cautionary gumpf about things being used in evidence, blah-blah-blah, all the while tip-tapping his fingers on top of a cardboard folder. Jessica knew it off by heart.

'Do you understand?' he finished with.

'Yes.'

Although Fordham was by himself, Jessica at least had some backup. Mr Percy – she wasn't entirely clear on his first name – was an old friend of her late father's. He'd been the family solicitor for as long as she could remember, though Jessica had never needed him for anything like this. He was in his early sixties, if not older, and surely close to retirement. A bit of a silver fox, with youthful looks, a sharp suit and a short, officious manner that made it sound like he was talking down to everyone – which he probably was.

'First things first,' Fordham said, still tapping the folder but not opening it, 'did you visit Greg Salisbury yesterday afternoon?'

'Yes.'

'Why did you do that?'

Before Jessica could answer, her solicitor leaned in. 'Are you saying there was any reason why she *shouldn't* have spoken to Mr Salisbury?'

'No.'

'Then she is surely free to visit whomever she wants?'

Fordham peered between the pair of them, leaving Jessica unsure if Percy was helping or hindering. If she had been on the other side of the desk, this would only be winding her up. 'I was trying to get a bit more of an idea about who Peter was,' she said softly.

'Because, prior to the night before last, you'd never met him...'

'Exactly.'

Tip-diddy-tap. Fordham's drumming was either deliberately designed to annoy her, or he couldn't help himself. Either way, it was irritating. 'I know we spoke about this yesterday but, for the benefit of the recording, I'd like to ask you about the events that happened that night.'

And so he did.

For the second time, Jessica told her version, complete

with details about the poster pinned to the phone booth; Peter's story about his missing sister; the way she left him in the town centre and how she checked into the hotel room. Even though she told the truth and left nothing out, it still felt as if she was tripping herself up because she knew that the poster was no longer there and that Peter didn't have a sister.

Fordham said little throughout, not pressing the points, nor making notes. He was one of those annoying types who kept everything in his head.

When she finished, he took a sip of water, returned the glass to the table and then raised it again for a second drink. He was prolonging things, wondering if she'd fill the silence with something stupid. It was a good trick, but one she was already familiar with.

Eventually, he started to lay down his hand. 'We've checked the CCTV next to the phone booth,' he said.

'And...'

'I really wish it could corroborate your story, but the camera isn't working – if it ever was. Unofficially, around two-thirds of those CCTV poles on the prom don't have a functioning device inside. It's more of a deterrent than a security measure.'

'That's convenient.'

'Not really.'

That was one more part of Jessica's alibi blown away.

'Whose blood was on the bumper of your car?' he asked.

'I don't know. I thought you were checking that? My best guess is some sort of roadkill.'

'Do you remember running over any sort of animal?'

Jessica shook her head. 'No.'

'When did you move your vehicle to the car park at the front of the hotel?'

'When I checked into the Prince Hotel.'

'Which was between six and seven in the evening...?'

'Right.'

Fordham was nodding along – he'd heard all this before. 'Did you move it after that?' he asked.

'No – I told you, I went to my room and stayed there. Then you woke me up the next morning.'

'We spoke to the receptionist – Brandon. He says he was on duty but spent some time in the back room and, of course, he needed to use the toilet on occasion. He says any guests could've left the hotel without him knowing.'

'I didn't leave.'

'What are you going to say if results from the lab come back to say the blood on your car is human—?'

Jessica didn't get a chance to answer because Percy leapt in: 'Don't answer hypothetical questions,' he said. '*If* your results say anything other than roadkill, *then* that might be an issue.'

There was a stinging silence in which Jessica felt as if she'd been rebuked, too. She was used to solicitors cutting across her – but never on her behalf.

'Someone might have splashed it there,' she mumbled.

'Jessica!' Percy reacted sharply, patting her shoulder, but it was too late.

'Why would a person do that?' Fordham asked.

'I don't know – why would Peter Salisbury tell me he had a sister that had disappeared? Why would my missing friend call me from a phone booth at the end of South Shore? None of this makes sense.'

Fordham hadn't flinched. 'What do you think's going on?'

'Don't answer that,' her solicitor said gruffly, but Jessica couldn't help herself.

'I came to Blackpool because I thought there might be a clue to Bex's location. I got a call from *that* phone booth opposite the hotel – you can check that, because that's what I did. All I did was come to look for her.'

'Have you found any trace?'

'No – I'd only just got into town when all the crazy stuff happened. I called the number on the poster and it all led to this.'

'Except that the poster you say you saw is no longer where you say you saw it.' Fordham rattled the sentence out like a tongue-twister.

'I don't know what to tell you,' Jessica replied.

Now his fingers had finished tip-tapping, he was instead nodding like a toy dog in the back window of a car. Jessica knew what was coming and he didn't disappoint.

'I suspect you already know this,' Fordham said, 'but Peter Salisbury does not have a sister, let alone one who's missing.'

'He told me he did – or whoever it was who introduced himself as Peter Salisbury.'

'Katy, wasn't it?'

'That's what he said.'

'There's no record of anyone with that name anywhere in the north of England. When did you find out she didn't exist?'

She met his gaze. 'Yesterday, when I visited Peter's father.'

'Are you sure this wasn't something you made up the day before to give you a reason for being with Peter Salisbury? A story of his missing sister tied in nicely with your missing friend – gave you a reason to be seen with him.'

Percy sighed, mouth open about to interject, but Jessica replied anyway: 'No.'

Fordham bit his bottom lip, still nodding. 'How about this? For whatever reason, you ran into Peter Salisbury on Black-pool Promenade. That part, I think, is something there's little dispute over. Perhaps you were on the street, maybe you were in a bar, perhaps it was one of those Internet dating things? Either way, you met up the night before last. Except that he wasn't who you thought he was. He was a bit touchy-feely, a little too friendly, wouldn't take no for an answer. There was a knife, one thing led to another and—'

Jessica's solicitor cut in with a scrape of his chair leg. 'All right, I think we'll leave it there.' He held a hand in front of her to stop her saying anything. 'You have no basis at all to insinuate that anything of the sort happened.'

'There's blood on her car.'

'Blood for which you don't know the origin.'

'But we will.'

Fordham was eyeing Jessica, ignoring the other man in the room. Something had changed in the past twenty-four hours. Fordham was likely having pressure put on him from above and the friendlier parts of his nature that seemed to believe her had dissipated. Jessica glanced up at the camera in the corner of the room, wondering if there was a superintendent on the other side.

'I didn't know him,' she whispered. 'We only met once and even then it was briefly. He told me about his missing sister, I told him about Bex, then we went on our way.'

'Except that he never made it home.'

'I've told you everything I know.'

Jessica turned to her solicitor and he leaned forward, fiddling with his wedding ring.

'If you're going to charge my client, Chief Inspector, then do so. Presumably, you're still waiting for results of your blood tests and I would suggest that, until they arrive, there's very little else to be said.'

Fordham nodded to agree and started to move his chair backwards when something obvious slipped into Jessica's mind.

'Do you have a picture of him?' she asked.

'Who?' Fordham replied.

'Peter Salisbury. Perhaps the person I spoke to was

someone else entirely? It's not like I asked for a passport. He told me his name and I took it at that.'

Fordham slipped the cardboard wallet from the table and removed a photo that he handed across. It showed a man sitting in a beer garden, pint glass on a wooden table in front of him. He was wearing a white vest and squinting slightly but had the same rough stubbly chin and short dark hair as the person with whom she'd walked along the promenade. Jessica stared at the picture, wanting it to be somebody different, but she realised she'd not had a good look at 'her' Peter in any case. It had been dark, she'd walked by his side and they'd both been bundled up in coats. When they'd faced one another, she'd gone out of her way to *not* look at him properly. All there'd been was one meeting of the eyes that had lasted barely a second before she'd felt compelled to look away. They'd spent less than an hour together. If he were in front of her now, Jessica wasn't sure she'd be able to identify him with absolute certainty.

'Is that the man you met?' Fordham asked.

'I think so.'

'Only "think"?'

'I suppose I didn't get much of a look at him. It probably is.'

Fordham reached out and took the picture from her, snapping the cardboard wallet closed. 'This photo came from Peter Salisbury's father. Mr Salisbury identified his son's body. If that's who you met, then that's the same person in the morgue.'

There was a moment of silence and then Jessica's solicitor stood sharply. 'I think we're done here,' he said.

ELEVEN

A breeze was fizzing across the sea, sending stinging spears at anything and everything in its path. Jessica was shielded behind Mr Percy's Mercedes in the car park over the road from the police station.

After fussing with his files, case and coat, her solicitor locked the vehicle and leaned against the outside of the driver's door. He fished into his pockets and took out a packet of cigarettes. 'Want one?' he asked.

Jessica stared at the enticing gift on offer. She'd not smoked since she was a teenager, but, bloody hell, she felt like one now.

'I shouldn't,' she said.

'Your mother would probably have me strung up if she knew I was offering you fags in any case.'

'I'm a grown adult.'

'Do you think that would make any difference?'

'Good point.'

Percy took an expensive-looking metal lighter with his initials on the front from his pocket. He snapped the top and lit the cigarette, taking a deep drag and holding it in his lungs.

'Everyone at the station's on those bloody e-ciggie things,' Jessica said, peering back towards the words 'BL CKPO L POLI E ST T ON' above the entrance to the building.

'Cowards,' Percy spat, with a grin that didn't seem to come naturally. 'If one is going to smoke, the least one can do is do it properly.'

'Bollocks to it.' Jessica held out a hand, eyebrows raised expectantly. Percy said nothing as he passed the cigarette across. Jessica inhaled, handed it back, and then coughed herself stupid.

Percy wasn't wearing glasses but still managed to appear as if he was staring over a pair towards her. 'How was that?' he asked.

Jessica was still spluttering: 'Awful. That's why I don't smoke.'

'I meant inside.'

'Oh. That was awful, too.'

'Did you expect anything else?'

'That Fordham bloke was a bit friendlier yesterday. There's normally an unspoken... *thing*... between our lot that we look out for one another.'

Percy was still peering over invisible spectacles. Jessica was voicing everything that those out of the force feared – one rule for them; another for everyone else.

'I didn't mean it like that,' Jessica added quickly.

Percy was like some sort of professional smoker – each drag perfectly executed with precision so that he could exhale for the same number of seconds every time. He held the stick like an expert, too, nestled between the V of his index and middle fingers of his left hand, even though he wrote with his right. Optimum multitasking.

'What are you doing now?' he asked.

'I'm not sure.'

'Go home to Manchester. Carry on as normal and don't

tell anyone you don't trust completely. You've been bailed for seven days, but the results will probably come back before then, so look out for my call. Until then, stay out of trouble. Do you have a union rep?'

'Probably. It might be Fat Pat... Patrick, even.'

'You might need to speak to him in case this goes... *badly*.' Percy stopped for another puff. 'From what I gather, Lancashire Police have already informed Greater Manchester Police about this.'

'So they said.'

'As far as I can understand, there's no threat to your job at this stage. They can't suspend you, because – in your own terms – all you're doing is "helping police with their inquiries".'

'It sounds even stupider when you say it.'

He nodded but didn't smile. After a glance over his shoulder towards the station, he dropped the fag end on the ground and trod on it.

'That's a thirty-quid littering fine,' Jessica said.

He ignored her. 'I'll put a few calls in and see if there's anything else I can find out. Are you heading home?'

Jessica squirmed. It felt like her dad asking if she was staying in for the night. 'I thought I might hang around in Blackpool for a day or two. I have a few days off anyway.'

At first she thought he was going to tell her off but, instead, he nodded. 'I'll talk to you before, but, one way or the other, I'll see you back here in a week to answer bail.' He opened the car door but didn't get inside. 'And Jessica...?'

'What?'

'Stay out of trouble.'

She wanted to tell him that he wasn't her dad, that he couldn't tell her off, but he was only trying to help. He'd known her since she was a kid.

'Um... you're not going to tell my mum, are you?'

It took a couple of seconds, but, this time, a grin did creep onto Percy's face. It disappeared almost instantly. 'Of course not.'

As he pulled away, Jessica stood in the car park watching. Her phone had been turned off while she was being interviewed, but she switched it on and waited a few seconds before the missed calls started to ping through. When she was sure it had finished buzzing, Jessica called Detective Chief Inspector Topper. He was her immediate superior at the Longsight station where she worked, someone she actually liked and trusted.

He answered on the first ring: 'Jessica?'

'Guv.'

He was flustered: 'I've been hearing... things.'

'Like what?'

He paused for a moment. 'How about you tell me what's going on?'

Jessica sighed, ambling across the tarmac towards the seafront and finding a spot in an empty bus shelter. 'It's a bit of a mix-up,' she said. 'Well... not a mix-up as such. I saw this bloke the other night and, after we'd separated, someone else stabbed him. He had my card in his pocket and I'm apparently the last person to see him. CID up here had a few questions.'

'Oh.'

'It's just a mix-up. Well...' Not a mix-up as such. Jessica went silent as she realised she was repeating herself.

'Is there anything I can do?' he asked.

'I don't think so. Things are going to have to play themselves out. It's all standard stuff.'

Jessica winced, again tailing off. This was anything but 'standard'.

'Are you *sure* everything's okay?' he added.

'Yep – I'm on leave anyway. I'll be back soon.'

She heard the click of his tongue, as if he was going to ask her – again – if she was all right. 'If you're sure,' he said instead. 'Call if you need anything.'

'I will.'

'I mean it, Jess. Call if you need me.'

'I will, sir.'

For a moment she wondered if they were going to exchange a series of 'no, you hang up' – but then she realised he'd gone.

The scratched plastic of the bus shelter rattled in the wind and then went still. The promenade and street opposite was nearly deserted, with only a smattering of shoppers and a road cleaner mooching up and down. An empty tram skimmed along the tracks close to the pier, passing close to the spot where Jessica had last seen Peter. This was the type of place that didn't come to life until it was dark.

Jessica knew she should take Percy's advice – go home and keep her head down – but she'd come to Blackpool to find Bex. Not only had she failed to do that, she couldn't escape the sense that this had been targeted *at* her. It wasn't some accident. If she went home now, it would change little. She would still be the last person to have seen Peter and Bex would still be missing.

Although the wind was still snarling and gnarling around the front, it wasn't actually that cold. Not for the north of England, anyway. Jessica set off along the street that ran parallel to the prom, using the row of shops and hotels to protect her from the breeze. She'd only walked a short distance when she saw the orange and white sandwich board outside a newsagent. It had the logo of the local newspaper across the top and a somewhat predictable headline: 'BODY FOUND ON BEACH'.

Jessica didn't know how many corpses were found on the

shore each year, but the statement seemed so definitive, so matter-of-fact, that it stopped her dead. It took her a few seconds to compose herself and then she entered the newsagent. She avoided eye contact with the man behind the counter. He was reading a magazine and listening to cricket on the radio. She could feel him watching her as she picked up a copy of the *Blackpool Gazette* and started reading, skimming the front page and then turning inside.

The details were largely sketchy – Peter Salisbury had been seen the night before last on Blackpool Promenade and had then turned up stabbed to death on a patch of rocks further down the shore. Police were appealing for anybody who may have seen him to come forward. There was a picture of the rocks on which he was found, Central Pier where he was last seen, and the photo of him in the beer garden. The rest of the article was the usual police-speak – 'investigation ongoing', 'following a series of leads', advising the public 'not to panic' – and so on. Those bloody press releases might as well be cut-and-paste jobs given the similarity in language. It didn't matter where the force was based geographically, there would be some hard-nosed press officer writing as if they were paid by the word. It may as well read, 'Blah, blah, blah – we're on the case, all right?'

Thankfully, Jessica's name was nowhere to be seen in the coverage. If it had been, that would mean it would be on the Internet, too. Once out, there would be no turning back. She'd be cached on various search engines from then until the end of eternity.

'You gonna buy that?'

Jessica turned to face the shopkeeper, closing the pages guiltily. 'Er, hang on...' She reached into her pocket and came out with a pound coin she didn't know she had. She paid, took her change and then headed back towards the front. The photo of Peter in the paper had left her with a thought that had previously washed over her. If he *didn't* have a sister, then the picture on the poster supposedly showing Katy must belong to somebody else.

TWELVE

Jessica was sitting on a bench on the seafront, ignoring the breeze and tucking into a bag of chips. They were proper chips, too – thick and deep-fried, dripping with vinegar and speckled with a person's daily allowance of salt. People could say what they liked about Blackpool, perhaps even the north as a whole, but bloody hell, northerners knew how to do chips.

She ate with her left hand, drying her fingers on the crumpled white paper as she used her phone with her right.

The Blackpool Police website was the usual type of disjointed mess so often associated with public bodies. There was a force logo, a pixelated image of the chief superintendent and some overwritten bollocks about how he was there to protect the local community. So far, so yawn-inducing. As well as a list of press releases about locking up valuables, reporting anything suspicious and the usual array of common sense pronouncements, there was a gallery of wanted criminals, links to the force's desperately undersubscribed social media pages and – finally – a link to an external site cataloguing missing people.

Jessica worked her way through the photographs on the

site, stopping whenever she reached a young white girl with long dark hair. 'Katy' might not be real – but there was every chance Peter, or whomever it was she'd met, had ripped off somebody else's missing person poster. It could have been a generic photo of someone taken from the Internet but, from what Jessica could remember, that wasn't how it seemed. It *looked* like the sort of picture that was so often found on missing persons' posters.

There were missing people of all shapes and sizes; all races; young, old – a true slice of the British public represented by the fact they'd seemingly upped sticks without a trace. As Jessica was beginning to think she was hoping for too much, she stopped with a chip halfway to her mouth as 'Katy's image filled her phone screen. It was the hooped earrings that stirred her memory. Jessica had forgotten about them until the picture was in front of her. The poster attached to the phone box had been low-quality, some dodgy black and white photocopy, but this was the original. 'Katy' wasn't Katy at all, she was someone named 'Henka Blaski'. In the colour image, she had brown eyes, a little too much make-up and greasy, olive skin. She looked like Bex, too – perhaps not if they were side by side, but it was in the shape of their faces, the hint of a shadow under their eyes, plus the colour and style of their hair.

As she looked at the mushy remains of her chips, Jessica was suddenly not hungry. She balled up the paper and dropped it into the bin next to the bench. More than ever, she felt set up. She wondered if that's why Peter had chosen this photo for the poster that was stuck to the side of the phone booth. Jessica was *meant* to see it, to make the connection. If it had been a photograph of a missing person who happened to be male, or black, or old, perhaps she wouldn't have phoned the number on the bottom? It had been subtle enough to manipulate her without being too obvious.

Someone wanted her to call Peter on the night he'd died.

So far, she'd been a passenger, but, as she stood, still staring at the photo of Henka, Jessica decided it was time to start fighting back.

She crossed the road, heading into the back streets away from the town centre. The further she went, the more run-down the houses, B&Bs and shops seemed to become. The promenade might be nice and shiny, but very few places stood up to scrutiny if the surface was scratched.

It didn't take long before Jessica found the type of newsagent she was looking for – a bit grimy, with a board at the front advertising international calling rates to a long list of eastern countries. She bought a cheap Nokia and a pay-as-you-go SIM card, using cash and putting fifty pounds of credit on it. The shopkeeper held each of her ten- and twenty-pound notes up to the light, checking for potential forgery, but barely looked up from the counter otherwise.

Back outside, Jessica grappled the SIM card and battery into the phone and held in the button at the top. Thankfully, the screen flashed white and turned on. There was around sixty per cent charge – plenty for now. She copied a handful of numbers from her actual phone across to the new one. When she was done, she called Izzy.

The sergeant took a few rings to answer and when she did, she sounded annoyed. 'Hello?'

'Iz, it's Jess.'

There was a pause. 'Oh... I thought you were some tele-marketer. Why are you using a different number?'

'It's a long story – I need a favour. Can you check the missing persons' database for someone named Henka Blaski?' Jessica spelled it out letter by letter and then added: 'She was last seen in Blackpool around two months ago and there can't be many – if any – with that last name.'

Jessica heard the scraping of a pen and then, 'Okay. What do you want to know?'

'An address if you can find it – plus anything on other family members. Brothers, sisters, mum, dad – that sort of thing?'

'Anything else?'

'I don't think so.' Jessica took a breath. 'It's just... when you've got it, can you call *this* number back? Forget my other one. I wouldn't ask if it wasn't important.'

'No problem.'

There was no small talk, no messing around. The call dropped, leaving Jessica staring at the blank screen. As she waited, she dumped all the phone packaging into a bin outside the newsagent and then started pacing, pressing buttons on the phone and trying to see what it could do. From what she could gather, there was basic Internet, texts, the phone itself, and little else. It didn't have a camera, an app store, or anything remotely up-to-date. It was bizarre how quickly technology became essential to modern living. Jessica couldn't imagine getting through a day without the spangly, clever things her phone – her *proper* phone – could do. When she switched that off, leaving her with the new one, she felt a tiny bit more vulnerable.

Jessica jumped as the new phone started to ring. She'd been willing it to, but the tinkling, annoying ringtone was something out of a dodgy eighties movie.

'Iz?'

'I've got you a name and address,' Izzy replied.

Danuta Blaski liked plates. *Really* liked them. Three of the four walls of her living room were covered with ceramic and china plates, all neatly arranged on shelves. There was a series of twelve celebrating Elvis Presley; another dozen with pictures of the British Royal Family; and many others with flowers, animals, and who knew what else. In between the plates, there were numerous Christian crosses. There was also a church created from glued matchsticks in the far corner.

Jessica was sitting in an uncomfortable armchair, sipping from a china teacup, afraid to move. There was a set of plates showing puppies worryingly close to the armrest and she feared being an errant elbow away from bringing the entire lot down.

Mrs Blaski leaned back into the sofa opposite Jessica, sipping from her own teacup. 'I'm so glad the police are still looking for my daughter,' she said. Unsurprisingly, given the name, she was of Polish origin and carried some of the accent, even though her English was seemingly perfect.

Jessica tried not to wince. She'd used her police identification to get into the house and it wasn't exactly true that the police were still looking for Henka Blaski. She supposed that *she* was now looking for Henka, even if unofficially.

After putting her teacup *carefully* on the sideboard, Jessica took out a notepad and pen and rested it on her knee. 'I know you've been through this in the past,' she said, 'but could you possibly tell me about what happened on the night your daughter disappeared?'

Some people would argue about having to repeat themselves – some always did – but Mrs Blaski didn't appear to mind. She sipped her tea and started: 'It was two months ago – a Saturday night. Henka used to see her friends – she was nineteen, you know what girls are like at that age.'

'I was young once.'

The woman smiled. 'Me too.' She was fidgeting on the sofa, tugging at her skirt and wriggling her shoulders against the backrest. With her skin tone and long dark hair, she looked a lot like her daughter. 'She was going out with her friends,' Mrs Blaski added. 'They were supposed to be meeting at somebody's house, but Henka never made it. You don't know what to think. Our first thought was that someone had taken her, someone bad.'

'Was there any sign of that?'

A shake of the head. 'No sign of anything. All her things are still upstairs. She just went.'

'Was there any build-up? Any arguments? Fallings-out with her friends or a boyfriend?'

'No,' she snapped, 'and she didn't have a boyfriend.'

Jessica wondered if she should ask 'girlfriend', but figured she was probably pushing it. The sudden annoyance had only appeared at the mention of a possible boyfriend.

'Was there anybody else she might have fallen out with? A best friend, something like that?'

'No. I did tell the police this. She was happy.'

Jessica reached into her bag and took out one of the missing posters she'd created with Bex's image on the front. She passed it across. 'I don't suppose you recognise her...?'

Mrs Blaski fumbled along the side of the chair for a pair of glasses, putting them on and then staring at the picture. She peeped over the top towards Jessica. 'Should I know her?'

'I'm not sure.'

'Is she English?'

'Yes. She might be in Blackpool.'

The woman peered down at the picture again, then shook her head and handed it back. 'Henka didn't really have English friends. We're a... tight community.'

Jessica didn't ask her to expand because Mrs Blaski had spoken a little *too* forcefully.

The woman muttered something in another language and then blinked innocently when Jessica peered up.

'Everything okay?' Jessica asked.

'My husband think the police don't care because Henka's Polish.'

'That's really not the case.'

'He say you find the English girls first.' Mrs Blaski glared at Jessica, daring her to confirm it.

After a moment, Jessica peered away, putting the picture of Bex back into her bag. This was an argument of which she wanted no part. There'd be no winners. 'Can I look at Henka's room?' she asked.

'People have been: men with gloves. They took stuff, then returned it.'

'Can *I* look?'

Mrs Blaski finished off her tea with a flourish, tipping her head back and then clanking the cup back onto the saucer. 'If you wish.'

Jessica liked Henka's room a lot. Sometimes, when a person had gone missing, their living space would be tidied up by frantic parents, or spoiled by search teams. Here, the teenager's room *felt* like something that a young person would live in. One wall was devoted to photographs that looked like they'd been taken on a phone and then printed on a sketchy inkjet. Henka was in most of them, smiling, carefree and happy. In many, there was another girl with her who had a similar skin tone and dark hair. They were in the park; on the beach; on the prom; at the Pleasure Beach. Doing normal things that kids did around the town. Perhaps unsurprisingly, given her mother's bristling at the suggestion of a boyfriend, there were no males pictured, except for an older man Jessica assumed was Henka's father. Jessica picked over the photographs, taking them in, looking for anything out of the ordinary, but it was simply a teenage girl being a teenage girl.

The only thing Jessica saw that was remotely noticeable was that Henka seemed to like wearing the same clothes. In at least a third of pictures, she had on small denim shorts and a red vest top with 'BABYLON' printed across the front in shimmering, presumably fake, jewels. From the look of her hair length and colour, the pictures had all been taken at around the same time, likely the previous summer. There was blue sky in the background, lush green grass and bright sandy beaches.

In a few others, Henka was wearing a green and white apron with some sort of bird logo stitched onto the front. She was sticking her tongue out to the camera in one and threatening to throw a tin of food at whomever was taking the photo in another. All the while, grinning, grinning, grinning. A happy-go-lucky young woman who had made England her home and was bloody enjoying it.

Around the rest of the room, there were soft toys, a sparsely filled wardrobe, trainers, some books and some candles. Jessica didn't want to make too much of a mess, so she trod carefully, returning everything to where she'd taken it from.

When she was done, she headed down the stairs to find Mrs Blaski waiting at the bottom, arms crossed. 'Are you finished?' she asked.

'Yes, thank you.'

'Are you going to find my Henka?'

Jessica took a breath, so wanting to say 'yes'.

'I'll try,' she replied truthfully, hoping it was a promise she could keep.

THIRTEEN

Jessica left the Blaski house and set off walking in an increasing spiral around the nearby streets. Danuta insisted that her daughter had few non-Polish friends and, if true, it meant she must be known in the local immigrant community.

It didn't take Jessica long to stumble across the 'Polski Sklep' next to a hairdresser's a few streets from the house. There was a large green awning overhanging the pavement with a circular bird logo printed in the corners, plus an A-frame board at the front listing something in Polish. Jessica headed inside, breathing in the smell of drying meats and sausages. As well as shelves of items with non-English labels, there was a deli counter with hams and kielbasas hanging from the ceiling. Jessica had to sup back the drool that was beginning to coat her tongue.

The young woman behind the counter was unquestionably the same person as in so many of the photographs lining Henka Blaski's wall. She was nineteen or twenty, slim, with similar hooped earrings to the ones Henka wore. She brushed down her green and white uniform with one hand, the long nails of her other click-clacking on the countertop as she flicked through the pages of a fashion magazine.

'Can I help?' she asked, peering up.

'Do you know Henka Blaski?' Jessica asked, knowing the answer.

The girl's fingers were splayed open on the magazine pages and froze where they were, her shaped eyebrows curving down in concern. 'Oh, God. You've not found a body, have you? Oh, God. Oh, God—'

Jessica held a hand up, shaking her head. 'No, sorry, it's not that.' She took out her police warrant card, again feeling guilty for using it when she wasn't working. The girl behind the counter barely looked at it and certainly didn't question the fact that it said 'Greater Manchester' instead of 'Lancashire'.

'What's happened?' she asked.

'I just want to ask a few questions,' Jessica replied. 'Nothing you won't have already gone over with the police.'

'Oh... I thought...' She tailed off.

'What's your name?' Jessica asked.

'Maryla.'

'I'm Jessica. I gather Henka also worked here?'

It was a bit of a guess based upon the picture of Henka in the same uniform that Maryla was currently wearing, but the young woman nodded.

'And you were friends?'

Another nod.

'Good friends?'

'I guess.'

'Can you tell me about the day she went missing?'

Maryla chewed on her bottom lip for a moment. It was coated with a thin, glimmering pink gloss. 'Why do you want to know?' she asked.

Jessica took out the poster with Bex's picture from her bag

and held it up. 'I'm looking for her and if I can find Henka, there's a chance I might find my friend, too.'

Maryla stared at the picture of Bex, showing no recognition. 'I told the police all I know. Henka was supposed to come to my house but never arrived.' She peered back down to her magazine and flipped a page.

'Her mother said she didn't have many non-Polish friends.'

There was a snort of derision from Maryla. 'Dan says lots of things.'

'She also said Henka didn't have a boyfriend.'

Maryla didn't reply, flicking another page, even though she couldn't have read the previous one.

'I saw her bedroom,' Jessica added. 'There are lots of photos of you there. The pair of you – years of memories, but not a boy in sight. No ex-boyfriends, current boyfriends, wannabe boyfriends. Nothing.'

Maryla shrugged. 'So?'

'So... I was nineteen once and boys were my life. Maybe boys weren't her thing, but being that age is about being crazy in love – even if that's with someone completely wrong.'

Maryla was back to biting her lip again. She looked up slowly. 'Boys were her thing.'

'So who was he?'

They locked eyes and Jessica could see the glimmer of fear in the young woman. 'I could get in trouble,' Maryla whispered.

'You won't.'

Maryla tried to step backwards, but Jessica reached forward and gently touched her wrist.

'It's okay,' she added.

'You won't get it,' Maryla said.

'Try me.'

'You're not... one of us.'

It could have sounded sinister but instead came out as if she was apologising.

Jessica kept hold of Maryla's wrist, not squeezing, simply letting her know that she was there. 'I'd like to find Henka, too,' she added, emphasising the other girl's name.

Maryla sighed, pulling her wrist away and crossing her arms. 'His name's Jacek,' Maryla breathed. 'You wouldn't understand. Henka's mum and dad are strict Catholics. Jacek's are Orthodox.'

Jessica nodded in the direction of what she thought was the sea. 'I think the Irish folks that live around here probably know a thing or two about Protestant–Catholic fighting.'

Maryla shook her head. '*Both* families were against them.'

'But they saw each other on the quiet?'

There was another shrug, followed by a wonderfully defiant, fists clenched, eyes narrowed, bring-it-on declaration of: 'If you like someone, you like 'em, right?'

Jessica couldn't help but smile. 'I'm not sure anyone could put it better than that.' The cogs were beginning to turn slowly. 'I'm guessing you were their cover?'

'I was Henka's – she'd tell her mum and dad she was out with me. Sometimes they'd call and ask to speak to her, so I'd say she was on the toilet, or whatever. Then I'd call her and she'd get back to them. I don't know what Jacek told his parents.'

'Did anyone else know they were seeing each other?'

'Everyone thought they'd broken up.'

'How long ago was that?'

Maryla unfolded her arms and counted on her fingers. 'A year, maybe? Her mum pretended it had never happened. His dad thought the same, but they didn't really talk about it. They were afraid of being found out.'

'Were they together on the night Henka disappeared?'

'The three of us were out together. We used to do that a

lot, just in case we were spotted. Henka would say she was with me and that it was a coincidence Jacek was there. Nobody ever saw us anyway, but she was paranoid.'

'Where were you?'

'On the seafront, near the pier. We were walking and talking, eating candyfloss. Not doing much.'

'What happened?'

Maryla took down one of the kielbasas from the rack behind her, slipped her hands into a pair of gloves and started chopping.

'They were weird that night – both of them,' Maryla said. She didn't look up, but there was a hint of brightness to her voice. Jessica guessed Maryla hadn't told this to anyone before. 'I'd hang around and then drift off later in the evening. We'd go to the tourist areas, where there are no Poles. Sometimes I'd meet a boy while we were all out, sometimes I'd do my own thing. Usually they wanted me there in case we ran into someone who recognised us – but not that night.'

'Did one of them say something?'

She shook her head: 'There was this sort of vibe, like I wasn't wanted. After a bit I went home by myself and left them to it.'

'That was the last time you saw Henka?'

Maryla gulped and nodded.

'What happened to Jacek?'

The atmosphere changed in a flash, as if someone had turned on a fan that was blasting cold air around the room. Maryla stared at Jessica, head at a slight angle. 'I thought you'd guessed – that you already knew. I thought that's why you'd come – because you'd put it together.'

'Knew what?'

Maryla paused, biting her lip. 'Jacek's missing too.'

Jessica stared at her, trying to figure out what it all meant and then she knew. Jacek and Henka had been reported missing separately and no one had put the pieces together. Nobody had tipped off the police that they were once a couple because both families were trying to pretend it hadn't happened. Maryla was the only one who knew.

'Why didn't you tell the police?' Jessica asked quietly, immediately wishing she hadn't.

'They never asked.' Her top lip flared, anger rising. 'They always assume missing Poles have gone home to Poland, never bother to look. No one cares about us. What's one missing Polish girl when you have nice, English ones to go looking for?' Her eyes widened, daring Jessica to dispute it.

'I'm sure that's not true,' Jessica eventually stuttered – but the delay had already said plenty.

Maryla picked up the knife again and started chopping another sausage, slamming the blade into the wooden block over and over. 'If that's true, then where are they?' she spat.

This time, Jessica did not have an answer.

FOURTEEN

Jessica had been shaken by Maryla's venom. Was it true that police forces, perhaps public bodies as a whole, put less focus on immigrant communities? She tried to treat everyone the same, but it was human nature to make certain assumptions about others who were different.

In other circumstances, she'd have phoned the local police and told them about the connection between Henka and Jacek. With everything that was going on – and DCI Fordham's attitude towards her – Jessica doubted it would go down well.

Instead, she headed back towards the centre of the town, figuring she'd take Darren's advice from the previous day. The Help the Homeless centre was hidden along a narrow, dusty alleyway a few streets away from the town hall. It might only have been a short distance but it may as well have been a different town entirely. Jessica found Blackpool to be a place riddled with confusion over its own identity. There were the illuminations, the bright shops, the attractions and the pubs. A shiny surface-dressing for those who didn't know better.

Beyond that, it didn't take too much exploring to find the boarded-up shops, the grimy pubs, the fly-tipped mounds of rubbish in the back ginnels. It was like two towns living on top of each other – one for the tourists, one for everyone else.

On the invisible border between the two towns lay the Help the Homeless drop-in centre. It inhabited an old pub that still had the faded sign high on the wall outside. Pinned to the door was a list of strict curfew times for when the place was locked for the night, plus a code of conduct saying that the staff who worked there were volunteers who would not tolerate abuse. Jessica headed inside, finding her appetite again as the smell of warm soup drifted around the enclosed space.

It took her a few moments to get her bearings, but the inside was warm and welcoming, teeming with people. The bar had not been removed from the pub and was being used as a long serving counter, with three people behind chatting to one another. There was a large metal urn with steam seeping from the top and a basket next to it. As Jessica watched, a man in a pair of jogging bottoms and a T-shirt walked across. He pointed to the urn, got a nod from one of the people behind the counter and then filled up a bowl with soup. He took a chunk of bread from the basket and then shuffled away to the corner, where he was sitting with a pair of other men around a small circular table.

Much of the room was laid out in the way it would have been when it was a pub. There were booths to the side and a dozen or so round tables with stools. People were sitting in small groups, some eating, some not, but all seemingly having a peaceful chat. Jessica soon realised that, as much as she was taking in the room, many of the people were watching her, too. Some would glance towards her, then look away; one or two were staring at her, silently asking who she was.

'Can I help you?'

Jessica jumped slightly as she realised there was a woman at her arm. She stepped backwards as they each apologised to one another.

'I'm Pam,' the woman added. She was a few years older than Jessica, dressed in a long white apron with her auburn hair bobbed underneath a net.

'Jessica. Are you in charge?'

The woman straightened herself, filled with pride. 'It's not as straightforward as that, but... I suppose so.'

'Is there somewhere we can talk privately? I'm a police officer.'

Pam slipped off the hairnet and began tugging her hair down into a loose ponytail. She frowned at Jessica. 'Is there a problem?'

'No... it's just... walls have ears and all that.'

Pam peered past Jessica towards a pair of booths on the side wall but she said nothing. With a flick of her head, she led Jessica towards a small circular table next to the hatch for the bar. It wasn't completely private, but there was nobody nearby. Already on the table was a steaming cup of tea and a plate piled with three slices of toast that was oozing with melted butter.

'I missed lunch,' Pam said, picking up a piece of toast and biting into the corner.

'What is this place?' Jessica asked. She hoped it sounded like a compliment, because it was. Away from the glitz of the promenade, this would be a lifeline for those less fortunate.

Pam continued eating, talking in between bites. 'It's a cross between a soup kitchen and a homeless shelter – largely funded through charitable donations, but we get some money from the council.'

'And you run it?'

She shrugged modestly. 'I founded it and keep things

ticking over. It's me who goes begging to the supermarkets and bakeries for their leftover food. "Run it" doesn't sound right.' She nodded towards the other three people behind the bar. They were all young, definitely no older than twenty. Two of them were pouring cups of tea for a pair of blokes who were presumably homeless. 'We're all equal here.'

'Where do people sleep?'

Pam finished off the first triangle of toast and pointed a thumb towards the roof. 'There are rooms upstairs. We can fit about twenty in, maybe a couple more depending on the gender split.'

Jessica glanced backwards – there were at least thirty people eating and drinking. 'How do you—?'

'First come, first served. It's the only way. Some of them grumble, but everyone knows how it works.' She sipped her tea. 'Why are you here?'

Jessica took one of the posters of Bex from her bag and held it out. 'I was hoping you might have seen her.'

Pam didn't reach for the poster. 'We have all sorts here – people who've fallen out with their husbands, wives or parents; young and old; men and women. Some are runaways, some locals. I never ask the questions, because it's none of my business. I just hope to provide them a roof.'

Jessica put the paper on the table between them. 'She's a friend.'

'I thought you said you were police.'

'I am – but I'm asking for me.'

Pam glanced down at the sheet, lips pursed. Her eyes narrowed and then she took a bite of toast. 'Most here don't want to be found.' She lowered her voice, tailing off and raising her eyes over Jessica's shoulder. 'Everything all right, Fran?'

Jessica turned to see a woman wearing a deerstalker shuffling from foot to foot a short distance behind her. She was in her twenties, hair bundled under her hat, clearly trying to listen in. 'Fine,' she replied.

Pam and Fran eyed each other, neither speaking until Fran spun on her heels and headed towards a noticeboard next to the front door.

When they were alone again, Jessica picked up the poster. 'Have you seen her? She's named Rebecca, but everyone calls her Bex.'

There was a slight – though deliberate – roll of the eyes. 'I'm not sure I'd tell you if I had, but... no. Not that I remember, anyway. Lots of people come in for a meal and then they don't come back.'

'Could you show this poster around for me? Or put it on the wall?'

Pam lifted her mug, deliberately holding it in front of her mouth as she spoke. 'People are watching. They've noticed you – you're making them nervous.'

Jessica fought the urge to turn and see who was looking at her, not that it really mattered. In a room full of hungry and homeless people, of course she stood out. A fair number would have already clocked her as police – if not that, then some sort of social worker.

'I'll go,' Jessica replied, standing but maintaining eye contact. 'Can you please ask around? My number's on the bottom.' She realised as she said it that the number on the poster belonged to the phone she'd switched off, but there was still voicemail.

Pam nodded. 'I'll see what I can do.'

Jessica kept her eyes on the ground as she hurried away from the centre. She'd had dealings with the homeless community in the past – it was where she found Bex in the first place – and she knew how places such as this needed to be left as a safe place for those who needed it.

She had reached the corner of the street, about to head back towards her hotel when a voice called 'hey' over her shoulder. Jessica turned to see Fran with the deerstalker jogging along the street, one hand cupped around her mouth.

'Hey,' she shouted again.

Jessica stopped and faced her. 'Hello...?'

'You really police?'

The skin on her cheeks was taut and she stood tall. Everything about Fran said that she was somewhere in her mid- to late-twenties, except for her eyes. They were dark and sunken into her face. With the hat covering her hair, and pale, greying skin, she looked like a skeleton. Either that, or one of the shoddy waxworks from Tussauds on the seafront.

'I am,' Jessica replied. 'How'd you know?'

'You look it. Bit stuck-up, like.'

Jessica didn't know how to reply, so she shrugged. She'd been called many, many things over the years – but never 'stuck-up'.

'I'm not *Blackpool* police, if that helps.'

'Where ya from?'

'I work in Manchester.'

Fran nodded along. She had her hands in the pockets of a thick army-green coat that matched her hat. 'You've lost your friend?'

Jessica failed to hide the frown of annoyance that she'd been overheard. 'That's right.'

'Who is she?'

'You really want to know?'

'I wouldn't ask otherwise.'

Jessica took another of the posters from her bag and handed it over.

Fran eyed the image and then peered up. 'She in trouble, or something?'

'Nope, she's just a friend who went missing.'

'And you think she's here?'

'Maybe.'

Fran folded and pocketed the poster. 'You some sort of do-gooder?'

'Not really.'

'God-freak?'

'Nope... why?'

Fran was bouncing on her heels in the same way she had done inside. A strand of light hair freed itself from underneath her hat and swayed across her face. She didn't seem to notice. 'God-freaks are round here all the time, offering our lot food and shelter *if* they accept Jesus. As if we have to talk about their God to get our reward at the end of it. When you're hungry, you'll say you believe in anything.'

'I'm not religious,' Jessica added.

'So, why'd your friend disappear? She have a boyfriend on the go?'

Jessica had no idea where the conversation was headed, but, for a reason of which she wasn't sure, Bex's story came flooding out. She told Fran everything – how Bex had gone to live on the streets after bad experiences with her mother; how she'd moved in with Jessica; how she'd left without a word or sign. She finished with an exhausted sigh. Fran hadn't interrupted once, instead bobbing on her feet and nodding.

'And the first time you heard from her was the phone call?' Fran asked.

'Right. It was traced to Blackpool. That's why I'm here.'

Jessica had no idea who Fran was, but the other woman spoke with the authoritative confidence of somebody used to being in charge of others.

'I've not seen your friend,' Fran said, 'but I'll ask around and look out for her. If she's spent any time on the streets around here, then someone will know her.'

'Thank you.'

Jessica wasn't sure if this was the end of the conversation. She took a small step backwards, but Fran moved towards her.

'Perhaps you can help me with something...?' she said.

'I, er...'

'Look, I'm friends with some of the girls who, y'know, live around here.' She nodded towards the homeless shelter, making her point. 'There's this guy who comes around the streets at night, offering money and trying to get the women to go with him in his car. My lot always say no – we look out for each other – but there are other girls, younger ones, who don't know what's what. I always worry they might say yes.'

Jessica turned to look at the web of alleys and streets behind. There were boarded-up shopfronts and a web of cut-throughs heading in all directions. Lots of places for people to shelter.

'*Your* lot?' Jessica repeated.

Fran didn't expand. 'Look, can you help or not? You say you're police, but—'

'I am.'

'So can you help?'

'I don't...' Jessica sighed, stumbling over her words. She'd come to Blackpool to look for Bex and somehow inherited a search for a missing Polish couple and now this. Not to mention all her own problems. 'What does this bloke in the car look like?' she asked.

Fran's features brightened. 'He's sort of... normal. Brown hair, thin... y'know... normal.'

That didn't really help.

'I'm not really sure what I can do. Have you tried the Blackpool police?'

She shook her head. 'No way. I don't trust that lot.'

'How come you trust me?'

Fran eyed her from bottom to top. 'You're *different*... d'ya

have a phone? Is that your number on the poster? Can I call
you?' She rattled off the questions in exhausting fashion.

'Yes, no...' Jessica took out the new phone and started
trying to find her new number.

Fran took a mobile from her own back pocket and held it
in her palm expectantly.

'You have a phone?' Jessica asked.

'Most of us do.'

'How do you charge it?'

Fran shrugged. 'I figure it out.' She read out her own
number, telling Jessica to type it into the phone and call her.
Moments later, the device in her hand started ringing. Fran
pressed the reject button and then looked up. 'We've got each
other's numbers now. I'll call you if I see him, okay?'

'How will I get here in time?'

'If you don't, you don't – but he cruises around for a while,
sometimes an hour at a time.'

Jessica repocketed her phone, wishing she'd said 'no'. She
took another step backwards and, this time, Fran didn't follow.
Instead, she flicked her head up.

'You really miss her, don't ya?' she said.

From nowhere, there was a lump in Jessica's throat. In all
the time that had passed since Bex had disappeared, with all
the people she'd spoken to, all the questions she'd asked, no
one had ever pointed out the obvious.

'Yes,' Jessica replied with a gulp.

'You f'real?'

'What do you want me to say?'

Fran continued staring at her for a moment, features
unreadable, and then she broke into a smile. She practically
skipped on the spot, reaching forward and looping her arm
through Jessica's. 'Come on, then. I'll take you on a tour of the
real 'Pool and we'll ask around about Bex. You're not going to

get much sense by yourself – not walking around looking like that.'

Jessica allowed herself to be dragged for a few steps. She peered down at her plain trousers and jacket. 'What's wrong with how I look?'

'It's how you stand, honey. All uptight and full of questions. Now, come with me and let's see what we can find out.'

FIFTEEN

Fran was a walking, talking guidebook for everything that wasn't on the official Blackpool tour. She steered Jessica well away from the tower, the piers and the promenade, gliding along a string of alleyways and inlets in a direction Jessica was pretty sure was taking them away from the sea.

'Are we heading away from the centre?' Jessica asked.

Fran still had a hold of her arm and was hustling along a cobbled path. 'You're smarter than you look.'

They slipped into a darkened ginnel with gloomy tree branches hanging low, dousing it in thick shadow. Jessica felt a moment of worry, but it was quickly gone as Fran sneaked through a gap in a sodden fence by lifting a rotting panel. They passed alongside a tall chain-link fence with train tracks on the other side and then emerged onto what looked like a dead-end cul-de-sac. More trees swayed above, leaving them in a heavy darkness as Fran let go of Jessica's arm and strode forward, crouching through a gap in a second fence and heading into an overgrown garden. The out-of-control grass was damp with dew or rain that hadn't had a chance to dry because of the eclipsing fence and trees. The ground was slightly mushy, but Jessica could feel a trail of small stones underfoot. They were following a well-trodden path.

Without waiting for Jessica, Fran approached a wooden door at the back of a house and knocked four times, pausing for a second and then rapping twice more. There was a clunk, a click and then the door swung inwards.

Fran turned back to Jessica, grinning as she stepped into the house. 'Come on then.'

Jessica ducked unnecessarily, almost walking into the back of Fran, who had removed her deerstalker, freeing a mane of very light hair. It was hard to tell if it was grey or blonde. As she took off her shoes, she grinned up at Jessica.

'Welcome to the Shanty,' she said.

It took Jessica a few moments to adjust to the dim lights. They were in a large carpeted living room, with pillows, cushions and throws lining the walls. A window at the front was blocked by a large piece of chipboard, with a crumbling sofa pressed against it. There were eight or nine women sitting around, all looking at her. Two of them were eating from tins; another was reading a battered paperback directly underneath the bulb in the corner.

'Say "hi",' Fran said chirpily.

'Er... hi,' Jessica said.

No one replied.

'Shoes off,' Fran said, pointing towards a neat row of footwear against the wall next to the door through which they'd come. Jessica tugged hers off and added them to the end of the line.

Fran took Jessica's arm again and pulled her through a side door into a kitchen. There was no fridge or cooker, but there was a microwave, toaster and kettle atop a blueish sideboard. The window was boarded up, but a yellowing bulb glowed above. Fran clicked on the kettle and then leaned against the sink.

'Where are we?' Jessica asked.

'I told you – the Shanty.'

Fran grinned. With her hair loose around her shoulders, she seemed a different person, freer and happier. It was definitely grey, almost white. Fran unhooked a hair tie from her wrist and tugged the silver strands into a ponytail.

'What's the Shanty?' Jessica said.

'It's a safe place. No one knows we're here and that's how we'd like to keep it.'

'You're squatting?'

It had popped out before Jessica had thought about what she was saying. Sometimes it was hard to be off-duty.

Fran grimaced for a moment, but it disappeared in an instant. 'No... well, maybe. The problem with squatters is that they're brazen about it. They annoy the neighbours, they make noise, they taunt the homeowners. With the new laws, the police come in and boot them out. The Shanty is different. We only usually arrive or leave when it's dark, or when we're sure there's nobody around. We have rules, too. No drugs. No men. No noise. We look out for one another.'

Now it had been pointed out, Jessica realised that everyone in the living room had been female.

'Why no men?' she asked.

This time the frown lasted longer on Fran's face. 'Why would you ask that? I said "no drugs" – you could've asked why we don't allow drugs.'

'I suppose, well... excuse the cliché – but drugs are usually bad.'

'And men?'

'Men aren't all bad.'

They stared at one another, Jessica afraid to add anything else in case she dropped herself in it. Fran's features were unmoving, unreadable.

'This place was abandoned,' Fran eventually said. 'Don't

you think it's immoral that there are all these empty houses, yet people have to live rough?'

Jessica didn't want to antagonise her: 'I suppose.'

'All these buy-to-let scumbags. They got houses below market price when Thatcher sold council homes off dirt-cheap, then flogged them on for huge profits. But what about us lot who were too young for all of that? We got screwed by the government, by the system. Now you have kids saving up for years so they can buy some two-bedroom rat-hole off some bloated fat Tory who kept voting Thatcher.' She spat in the sink. 'Fucking Tories. Fucking Blair. Bastards, the lot of them.'

Jessica bit her tongue to stop herself speaking. She wasn't sure how she felt about any of that but doubted replying would make it better.

The tension was broken with the click of the kettle. Fran opened a cupboard door and took out a pair of chipped mugs. She poured in some long-life milk, dropped in a teabag from a large bag of PG Tips and then swilled it around with the water, using the same teabag to make both. She passed Jessica across one, saying far more softly: 'We're out of sugar.' She pushed past Jessica through the door and added: 'Come on, let's go and introduce you.'

Back in the living room, Fran and Jessica sat on a pile of cushions in the corner underneath one of two uplighter lamps. They were by themselves, though in a single room containing nine people, there was little degree of privacy.

Fran plumped up a pair of pillows and leaned backwards, cradling her tea. Jessica copied until they were pressed closely together.

'There are all sorts of girls here,' Fran said. 'Some lost their jobs, some fell out with their parents. Some got pregnant but things didn't work out. Everyone has a story.' She raised her voice, 'Hey, Ruth – come and say hello.'

The young woman in the opposite corner who was reading

underneath the other lamp clambered to her feet. She was late-thirties with short brown hair, wearing a large sweatshirt with 'Green Bay' across the front. She offered a weak smile as she sat next to Fran, resting her head on the younger woman's shoulder.

Fran introduced them both by name.

'Hey,' Ruth said.

'Hi,' Jessica replied.

'Show her your photo,' Fran said.

Jessica unfolded the poster of Bex and passed it across.

Ruth held it under the light and stared, but shook her head. 'Never seen her,' she said, handing it back. 'Sorry.'

'Thanks for looking.'

Ruth seemed uncomfortable making eye contact. She nuzzled further onto Fran's shoulder, gaze firmly on the floor. 'What's it like out there today?' she asked.

'Quiet,' Fran replied.

'Good.'

There was a moment of silence and then Fran added: 'Can I tell her?'

Jessica thought Fran was talking to her, but it was Ruth who answered. 'Sure.'

'Ruth's a smart, smart cookie,' Fran said. A hint of a smile crept around the corner of Ruth's mouth. 'She was running a business creating banners, labels, stickers – all sorts like that – when her boyfriend and business partner upped sticks and took the money off to Spain. He left her tens of thousands in debt. There were bailiffs, repossessions...' She tailed off, flicking her shoulder slightly to make Ruth sit up. 'But you came through it, dint ya, honey?'

Ruth's smile had shrunk and she picked up her paperback again. 'I think I want to get on with my book.'

Fran squeezed her arm and then jumped to her feet, indicating for Jessica to do the same. 'C'mon – I'll give you the tour.'

Jessica followed her out of the living room into an unlit hallway. She heard the creak of the stairs before she saw them and then fumbled for the banister, trailing Fran upstairs. Through her socks, it felt like bare wood underfoot, but there was no light to tell for sure. By the time Jessica's eyes had started to adjust to the gloom, they were on the landing and Fran was knocking on a scratched wooden door off to the side. A muffled 'come in' sounded and then Fran led Jessica inside.

Three single mattresses were resting against one wall, with a fourth against the opposite wall. A steel-frame bed was pushed into an alcove, while, against the final wall, there was a pair of wardrobes. The window was boarded up, like all the others, but a bulb glowed above the centre of the room, leaving curved shadows in the corners. Jessica's eyes were beginning to hurt from the effort of straining. The whole house was cloaked in the same dim yellowness of ancient thirty-watt bulbs, the type of which Jessica's dad – probably many dads – used to have in their shed.

A waif of a girl was sitting cross-legged on the bed reading a tattered *Vogue* magazine. She had long black hair that was held backwards by a green stripy bandana.

'This is Ellie,' Fran said. 'Ellie, meet Jessica.'

They said 'hi' to one another and then Fran sat next to Ellie on the bed.

'Ellie is the *real* genius of this operation, aren't you, honey?' Ellie bit her bottom lip, but it wasn't enough to disguise the smile. She was younger than Fran, perhaps still a teenager. 'Ellie's our in-house electrician. She's the one who got the lights working again, plus hooked up the power so we can make toast, use the microwave and charge our phones.' Fran winked at Jessica, answering that particular unspoken question from before.

'It wasn't that hard,' Ellie said.

Fran patted her on the back and then stood up again. 'Rubbish – without Ell, we'd be in the dark. We'd have to take the boards off the windows and then people would know we were here. She saved us all.'

Ellie grinned wider, saying nothing.

'Show her your poster,' Fran told Jessica.

Ellie gazed at the picture of Bex but soon shook her head, offering a whispered 'sorry'.

'You'll keep an eye out, yeah?' Fran asked.

'Course.'

'Good girl. We'll leave you be.'

'We need some spare fuses,' Ellie said as Fran headed towards the bedroom door.

Fran turned back: 'No problem, honey. I'll see what I can do.'

Back on the landing, with the door closed, Fran lowered her voice, leaning in so that only Jessica could hear. 'She's twenty-two. Bit of a daddy's girl when she was a kid – into DIY and fixing things. Her parents died when she was a teenager, but she'd got herself together and was training as an electrician. That's when her husband raped her. She went to the police but they botched the tests. She had nowhere left to go and ended up on the streets.' She stopped to catch Jessica's eye. 'Still think we should trust the police?' Fran paused. 'Or men?'

'Not all men are like that,' Jessica whispered back, but Fran had already made her mind up.

'Maybe in your world.'

She broke into a forced smile and crossed the landing, knocking on a second door and getting a 'come in'. The second bedroom was much like the first, with two more wardrobes, one double bed, one single and a pair of mattresses on the floor. Someone had painted a series of swirls and swishes on the walls as well as a spiralling pattern of flowers. There was a table in the centre covered with unlit candles and an incense stick. A woman was lying on the double bed. She was the oldest Jessica had seen in the house – probably fifty-something, with a straggle of grey-black hair. She took out a pair of earphones and sat up.

'Oh, hi...' she said, eyeing Jessica.

'This is Jessica,' Fran said cheerily. 'Jessica, this is Melissa – Mel. She's a massive star of the household. She's like a mum to everyone. It wouldn't be the same without her.'

Melissa smiled weakly. She had large shoulders bulging through a thin long-sleeved top and a tattoo on her neck. She yawned, flapping a hand in front of her mouth. 'Couldn't sleep last night.'

'We'll leave you be,' Fran replied, brushing Melissa's arm and then motioning to Jessica for the poster. 'Can you look at this first?' she added.

Melissa eyed the picture of Bex but shook her head. 'Not seen her,' she said, lying back onto the bed.

Fran and Jessica headed into the hallway, clicking the door quietly closed behind them. Fran leaned in, lowering her voice again. 'Mel was in the army. She had PTS and a breakdown. Ended up on the streets. No one wanted to help, so we brought her here. We're her only family. You've gotta look after each other.'

She pushed her way into what turned out to be the bathroom. The ceramic bath was crusted with limescale and, because of a missing tap, there was a pair of pliers attached to the spindle sticking out of the top. The tiles had once been white but were now crusted with brown and the sealant was peeling away. Against the wall was a line of shampoo bottles and a small stack of colourful soaps.

Fran sat on the corner of the bath, nodding for Jessica to close the door. There wasn't much room, but Jessica went with it, figuring this was one of the few places in the house that people could talk in private.

'You know nobody cares about us, don't you?' Fran said.

Jessica wanted to argue but had no idea what to say. As a group, perhaps that was true; as individuals, Fran certainly believed that.

'The council couldn't give a shit, the government don't care as long as we're not on their unemployment statistics, the police want us off the streets so it all looks nice and tidy. We're the forgotten.'

'Someone must care.'

'Who?'

'I don't know, I... there's that homeless shelter where I met you...'

Fran shrugged. 'That's, what, twenty beds? Do you know how many there are living on the streets?'

Jessica shook her head.

'Hundreds – and that's at the moment. In the summer, there are all these fake homeless, begging for money from tourists and making a living.'

'Really?'

'*Really.*'

'That's just... wrong.'

Fran rolled her eyes. 'That's life. You telling me Manchester's any different?'

'I guess not.'

Fran held out her arms, not needing to say 'I told you so'.

'What about you?' Jessica asked.

The other woman peered away, folding her arms. 'Huh?'

'How did you come here?'

Fran opened her mouth but clucked her tongue into her teeth, weighing Jessica up, then she held out a hand. 'Look, if you give me some of those posters, then I'll ask around about your friend, but I'm pretty sure she's not in 'Pool.'

'Why'd you say that?'

'Because I know a lot of the girls around town – even the ones who don't live here.' She took a handful of the posters from Jessica. 'You know I've trusted you big time, don't you?'

Jessica nodded. 'I know. I appreciate it.'

'You've got to keep quiet about this place.'

'I don't even know where we are.'

'Good.' Fran stood up. 'You should go.'

Jessica felt it was time, too. She had a strange sense about the house... the Shanty. It was hard to explain, but it was almost religious, as if there was something special happening here bringing the vulnerable women together. They had a bond that Jessica wasn't a part of. Fran was the glue keeping them all united. She'd called Ruth a 'smart cookie', Ellie a 'genius', and Melissa a 'star'. Everyone would have a nickname and be made to feel special because that's what they needed.

'Call me if you see that man again,' Jessica said, patting the phone in her pocket.

'I will, honey,' Fran replied, taking Jessica's arm once again. 'And if you ever need me, you know my number.'

SIXTEEN

Jessica wasn't sure if Fran deliberately took her on a labyrinth loop away from the Shanty to conceal its location, but, either way, she had no idea where she was. By the time Fran said goodbye and pointed Jessica in the direction of the tower, the dark clouds had flowed over the top of the town and the sun was blocked from view. It was late-afternoon but already getting dark. In the distance, the illuminations glowed; the tower sparkled. Tourists would be cruising up and down, stopping in the arcades and the cafés. That was the overground world, but she had now seen the underground. Two worlds living atop one another.

She found her way back to the Prince Hotel, where Brandon was standing behind the reception counter, tapping away on his phone. He offered a brief 'hi' and then returned to what he was doing as Jessica headed up the stairs.

As soon as she opened the door to room seven, Jessica felt something was wrong. She stood on the threshold, half in, half out, scanning the space. The curtains were still open; the *Best of Blackpoo* book was on the counter... but there were little things. Jessica had left a pile of newly bought folded clothes on the chair but they now seemed slightly crumpled. The second pair of shoes, her work ones with the slight heel, were lined up perpendicular to the wall, when she had simply kicked them off. The maid had been in to make the bed – but would she have moved Jessica's notepad from the bedside table onto the bed itself?

Jessica edged into the room, looking for other signs that somebody had been through her things – but she had brought so few possessions that it was hard to tell. Anything important had been in her bag with her. There was a noise behind, in the corridor, and Jessica spun to see a short woman in a white cleaner's uniform heading for the stairs.

'Hi,' Jessica said, moving out of the room.

The maid had slightly tanned skin and dark, wiry hair. She was wearing a light purple uniform, the shade of those grim Parma Violet sweets. Jessica had always hated them – she'd never met anyone who liked them – and had an aversion to the colour. The maid stared at her with wide brown eyes. 'No English,' she said with an Eastern European accent.

Jessica pointed towards her room, sweeping up with an invisible broom like someone playing charades. Or like a nutter on the streets. 'Did you clean in there?'

'No English.'

Before Jessica could ask anything else, the maid bowed her head and hurried down the stairs. Jessica waited for a couple of minutes and then unclicked the catch on the bedroom door, locking it behind her. She returned to reception, leaning on the counter and getting Brandon's attention.

'Everything all right?' he asked.

'Not too bad.'

'The police were in, I thought—'

'It was a misunderstanding. They thought I'd seen something, but there wasn't much I could tell them. It's all sorted.'

'Oh... good stuff. I've never talked to the police before. It was all a bit, well... exciting.'

'I suppose it can get a bit dull around here... how many guests do you have staying in the hotel at the moment?'

He put down his phone, humming as he thought about it. 'Not many – six or seven.'

'And there can't be many staff around for those numbers?'

'There's a few maids who do all the hotels on this rank, plus the kitchen lot. There's Mr Eckhart, too. It's usually quite quiet by this time of day.'

Jessica grinned. 'You've got the place to yourself then?'

'I suppose.'

She turned to go back up the stairs and then stopped, patting her pockets but being careful not to accidentally jangle the room key. 'Shite, I've left my key in the room and locked myself out.'

Brandon smirked at her. 'It happens to someone at least once a day. Hang on.'

Jessica moved quickly once he'd gone into the back room. She shuffled around to the far end of the counter, giving her a clear view through the door. Brandon was standing a couple of metres away next to a safe that was at chest height on a shelf. He made no effort to conceal what he was doing, typing '1', '2', '3' and '4' into the front panel and then levering it open. Jessica quickly sidestepped back to where she was as he turned and moved back to the main desk.

'What are you grinning about?' Jessica teased.

'Skeleton key,' he said with a flirty wink. 'I always get a bit excited at using it.'

'There's only one actual key per room?'

'There are three – one for the guest, two in the back office, plus two skeleton keys that fit all doors. The maid has to sign the key in and out every morning. She's just returned it now.'

Brandon edged around the counter and headed for the stairs, key thrust in front of him like a knight with a lance.

'The maid said she didn't speak English,' Jessica said.

Brandon peered conspiratorially over both shoulders and then leaned in to whisper. 'I don't think Mr Eckhart likes foreigners. He's always going on about them coming over here and all that. Doesn't stop him hiring 'em, though. Lower wages, probably. I think the cleaners are Polish.'

When they reached room seven, he unlocked the door and then swung it open for her.

'Your palace awaits,' he grinned. 'Keep hold of your key in future, yeah?'

Jessica almost reached for it in her pocket, but she stopped herself, brushing his hand with hers as if she hadn't meant to. 'Will do.'

SEVENTEEN

Jessica waited until she'd heard Brandon's retreating footsteps and then closed and locked the door behind her. She checked under the bed, in the drawers and the wardrobe, looking for anything... *different*. She wasn't sure what. When she found nothing, Jessica refolded the clothes on the chair, returned the notepad to the nightstand and then lay on the bed. Aside from the maid, someone else had been in the room. There might not have been many of her possessions to go through, but whoever had entered wouldn't have known that. Whoever it was had access to the safe behind reception, meaning it was likely either Brandon or the owner, Luke Eckhart. It might have been Brandon – but she doubted it.

She crossed to peer out of the bay window towards the phone booth that had started all this. It was still there, unassuming and probably unused. It wasn't quite evening, but there was a hazy greyness clinging to the edge of the town. The sea was a murky black, the sand a damp brown. The twinkling lights glistened at the other end of the prom, but it was truly dank.

Jessica sat, watching as a white van in the car park tooted

its horn. In unison, five women in matching violet uniforms hurried across the tarmac from the rank of hotels. The van was speckled with a crust of mud along its bottom half, but there were no other markings. One by one, the women helped each other into the back of the van, before the doors clanged shut. There was a screech of tyres and then the vehicle shot off, doughnutting around the car park and then joining the main road without indicating. Jessica wrote the number plate across the top of one of the posters with Bex's photo. It was probably some sort of agency providing cleaners around town, but there had been so much weirdness in her life over the past couple of days that she figured she never knew when it might come in handy.

She plugged her new phone into the wall and switched the old one back on. It blinked and beeped its way to life and then flashed through half a dozen missed calls, none of which were from numbers she recognised. There was a voicemail from Darren, saying that he'd shown her posters around, but that was it. Jessica wondered if the missed calls were from people who'd seen her posters, who might have seen Bex. She called the first, but there was a recorded message saying that she'd been called by the bank and, if she could let them know when she'd be available, they'd get back to her. Caller numbers two and three didn't answer, while number four was a telemarketing company. Typical, really.

Jessica was about to set the phone to charge when the screen flashed and it started to ring. The number was someone's mobile but not one she recognised.

'Hello?' Jessica said.

'Oh, er, hi...' It was a young woman's voice and, for a moment, Jessica thought it was Bex. It had the same mix of youth and wisdom, with the hint of a northern accent. 'I, er, saw your poster,' the voice continued.

It wasn't Bex.

Jessica felt a twinge in her chest, a thump of defeat, before she realised what the call might mean. 'Oh, right,' she said. 'Have you seen her?'

'Who is she?'

'She's my friend. She's been missing for a few months.'

The voice coughed, sounding nervous. 'I don't know her name, but I think I've seen her around.'

'Where?'

'I, um...' Another cough. 'I don't really want to talk on the phone. Can we meet?'

If there had been alarm bells in the room, they'd have been off the charts, with huge orange lights flashing on and off.

'I don't have any money if that's what you're after,' Jessica replied.

'I don't want money.'

'Why can't you tell me on the phone?'

'It's complicated. I'd rather show you.'

'Show me what?'

The voice sighed. 'Look, if you don't want to meet, then we don't have to. I was trying to be nice. I—'

'No, wait.' Jessica didn't want her to hang up. 'Okay, fine. We can meet. Are you in Blackpool?'

'Yes. Do you want to meet in the centre somewhere? On that square bit next to the tower. Seven o'clock. I'll wear a red coat.'

'All right. I'm Jessica, by the way. What's your name?'

Jessica waited for the reply but it never came. It took her a moment to realise the other person had hung up. It didn't seem right, didn't *sound* right, and yet Jessica had brought this on herself by posting her phone number so publicly. It could turn out to be some sort of robbery, but the caller had suggested a very public place. Would she lead Jessica to somewhere deserted and then do who knew what? Would she have people lying in wait?

Or perhaps she really had seen Bex around?

Meeting whoever had called on the square next to the tower wouldn't be too big a deal and there would likely be people around. Jessica could refuse to go anywhere until the girl had told her what she knew. If it was a scam, the girl would take off.

There was only one way to find out.

The evening wasn't as chilly as when Jessica had first arrived, with the wind finally taking a night off. Given the time of year, it was perfectly pleasant, with barely even a need for a jacket. Jessica headed along the prom, now as familiar with the local layout of the streets as she was with the area around her house in Manchester. As she reached a roundabout, there was a small crowd of people, pointing and using their phones to film a man who was pacing around the circumference of the central reservation. He was pumping a banner up and down into the air, with 'HIRE ME' emblazoned across the front and a phone number underneath.

She stopped to watch him for a few moments as most of the rest of the crowd moved on, easily entertained. Jessica didn't know what to say, so she was about to get going when four vest-wearing thugs with big shoulders swaggered into place next to her. Two of them were drinking from cans of lager while another cradled a cardboard case of beer under his arms.

'Look at this bell-end,' one of them sniggered. He was bald, veins throbbing in his pitbull neck as he raised his voice, shouting at the man on the roundabout. 'Oi, you!'

The man with the banner turned. He was likely still a teenager, rakish, but wearing a suit with shined shoes and smart, smoothed-down hair. By acknowledging their presence, he'd already got himself in trouble.

'What you doin'?' Pitbull shouted.

'Nothing...'

'You want a job?'

'Er, yeah...'

Pitbull reeled back and lobbed the can of lager towards the teenager. He jumped out of the way, but it slammed into the ground, exploding and spraying him with beer. In an instant, the other man with a can threw his too. This time it thwacked into the teenager, exploding on his back in a fountain of foam.

'Wa-hey!' Pitbull shouted. One of his friends took out a can from the crate and rocked back, but Pitbull wrenched the beer from his grasp. 'Don't be a prick – this has got to last us all night.' He blew a kiss at Jessica and then cracked open the can, swaggering along the prom as if he had a pair of grapefruits between his legs.

A few cars continued around the roundabout as if nothing had happened, but when there was a break, Jessica crossed the road until she was on the central area with the young man. When he turned and saw her, he flinched away until she held up her hands.

'It's okay,' she said.

He was gulping back tears as he packed his banner down into a bag. There was beer dripping from the back of his hair, running along the seam of his suit. 'Bastards,' he muttered.

'Do you need a hand?'

He shook his head. 'I'm going home. I knew this was a stupid idea.'

'Whose idea was it?'

He stood up, trying – and failing – to brush down his sopping jacket. 'Mine. There are no jobs around here. I worked in a hotel over the summer and my girlfriend was in a café. We both got laid off last month. I don't want much – just something that pays minimum wage – but there are all these cheap foreigners over here.' He humped the bag over his shoulder and it squelched into his back. 'You know of anything going?'

Jessica shook her head. 'Sorry.'

'Fine.'

Without another word, he stomped off, heading away from the lights, away from the prom, into the darkened back streets of the town. Jessica watched him go, admiring the effort.

She made her way back to the prom and then crossed over when she reached the tower. There were more people out compared to the evening she'd been in this area with Peter Salisbury. Some kid was lumping around an oversized dinosaur that was twice the size of him, with many more scoffing ice creams and candyfloss as they excitedly made their way up and down.

Jessica continued to the square next to the tower, sitting on a bench and waiting. A steady stream of people was heading towards the nearby theatres, tickets clutched, best shoes on. Some kids were loitering in a shop doorway passing a cigarette between them, before getting bored and moving onto their next place. A woman with a scruffy supermarket bag for life overflowing with clothes asked Jessica if she had any change. A man asked her for a light.

There was no girl in red. Five to seven. Seven o'clock. Five past. Ten past. Nobody came. Nobody rang. Jessica tried calling the number that had contacted her, but there was no answer. Quarter past. Twenty past.

Jessica waited until it was a few minutes after eight. The theatre crowd had disappeared to watch their shows, the tourists were either back in their hotels, or out having a meal somewhere. The square was quiet and Jessica was alone.

EIGHTEEN

Jessica was struggling to sleep in the hotel bed. It wasn't uncomfortable as such, but it wasn't hers. The mattress was softer, the pillows squishier, and it didn't smell of home. She wasn't a great sleeper at the best of times, and this was only making matters worse. Jessica woke up half a dozen times through the night, wondering where she was and then forcing her eyes closed in a desperate hunt for a bit more kip. She eventually gave up at half past seven, checking both phones to see that nobody had bothered contacting her and then heading downstairs for breakfast.

Luke Eckhart was behind the reception desk, still single-finger typing on his keyboard. His shirt was unbuttoned even lower than the previous time Jessica had seen him and the abundance of chest hair made it look like he'd taken up rug-smuggling. He tugged at his moustache and scowled up at her, which she figured was probably a standard greeting as opposed to one he reserved specifically for her. Other than them, everything was quiet.

'Morning,' Jessica said cheerily.

'Yeah,' he replied, peering back down.

'How are things?'

'Fine.'

'I was wondering...' she waited for him to acknowledge her, 'which of the hotels are the best?'

'What?'

Jessica motioned towards the rank they were on. 'You own a few of these hotels, don't you? Is this the best one to stay in?'

He clenched his teeth together. 'They're all tip-top.'

Perhaps shit-top, she thought.

'Do you live nearby?' she asked.

His forehead creased into a V of overlapping valleys. 'Bit nosy aren't you?'

'Sorry.' Jessica reached into her pocket and took out two twenty-pound notes. 'I wanted to pay for another night. Cash okay?'

Ching-ching! His eyes sparkled like a jackpot machine.

'I only wanted to make sure I'm staying in the best possible place,' she added.

'You won't do better than here,' he said, somehow managing to keep a straight face. He licked his lips, stretching for the cash as Jessica passed it across. He offered something close to a smile and then disappeared into the office and quickly back out again. He seemed as if he was about to say something when the door swung open and two women in purple maid uniforms walked in. They each dropped their heads, not making eye contact as they went through the connecting door into the café.

Jessica took a step backwards to give herself an angle to see through the front door. She heard the snarl of the engine before she saw it, but the white van was again tearing off the car park towards the main road.

Eckhart was frowning once more. 'Same time tomorrow?' he grunted, trying to sound inviting, even though his facial features weren't matching his words.

'Probably,' Jessica replied, stepping away and heading for the breakfast room.

An older couple who were up from Cardiff for a week were the only other guests present. They were staying in the Excalibur next door and proceeded to tell Jessica that they had been coming to Blackpool every summer for the past forty-nine years. She wasn't sure whether to congratulate or commiserate, but they seemed happy enough.

'It's where we came for our honeymoon,' Bronwen said.

'Is it better now or then?' Jessica asked, after finishing a mushy mound of black pudding.

Bronwen looked to her husband, Alf, who scratched his greying head. 'Bit of both,' they replied in perfect unison before taking each other's hand. They told Jessica of how the seafront used to look, before the wall was built; of the ancient trams; the fairground music that used to hang on the breeze and the way every square inch of beach was claimed during the summer months. They'd started coming in the winter a decade ago, put off by the noise and heat of July and August.

For a short while, Jessica forgot everything else that was going on. She happily ate, drank tea and allowed herself to be charmed by the older couple with a lifetime of stories. It was only when they started bickering in the way that only elderly couples could that Jessica remembered how much she had to do.

'I've not eaten butter in years,' Alf said, holding the incriminating tiny tub of butter in the air.

'Yes you have,' Bronwen replied.

'No, margarine. That poly-statue stuff.'

'We have butter in the fridge at home.'

'Since when?'

'Since always.'

Alf rocked back in his seat, eyes wide with shock as if he'd just found out he'd won the lottery. 'I don't even like the stuff—'

It might have been rude, but Jessica cut in before the great butter–margarine debate could rage any longer. 'Can I ask you a question?' she said.

Bronwen and Alf both turned to face her, argument forgotten in an instant. 'Of course, dear,' he said.

'What are the rooms like in the Excalibur?'

They peered at each other again, before both replying: 'It's fine.'

'Well, it's not bad,' Alf added.

'We've been in better,' Bronwen chipped in.

'It's clean,' he said.

'Always clean,' she confirmed.

'They could do with better biscuits,' Alf said, earning a small backhanded clip across his arm.

'The maid never says "hi",' Bronwen said. 'I don't think she speaks English. Still, it's cheap.'

'Cheap and cheerful,' Alf said.

'That it is.'

Jessica thanked them for the time and was about to return to the table containing small cereal boxes when the door leading to the Prince opened. The man sauntered across the café, nodded a silent hello to the Welsh couple, and then sat himself at Jessica's table.

'Morning,' he said.

'What do you want?' Jessica asked, knowing Bronwen and Alf were listening to every word.

Detective Chief Inspector Fordham looked at the remains of Jessica's cooked breakfast and the dregs of the bran flakes clinging to the bottom of her bowl. She rarely ate breakfast at home, but stick her in a hotel, include it in the bill, and she'd eat everything going.

'That looks good,' he added.

'You here to have a conversation about breakfast?' Jessica said, not bothering to hide her annoyance.

'Shall we step outside?'

With little choice, Jessica dumped her cutlery in the bowl and stood. She said goodbye to Bronwen and Alf and then followed Fordham out of the front door onto the car park. He was again wearing the long coat and only took his hands out of his pockets to push the door open and hold it for her. He'd had a shave but was really the master at the art of the casual tie. The knot was small and halfway between his top two buttons. Not too high, not too low. A really professional job.

He led Jessica over to the wall on which she'd been sitting when they took her car away. They sat next to each other, facing the sea, listening to the breeze and the waves.

'What have I done this time?' Jessica asked, only half joking.

Fordham sighed, scratching at his chin, mourning for the stubble that was no longer there. 'Do you know the name Sophie Johns?' he asked.

'Never heard of her.'

'She's missing.'

Jessica shook her head. 'I've still never heard of her.'

'Funny,' Fordham replied, sighing once more. 'We've got her mobile phone and the last number she called was yours. The last person who called her was also you.' He turned sideways, waiting for Jessica to do the same. 'Want to explain that?'

NINETEEN

Jessica explained that she had given out some flyers in the town centre, asking for people to call if they'd seen Bex. The girl now identified as Sophie had done just that: they'd arranged to meet by Blackpool Tower the previous evening, and then Sophie hadn't turned up. A simple explanation, easy-peasy, where's the problem?

She unfurled one of the flyers and passed it across. Fordham eyed it, turning it over to look at the blank rear and then folded it into his own pocket.

'It's really not your week, is it?' he said without a hint of humour.

Jessica didn't reply. She was rocking on the wall, lifting her feet off the pavement and trying to balance using only her arse. She felt like she had to be doing something with her body because her mind couldn't figure out what was going on. The first time, with Peter Salisbury, might have been a coincidence. Now that a second person had disappeared having last been in contact with her, it could only be a concerted attempt to frame her. Someone knew how to play her – and they were doing it perfectly.

Fordham let the silence sit for a few seconds and then couldn't help himself: 'Sophie was working at the Honky Tonk Diner yesterday,' he said.

'Where's that?'

'Down the street from the Winter Gardens – it's hard to miss with the oversized electric guitar sticking out of the top.'

Jessica remembered walking past it without clocking what it was called. It was in the centre, easily within walking distance of Blackpool Tower.

'That was the last time anyone saw her,' Fordham added. 'She called you within minutes of finishing her shift. You're the last person she contacted. We got the call from her parents late last night. Usually, we'd wait to see if she went home – but they had that phone tracker thing.' He wafted a hand in the air. 'You have that on your phone?'

'I went through a stage of always losing it, so I set up my laptop to make it ring.'

He patted his pocket. 'Bloody clever these things. In the old days, we'd have left it and then scratched around trying to find her. Anyway, her parents hadn't heard from her, so did that "find my phone" thing. They traced it to some side street close to the Honky Tonk. When they went down there, they found the phone in a wheelie bin, but no sign of their daughter. That's when they called us. One thing led to another and here I am.'

'Here you are,' Jessica whispered.

'That's two people: one dead, one missing. The connection is you.'

Jessica was shaking her head.

'Then there's your other friend, too – what's her name?'

'Bex.'

'Rebecca Kellock. She's been missing for three months now.'

The sound of Bex's full name made Jessica shiver. She'd

only heard it once or twice in the past and it was too official, too real. Rebecca Kellock wasn't the name of the girl with whom she'd lived.

'The only reason I'm here is because I'm looking for Bex,' Jessica said.

Fordham nodded and she wondered if he was thinking what she would be if the roles were reversed.

'It's too clean,' Jessica said. She waited for him to reply, holding her breath, hoping he'd nod and say she was right. He said nothing.

From the centre, there was a gentle hum of traffic. Ahead, over the sea wall, there were waves licking at the shore. Nearby, there was a click-click-click of the Big One roller coaster being hoisted into the sky, ready to hurl the train down its steep incline. Jessica hadn't even realised it was open at this time of year. She wondered if they were testing it.

They sat in silence listening to the resort. She willed Fordham to break the impasse, but he was better at this game than she was.

'Someone's trying to make me look bad,' she eventually said.

'Who?'

'I don't know.'

'Do you have enemies?'

'We all do, don't we? Especially in this job.'

'Want to give me any names?'

Jessica thought of the people she'd helped to put away over the years: Randall Anderson, Dennis Doherty, Edward Marks. Then there were the ones who got away: Brenda Gale, Zippo-rah, the Hyde family, plus Pomeroy and his cronies. Where would she even start?

'I don't know,' she said.

Jessica was suddenly aware of Fordham's breathing. There

was a slight tickle at the top of his throat, as if he had a secret cigar habit. In and out. In and out.

'We've got the post-mortem back on Peter Salisbury,' he said. 'He was stabbed in the neck – but we already knew that. The person managed to get close to him – someone he knew, trusted, or was comfortable with. They were standing in front of him, a little shorter but not too much.'

In other words, someone close to her height.

'They're still picking over the body for DNA.'

Fordham glanced across to her, not needing to ask the question.

'I've never denied I was with him,' Jessica replied. 'There might be one of my hairs stuck to him.'

'Someone swabbed him with bleach. He or she knew what they were doing, knew how to hide any trace of what they'd done.'

'It wasn't me.'

'This person had seen bodies before. They knew how to tidy up their handiwork.'

'It's not me.'

Jessica was too late to catch the repetition.

Fordham turned to face her. For a moment Jessica thought he was going to take her hand as he angled forward. Instead, he twisted the face of his watch and leaned backwards, waiting for Jessica to hold his gaze.

'What's going to happen if Sophie turns up dead?' he asked.

'I didn't kill anyone. Why would I?'

'We're still waiting on those blood results from your car, plus we're looking into Sophie's final movements. Why did she call you?'

'I told you – she'd seen my poster of Bex and she wanted to meet.'

Fordham pushed himself up and straightened his long

coat. He tightened the knot of his tie but didn't bother to move it any higher on his neck. When he put his hands in his trouser pockets, the tails of his coat were caught by the breeze and flapped behind him. He'd make a good silhouette.

'Don't go anywhere near Sophie Johns' parents,' he said. 'This is me *telling* you that they're off limits. No grey areas, no misunderstandings. If you try to talk to them, you'll be arrested and we'll keep you in. Understand?'

Jessica stared past him towards the ocean. 'Absolutely.'

TWENTY

With his point made, Fordham sauntered off along the promenade, hands still in his pockets. Jessica concluded that if he wasn't playing with himself through the trouser material, then the most serious relationship in his life must be between him and the mirror. He really did have a look-at-me vibe about him, like some bloke wearing a bright green suit at a wedding. There was always one. He probably spent fifteen minutes getting his tie into the perfect position every morning. She could imagine criminals – *real* criminals – absolutely hating him.

Jessica watched him walk away, wondering if he'd turn to look at her, but he didn't. After a couple of minutes, he disappeared behind an approaching tram and then she lost him in the crowd. She found him almost impossible to read: friendly one moment; a bit of a dick the next. Perhaps he was playing her, waiting for her guard to drop when he'd trick her into saying something stupid. There was also a chance that he was as bemused as she was, trying to figure out how it all slotted together. He'd definitely be getting it in the neck from some superintendent somewhere.

When she was sure Fordham wouldn't be returning, Jessica headed back into the hotel. She ignored the breakfast room, passed the reception desk without saying anything to Eckhart and continued up the stairs. She was about to head into room seven when she heard a shuffling at the far end of the corridor. A maid was wrestling with a vacuum cleaner, hauling the snaking arm and dragging it through an open doorway among a muffled barrage of what Jessica assumed were foreign expletives. If they weren't, they should be, given the venom with which they were spat.

Jessica made her way slowly along the corridor. After depositing the vacuum cleaner into the room, the maid was facing the other way, trying to yank a cleaning cart backwards. The wheels were stuck on a ridge of carpet and refusing to budge. Jessica rounded the cart and motioned to help, offering to lift the other end. The maid's caterpillar eyebrows rocketed, her dark eyes widening with such fear that Jessica took a step back and held her hands up to show she meant no harm.

'Do you want a hand?' she asked.

'No English.'

Jessica motioned towards lifting the cart again. 'I can lift this end, it's not a problem.'

The maid shook her head furiously. 'No, no, no.'

She was staring at the ground, avoiding any amount of eye contact, so Jessica took the initiative. She hoisted up the back end of the cart and pushed until the wheels bumped over the bulge in the carpet. The maid stepped back, squeaking something in her native tongue.

Jessica again held her hands up, showing her palms. 'No worries, see. Are you okay?'

'No English. No English.'

The maid glanced sideways at her, sneaking a quick peek from the corner of her eye and then looking away again. There was a tiny fraction of a second in which they locked eyes and Jessica saw understanding.

'You can understand me, can't you?' she said.

'No English.'

Jessica delved into her pockets, hunting from one to the other until she found a folded-up flyer with Bex's photo. She held out her arm, ensuring it was in a position where the maid couldn't avoid looking at it.

'Do you know this girl?' Jessica asked.

She expected a shake of the head and another string of 'No English' responses, but the maid's eyebrows again shot upwards, meeting in the middle of her creased forehead. It only took her a second to regain composure, but she'd already given herself away.

'You know her, don't you?' Jessica said, unable to mask the excitement in her voice.

'No English.'

'Was she a guest here?'

'No English.'

Jessica reached forward, placing a hand on the maid's shoulder, hoping to reassure her. It had the opposite effect, with the woman leaping backwards and letting out a small scream.

'No English,' she repeated, far louder this time. 'No English. No English.'

There was a small thump from the top of the stairs and Jessica turned to see Eckhart bounding towards them. His face was red, arms tense as he struggled to control his temper.

'Everything okay here?' he asked, addressing Jessica. She slipped the flyer back into her pocket, hoping he hadn't noticed. 'Is there a problem with your room?' he added.

'Not at all.'

He peered between Jessica and the maid like a headmaster with two naughty students, waiting for one of them to confess.

Neither of them spoke, with the maid smoothing down her uniform and then plucking a towel from the cart, looping it over her arm, ready to get to work.

'I'll get back to my room,' Jessica said, dipping around Eckhart's hand on hip and disappearing through door number seven.

Jessica spent an hour in her room doing very little other than using the Internet on her phone to find out what had been going on in the rest of the world. What she really wanted to do was to talk to the maid further – but she doubted she'd get anything other than the 'No English' response, plus she didn't want to bump into Eckhart again.

When she finally ran out of things with which to amuse herself, Jessica left her room and edged down the stairs. She crouched, peeping towards the reception desk, which was – thankfully – empty. She hurried through the front door onto the car park and then headed to the Saint Andrew's hotel at the furthest end of the rank. There were wooden boards across the entrance, with sooty scorch marks embedded into the sandstone around three of the downstairs windows. As well as the large banners declaring it a hazard, there was an A4 sheet of paper stuck to the wood across the front door. It was covered with transparent tape, protecting it from the elements, and listed the reasons why the hotel had been shut down.

It was full of the type of legalese so adored by councils and public bodies. If a press officer or lawyer threw enough long words at a statement, chances were that normal people wouldn't bother to read it.

From what Jessica could tell, 'significant concerns over the structural integrity of the aforementioned building' seemed to be the most pressing problem. It was probably a fair concern – because getting a good night's sleep would be tough if there was a chance the entire building could come crumbling down on a guest's head.

She skim-read the rest of the information, before she spotted the name at the bottom – Luke Eckhart. He *did* own the place, after all. It was no wonder he was so concerned about money, considering he had a condemned building on his hands. Whether it was knocked down or refurbished, it was going to cost him a few quid.

Jessica moved onto the Seaview Pleasance next door, which had a flashing neon sign in the front window advertising 'vacancies'.

The young woman behind the counter was local and overly enthusiastic about selling the hotel as a place to stay. She was likely still a teenager, probably on minimum wage, definitely overworked, considering the stack of papers behind the counter. Jessica asked her about the price of a night and was offered the same cash discount she'd been given at the Prince. She showed Bex's photo but got a shake of the head and a 'sorry'.

It was a similar story in the Excalibur and the Sunshine Resort: young people manning the front desk, a potential cash discount, no recognition of Bex.

As Jessica emerged from the final hotel into the car park, she turned back towards the Prince, only to see Eckhart standing at the front door. He had both hands on his hips, scowl fixed on her. Jessica turned her back on him, walking slowly across the tarmac towards the seafront. She crossed the road, determined not to look backwards and acknowledge the hotel owner. As she looked up, Jessica realised the phone booth from which Bex had called her was directly in front of her.

Back to the beginning.

Jessica lifted the receiver, dropped in a fifty-pence piece and called her home number. If Eckhart was still watching, then he would have to guess what she was up to. The phone rang and rang, before the answer machine eventually kicked in. Jessica heard her own voice telling the caller to leave a message. It was short and breezy, recorded in a hurry. Her voice was huskier than she realised, deeper, as if she had a cold. Or perhaps she always sounded like that?

She listened, waiting for a couple of minutes, still not turning back towards the hotel. As she listened to the silence on the line, it dawned on Jessica that perhaps Bex had brought her here – specifically *here* – for a reason. Something was going on in Eckhart's hotels that nobody else had noticed. She couldn't explain everything that had happened with Peter Salisbury and Sophie Johns, but, if Bex had stumbled across whatever it was Eckhart was up to, maybe that was why she'd called?

Jessica removed a handful of Bex's flyers from her pocket, searching for the correct one. At the bottom was the sheet on which she'd written the number plate of the white van that dropped off and picked up the maids each morning and afternoon.

At least one of those women knew who Bex was, even if she'd only seen her briefly. Finding out where they were being bussed in and out from would be a good start, but Jessica couldn't go through Izzy. All police checks of the number plate database would be logged and she didn't want to risk getting her friend in trouble.

She needed help from outside the force – which meant it was time to call a face from the past.

TWENTY-ONE

A woman's voice answered the office phone, offering a too chirpy, too self-satisfied 'hello'. Even with the one word, the Mancunian accent was thick.

'Hi,' Jessica replied. 'I'm looking for Andrew Hunter.'

'This is Hunter Investigations,' the voice replied.

'Yes, but I'd actually like to talk *to* Andrew.'

'Mr Hunter is busy right now, but I can help. If you'd like to give me a few details—'

'Is he actually there in the office?'

There was a short pause and then: 'I'm sorry, who's calling...?'

'Tell him it's an old friend.'

There was a ruffling and then the sound of voices muffled by a hand over the receiver. Jessica had no idea to whom she'd been speaking, but if Andrew had a secretary, then he was moving up in the world. The last time she'd met him, he couldn't even afford proper chairs. He was a private investigator who'd entangled himself in one of Jessica's cases involving a teenager that had seemingly killed herself. She thought him a bit clumsy, annoying even, yet there was something about him in that he genuinely seemed to care for the people with whom he was working.

They'd not seen each other in years, but she'd always kept his number, figuring the day might come when she needed a favour.

The stifled sound of chatter on the phone was replaced by a man's voice. 'Hello, this is Andrew Hunter. Can I help you?'

'Wow,' Jessica replied. 'You've *really* been working on your phone manner. That was very posh.'

'Er... who is this?'

'It's your absolute, all-time favourite police inspector. Think incredible charm, Hollywood good looks, rapier wit...'

Silence.

'Is this a wind-up?'

Jessica huffed her annoyance. 'I obviously left a lasting impression then...?'

'Megan?'

'Who the hell's Megan?'

More silence.

'Oh...' he said. 'Jessica.'

'You could sound a little more pleased.'

Andrew either laughed or breathed, it was hard to tell over the phone. The new one Jessica had bought sounded far tinnier than her actual one.

'Everything okay?' he asked.

'Is this line secure?'

He lowered his voice. 'I'm not sure there's much I could do if MI5 are listening in, but we do check for bugs in the office every now and then. What do you want me to say?'

'I need a bit of a favour,' Jessica said. 'You owe me one for not tipping me off about that whole devil cult in the woods thing, so this can make us even.'

This time he definitely laughed. 'Ah, Jessica. I forgot what it was like to work with you. I do keep an eye out for your name in the paper. Every now and then I'll see you there, pulling a face.'

'I don't pull faces.'

'Perhaps that's your "Hollywood good looks"? Anyway, I figured the day might come when I'd hear from you again. What can I do for you?'

Jessica was sitting on the sea wall, a couple of hundred metres past the hotels, well out of sight if Eckhart was still trying to watch her. A handful of tourists were passing up and down the promenade, but nobody was paying her any attention.

'This is going to sound dramatic,' she said, doing her best to make it sound undramatic, 'but someone's out to get me.'

She half expected Andrew to laugh – it *did* sound ridiculous – but he didn't. She could sense the anticipation in his voice.

'Go on,' he replied.

'I'm in Blackpool and things are a mess.'

Jessica spent the next few minutes talking him through everything that had happened since she had arrived. The more she spoke, the more ridiculous it all sounded. He queried a few points and asked her to expand, but she told him everything she could. It felt good to finally hold nothing back and tell someone the full story. She wondered if she should have gone to him to help find Bex in the first place. It was the type of thing in which he specialised, and yet to do so would have admitted defeat. After all, it was the type of thing in which *she* was also supposed to specialise. If she'd stuck her pride to one side, perhaps she wouldn't have ended up like this.

'If you're busy with a case, there's no problem,' she finished with.

'I can find time.'

'I only need a few details – who owns that number plate

and where do they live? I take it you can get hold of stuff like that?'

'I have my ways. Are you sure that's all?'

'Yes... well, hopefully. I don't know. Will you call this number back? Forget any other ones you have for me.'

Jessica could hear the scrape of a chair in the background and the sound of the woman's voice who'd answered the phone.

'I'll see what I can do,' he said. 'If you want me, call the desk number you have, then press one as soon as it rings. It'll redirect to my mobile. I'll call you back, but give me a little time. I am in the middle of something. Are you sure that's all?'

'I suppose there is one other thing?'

'What?'

'Thank you.'

'Don't mention it.'

TWENTY-TWO

While Andrew got to work, Jessica figured she'd be proactive by herself. DCI Fordham had specifically told her to stay away from Sophie Johns' family – but he'd said nothing about her friends. Besides, he'd told her where Sophie worked, practically begging Jessica to stick her nose in.

It was barely midday, but the Honky Tonk Diner was already rammed with families tucking into the 'world-famous all-day American breakfast'. For less than a fiver, it was perhaps no surprise, even if 'world-famous' was pushing it. Jessica doubted there were many south-east islanders desperate to escape their Pacific paradise in order to tuck into a mound of eggs and bacon close to Blackpool's seafront.

The restaurant was a clear rip-off of the Hard Rock Café, with an enormous electric guitar poking out from the roof and an outside paint job that was either reminiscent of piano keys or a sun-faded zebra.

Jessica pushed through the double doors, which were sliced into a garish fading musical note, and waited in the area close to the welcome counter. She smiled at the hostess and asked for a few moments as she took out her phone and pretended to have a conversation. As she did that, she scanned the room. The kitchen was open-plan on the far wall, with the rest of the restaurant split into two by a 'wall of fame' that was plastered with photographs of rock stars, few of whom had likely heard of Blackpool, let alone eaten there.

As with so many of these places, there were few staff and the poor sods on duty were vastly overworked. Jessica watched a skinny lad skid his way out of the kitchen, balancing a metal tray laden with half a dozen plates piled high with meat, eggs and potatoes. He spun on his heels, sashayed around a small child and then hurried towards the family who were sitting in the window. On the other side of the room, there was a young woman who was probably still a teenager. Her blonde hair was wound into a bob and held back by a crimson bandana that matched the colours of the restaurant. A blue biro was tucked behind her ear, a loose strand of hair looped around it. She crouched next to a table to ask a young boy if he was enjoying his meal, winked at his mother and then skipped back to the counter to fetch a tray of drinks.

Jessica knew almost nothing about Sophie Johns, but, if she worked here, chances were that she'd more likely be friends with the blonde girl than the skinny lad on the other side.

She put her phone away and caught the eye of the hostess – an older woman with short grey hair, a name badge reading 'Irene' and a drowsy gaze that meant she'd likely been up for hours. Jessica was capable of many things, but spending hours smiling and saying hello to strangers was not one of them. She'd crack within an hour, especially if there was some bratty little kid full of entitlement.

'Are you ready?' Irene asked.

'Hungry,' Jessica replied with a grin. It wasn't strictly true. She'd already had one breakfast.

Irene picked up a menu and took a step towards the half of

the restaurant being served by the young man, but Jessica pointed towards a table on the other side, close to the kitchen.

'Can I sit there?' she asked.

For the merest fraction of a second, Irene's features bristled with annoyance, but then the smile returned. 'Of course.'

She led Jessica to the selected spot, passed across the menu, recommended the waffles and then introduced the blonde server.

Lorna planted a pair of plates on a nearby table and then breezed across the floor, full of smiles and hair twirls. She also recommended the waffles and filled Jessica's mug with coffee, before saying that she'd return shortly.

Jessica took out one of the flyers with Bex's face on the front and laid it flat on the table. She scanned the menu but continued to watch Lorna over the top. The young woman was effortless, drifting from table to table; carrying food and drinks, saying hello to the kids, gently batting an eyelid towards the receptive single men and generally doing half a dozen things at the same time.

A few minutes later, Lorna returned to the table, still smiling. 'Have you decided what you want to eat?' she asked.

'Seeing as you said the waffles were good, I may as well go with them.'

'Blueberries and cream on top?'

'That sounds incredible.' Jessica motioned towards the poster on the table. 'Can I ask a weird question? I was wondering if you might recognise my friend? I think she could have been in here once or twice.'

Lorna stared down at the paper and then picked it up. She shook her head slowly. 'Sorry, I don't know her.' She took a small step backwards, but the smile had gone, her lips pressed together as if she was about to say something.

'You okay?' Jessica asked.

Lorna handed back the page. 'Yes, it's just... it's strange that your friend's missing.'

'Why?'

She glanced towards Irene, who was busy shepherding a couple onto the other side of the restaurant. 'Because my friend disappeared last night. Her name's Sophie.'

'She just disappeared?'

'She finished her shift and nobody's seen her since. I got a call last night asking if I'd seen her and that the police wanted to talk. She was due in today... but I suppose that doesn't matter now.'

'Was there any sign she was unhappy?'

Lorna glanced towards Irene again and shook her head. 'Not really – but it was only two days ago that they found out Peter had died.'

Jessica bit her lip to stop the gasp escaping. 'Who's Peter?' she asked, narrowly keeping her surprise in check.

The waitress flipped the loose strand of hair behind the pen. 'One of our regulars. He used to come in a few times a week, sometimes with his friends, sometimes by himself. Sophie had a thing for him.' She blinked rapidly, pinching the bridge of her nose. 'Sorry, I'll go sort out those waffles for you.'

TWENTY-THREE

With Foo Fighters in the background and a plate chocked with waffles, cream and blueberries, Jessica should have been a lot happier than she was, given the new information.

Peter Salisbury was dead, Sophie Johns was missing – and they knew one another. DCI Fordham and his mob would have to be complete idiots to have missed that. Not that a CID team overlooking the obvious was completely out of the question.

Jessica picked at her food, finishing off the coffee and its refill until her head was buzzing with ideas and conspiracies.

And caffeine, definitely caffeine.

Sophie claimed that she knew Bex, which could have provided some sort of link to the diner – and Peter was a regular. Was Bex really connected to this place with its rows of mass-produced gold discs, endless posters of rock stars who'd not visited and musical instruments that were never played? If so, how? Did she eat here? Hang around? Work? Even at the end of the tourist season, with winter well on its way, this place was packed. She wasn't a full-on paperclip face, but with her piercings and tattoos, someone would know her.

When Lorna came across with the bill, Jessica again asked her to look at Bex's flyer. She did so without complaint but shook her head once more, replying with a genuine-sounding 'sorry', before taking the poster and saying she'd ask around. Jessica believed she was telling the truth and, aside from interrogating everyone present, there was little else she could do.

Jessica left the Honky Tonk and crossed to the cashpoint opposite. She fed it her bank card and removed the daily maximum of cash. She had just finished separating the notes into her various pockets when her phone started to buzz. Andrew's name was on the front. 'Hi,' she said.

'You okay to talk?' he asked.

'Give me a minute.'

For a reason of which Jessica wasn't quite sure, there was a brass band set up across the street. They were rump-a-pump-pumping their way through a tune she vaguely recognised but had no idea of the name. She skirted away from them, heading into a narrow street and finding a spot underneath the awning of a tat shop that had gone out of business. A faded green '50% off EVERYTHING' banner was welded to the scratched window with a mixture of dust, dirt and rain.

'Sorry about that,' she said.

'You got a pen?' Andrew asked.

Jessica dug around in her pockets and then sat in the doorway. She cradled her phone between her shoulder and ear while resting the flyer with the white van's number plate on her knee. To an unknowing passer-by, she might appear homeless.

'Go for it,' she said.

'That van's registered to someone named Vince Waverly. I'll give you the address.' Andrew read it out, postcode and all, as Jessica wrote the details underneath the number plate.

'Any idea where this is?' she asked, not recognising Poulton-le-Fylde as a real place name. It sounded a bit French.

'About four miles outside of Blackpool centre,' Andrew replied. 'It looks a bit, well... *farmy* on the map. Middle-of-nowhere, bodies-under-the-patio-type thing.'

He laughed but Jessica didn't. It was a bit close to home for her liking.

'Do you want me to email or text you the details?' he asked.

'No, you never know who might be keeping an eye on it.'

She heard him tut. 'How much trouble are you in?' he asked.

'None... well, hopefully none. I don't know.'

'Do you need some help?'

'I'll sort it. Thanks – I owe you one.'

The taxi pulled up alongside something that couldn't really be called a kerbside. For one, there was no kerb; for another, the grass along the edge of the road was so long and wild that it was more of a *jungle*-side.

'You sure you want dropping off here?' the taxi driver asked.

Jessica peered through the windscreen at the long stretch of crumbling single-track road and the desolate expanse of grass and bushes on either side. She trusted that Andrew Hunter knew his stuff, but if this was some sort of joke...

'Here's fine,' she replied, handing over cash and climbing out.

'Do you want me to wait, or anything...?'

The driver wafted a hand to indicate the nothingness around them. Clearly he thought she was some kind of nutter – either that or some dogging fanatic without a car. It looked that sort of area.

'I'm fine,' Jessica said, closing the door. The driver offered a 'suit yourself' shrug and then did a U-turn before haring back the way they'd come.

'Bloody Andrew bloody Hunter,' Jessica muttered, taking out her phone to see if he'd sent her any further details. Then she remembered that she'd told him not to.

She turned in a circle, but there was little to see other than the tall grass growing into the verges. With the recent wet weather, the twisting mound of marshland and plant life had sprouted endless shades of green. The remains of an overnight frost glistened on the ground as the chilled sun hung low in the sky. Jessica tried standing on it, but the soil was sandy and soft, perhaps not a surprise, considering how close they were to the coast. It was disconcerting how near they were to Blackpool with its people, lights and noise; yet here, there was nothing except wilderness.

Andrew might have joked about this being an area in which bodies were buried, but he didn't know how unnerving that now sounded. If Jessica ever needed to bump somebody off, she'd be getting rid of the body here. No one would ever find it.

She started to walk in the direction away from where the taxi driver had come. She'd only gone a few metres when the hedges parted, revealing a thin, rocky track that stretched through a dark overhang of trees. It was a tunnel to... somewhere.

Jessica's first footstep along the lane went straight through a pile of twigs into a pool of muddy water. It spilled over the top of her shoe, drenching her sock. Her second step had a distinct squelch to it as well.

'Andrew bloody Hunter,' she repeated to herself.

The temperature in the shadow underneath the trees was at least a couple of degrees colder than on the other side. Crispy white mounds of frost were defiantly clinging to the edges of the path, inviting Jessica to slip on her arse.

She carefully passed underneath the natural tunnel, emerging onto a gravelly courtyard. It was only a few metres away from the road, but a large farmhouse was completely hidden by the greenery. If anyone were home, Jessica would have been in clear view, so she scooted back to the cover of the trees, keeping tight to the boundary and edging her way around the perimeter of the farm.

The farmhouse was huge, with long rows of windows over two storeys, plus a tall sloping roof, meaning there was probably a sizeable attic, too. It was at least three times the size of her three-bed Manchester terrace.

A short distance away, there was a barn that was comfortably as big as the house. There were few windows but massive doors at either end. The buildings were covered in a thin layer of grime, with dust and grit carpeting the paved areas in between.

Jessica continued around the line of the hedges until she reached an opening into a vast field. She didn't know what type of farm was operating, but there was no sign of animals, so it was likely crops. If that were true, then why were the adjoining hedges so overgrown? Even in winter, surely a farmer would take care of his or her land? When she peered closely, Jessica could see that there were tracks across the ground where something would have been planted and harvested, but it didn't look as if anything other than grass and weeds had been doing so for a long a time.

She crept closer to the barn, constantly peering towards the house in case the owner emerged. There was nobody, not even the hint that anyone had been there recently. Even the trees were still. It was so eerie that Jessica was shivering, imagining movement where there was none. If it were dark, dusk even, this would be prime horror-movie territory. She'd be the shrieking lone female being pursued by some maniac with a mask and a weapon. The Blackpool Chainsaw Massacre.

There was a thick bar and padlock across the front of the barn, so Jessica moved around the side close to the hedgerow until she was at one of the windows. The glass was single-pane, ancient and rickety in a rotten, damp wooden frame. Nearby, a second window was clear of glass, with the hedge growing through the open space. Jessica peered through the gap, half expecting to get an 'oi' from an unassuming farmer.

Nothing.

All she could see was a tractor parked in the centre, with bales of straw and some tools clamped to the far wall. Vertical metal bars were bolted into place in another corner – probably some sort of secure storage area – and there was lots of empty space.

Jessica finished squishing herself through the gap between barn and hedge until she emerged close to the house. Her feet were now cold and *really* wet from the loop she'd done walking in the mush. She pulled her jacket tighter but couldn't stop her teeth from chattering. The word 'barren' was invented for places like this: sprawling farms hidden behind swampish jungle along a single-track road in the absolute middle of nowhere.

She thought about knocking on the front door – how much harm could it actually do? – but there was something about this place that stopped her.

Fear.

It wasn't an emotion she felt that often. That part of her make-up had been hammered away at by years of running into stupid situations, of dealing with men and women who'd tried to intimidate and bully her. She'd become desensitised, and yet this place was so... nothing... that she felt certain there had to be *something* going on.

There was nowhere to hide if anyone happened to be watching from the house – but Jessica continued along the hedgerow until she had a view of the back of the house. At some point, this would have been a pleasant garden, but the grass was even more overgrown than around the rest of the property. In the centre of the lawn was an old swing, the chain wrapped around the top. It had rusted years before, as had the swingball post that was planted in the ground nearby.

Nestled between the lawn and the house on a patch of gravel was the white van that arrived at the hotels to drop off the maids each morning and evening. The lower half was coated with the same sort of grime that infested the rest of the farm. Seen in the context of the desolation, it was even stranger. Did the maids live here? Were they picked up from somewhere?

Jessica shivered, but this time it wasn't the cold. She glanced towards the house, but there was nobody at any of the windows. The walls were free of cameras and the hedge that skirted the rest of the property offered nothing but darkness. She felt watched, turning in a circle, half expecting there to be someone on her shoulder.

There wasn't.

She moved slowly across the gravel, unable to prevent the bottom of her shoes from scrunching on the jagged stones. It was only as they crunched together that she realised how quiet it was otherwise. At the hotel, there was a constant buzz of the ocean, tourists, cars... a living, breathing town. Here, even the birds had sodded off.

Jessica peered through the front windows of the van, but there was little to see other than a screwed-up Ginsters wrapper, two red-top tabloids and half a dozen air fresheners. All very normal. She made her way back to the hedge more quickly this time, wincing at the noise she was making until she was back under cover.

Silence.

She thought about the maid at the Prince Hotel and her expression upon seeing Bex's photo. Jessica was convinced the woman had known Bex, that the 'no English'-thing was to stop her having to talk to anyone. She was connected to this van, this place.

But had Jessica seen only what she wanted in the maid's face? Perhaps it had been confusion? Fear, even? It wouldn't be the first time – everything about this trip had been based on a phone call from someone she *thought* sounded like Bex. There was no proof, no rerun. Now she was at a remote farm, examining rubbish in the front seat of a van and listening to the wind.

Jessica was between the house and the barn, with the arched entrance on the other side of the courtyard. It would take her ten seconds at most to dash across and be back on the road. Then she could begin the walk back to the town centre. She eyed the house once more, seeing nobody and figuring the direct route was preferable to sloshing the long way round the property. Jessica took a couple of steps onto the yard, still watching the house, ready to run, and then...

Thunk!

The noise had come from the barn, something hard bashing on wood, like someone was cutting down a tree. She was level with one of the barn windows and stepped across, peering through the murky glass towards the wide-open space. The tractor was still in the centre, the straw around the edge untouched. There was nobody there, let alone anyone making a noise.

She cupped her hand across the top of her eyes to eliminate the glare, squinting towards the corners, yet there was still nothing. The sound had come so out of the blue that she could almost still hear the echo, reverberating around the farm. *Thunk, thunk, thunk, thunk...*

It took her a moment to realise that the noise was real. She spun, but the man was already within a couple of metres of her. He was fifties, maybe early sixties, but still built like a mutated bulldog, all padded out with a thick waxed jacket, dark jeans smeared with grease and oil and steel-capped boots. His grey prickly beard masked much of his mouth, but his gruff tone told enough of the story.

'Who the hell are you?' he asked.

TWENTY-FOUR

Jessica tried to step backwards away from the man, but there was nowhere to go. She was pressed against the window of the barn, staring up at the man who towered over her by a good six inches. His fists were balled, ready to attack and, for some reason, she was fixated on the hairiness of the backs of his hands.

'This is private property,' he added.

'Um... yes.'

He leaned close enough that she could see the flecks of grey in his otherwise dark beard.

'Well?' he demanded.

'I... er... I'm going door to door in the area looking for my friend.' Jessica scrambled into her pocket and pulled out one of the flyers showing Bex. She offered him one but he didn't take it.

'Door to door? Not many doors round 'ere.'

'I know. I've been walking a lot. There's not much out here.' She offered a friendly giggle, but he didn't even crack a smile. She held the flyer higher and he glanced down quickly and then returned his glare to her.

'Not seen her,' he said.

'Could you look again?'

He flicked his gaze towards the poster and almost instantly back up, shaking his head. 'Told you – not seen her.'

She pushed it into his hand. 'Can you *please* have a proper look? I—'

He snatched the paper away, ripping it in half and screwing it up one-handed, before leaning in even closer. She could smell the coffee on his breath. 'Do you want me to call the police? I told you, I've *not* seen her.'

The man stepped backwards, giving Jessica space to move. As she took a step towards the dark arch that led back to the road, there was another bang from the barn, louder this time. She twisted to peer through the window, but the man gripped her shoulder and pulled her backwards.

'What do you think you're doing?' he demanded.

'What was that noise?'

'None of your business.'

Jessica took another step towards the road but was interrupted by a shrill grating that made her wince. She jumped away as the large barn door swung outwards, hinges creaking with complaint.

A younger man emerged, wiping his hands on his checked shirt that had the sleeves rolled up. He jumped as he spotted the bearded man. 'Jesus, Dad, what you doing there? You nearly—'

He stopped speaking when he noticed Jessica, eyebrows deepening to a frown. They were unquestionably father and son, with matching build, dark hair and brown eyes. The younger man's beard was coming along gradually but failing to live up to his old man's standards. There were fewer greys but none of the bushiness that only came with years of practice.

'Oh,' he said, straightening himself and re-wiping his hands. 'Who's she?'

'*She's* leaving,' the older man replied, turning back to the house. 'Make sure she finds the road and keeps going.'

'Right...' The younger man stepped between his father and Jessica and nodded at the darkened arch. 'C'mon...'

Jessica had little choice but to follow. She glanced over her shoulder towards the barn and the older man, who was now in the centre of the courtyard glaring at her.

'I don't think your dad likes me,' Jessica said.

To her surprise, the younger man laughed. He scratched his beard and then put his hands in his pockets. 'Dad don't like many people, 'specially not on the farm. Why you 'ere?'

Jessica realised she was still holding the ripped flyer. She folded it into her pocket and took out a fresh one, passing it over. 'I'm looking for my friend.'

He took the paper, but they had passed under the tree arch and it was too dark to see anything. Jessica's foot again sank through the surface into a puddle. The water was once more in her sock and she could feel the silty grit being crushed by her skin.

'Puddle there,' the man said.

'Huh?'

'Puddle. You stepped in it.'

'Oh, right...'

He laughed and it took that for her to realise he was joking. A moment later, they were back on the road where the taxi driver had dropped her off. Jessica was wishing she'd asked him to hang around.

She blinked her way into the light and turned to face the man. He was attractive, in that rugged sort of way: the type of bloke who looked like he spent his days living in caves, chopping down trees and climbing mountains. There was grease on his cheek, more on his bare arms. He was clearly too masculine to need sleeves when it was this cold. He stared at the poster of Bex, bottom lip pouted, but his expression was hard to read, partly because he had so much facial hair.

'Why you asking here?' he said.

'I'm going door to door.'

'Not many doors 'round 'ere.'

'Your dad said that.'

He peered up from the poster to stare at her properly. 'So what ya doing out here?'

'I told you – door to door. There aren't *many* doors, but there are plenty of farms. My friend might have been looking for work, fruit-picking, manual labour, that sort of thing.'

Jessica had no idea where 'fruit-picking' had come from – but she impressed herself at how plausible it sounded.

'Not much fruit-picking at this time of year.'

'I know, but that doesn't mean nobody's seen her.'

He shrugged and handed the paper back. There were smudged words written on the back of his hand but Jessica couldn't make any of them out. 'Fair enough,' he said.

'Have *you* seen her?' she asked.

'Nope. Nice piercings, though.' They stared at one another before he turned away back to the farm.

'What's your name?' Jessica asked.

'Waverly. Max Waverly.'

That matched the name Andrew had passed on, meaning Max's father – Mr Hairy Hands – was probably Vince.

'I'm Jessica. Can I leave you one of my posters just in case?'

She offered him one of the flyers and Max took it without looking. He folded it into the front pocket on his shirt, his shoulders dropping slightly as he cracked a smile that didn't suit him. 'Sorry 'bout me dad, like. He's paranoid 'bout being robbed. You see all this stuff in the papers 'bout rural crime, plus gangs and that. We're a bit remote out 'ere, so you never know what might 'appen. Police are useless and, even if they weren't, it'd take 'em ages to get 'ere.'

'I understand.'

He nodded, stepping towards the hedge and then turning back. 'You need a lift or owt?'

'I'm okay.'

He shrugged a wordless 'fair enough' and took another step away before Jessica had a thought.

'Do you ever go to Blackpool town centre?' she asked.

'Aye, sometimes. Always packed, like.'

'Do you know the Honky Tonk Diner?'

'The 'onky Tonky what?'

'It's a restaurant in the centre of town.' Jessica nodded in the direction of what she thought was Blackpool. 'There's a big guitar over the door.'

'Don't ring a bell.'

He turned away quickly, caught in an obvious – and need-less – lie. Anyone who'd visited the town would have a recollection of the diner, even a vague one. For someone who lived locally and visited the centre semi-regularly, it would be impossible to miss. Max shuffled away quickly, reaching into the hedge and pulling across a gate that had been hidden by the foliage. The metal was brown and crusty, with a large faded red semicircle arched across the top.

'Good luck finding your friend,' he said, lifting the bolt to clamp the gate in place. As he raised his arm, Jessica was able to see his thick Popeye inner arms. At first, she thought they were smeared with oil, but her heart skipped as the truth dawned. The lines spiralled outwards, the shape now obvious.

He had a spider's web tattoo that matched the one on Bex's arm.

TWENTY-FIVE

Jessica had spent so long looking at the various photographs of Bex that the spider's web tattoo was imprinted on her mind. It was one of the first things Jessica had noticed when they'd first met in a greasy late-night café. At the time, Bex had shrugged off a question about where she'd got it and it hadn't mattered. Through the course of her police work, Jessica knew a little about tattoos – and Bex wasn't someone who was heavily into the ink scene. She had her piercings and marks because she wanted them, not to make any sort of statement. The web on her inner arm was the only one of its kind Jessica had seen, but she'd never thought it was the type of thing that could be one of a pair.

She ripped her gaze away from Max and hurried along the deserted track, not daring to look back. It was hard to get her head around it all. Bex had called her from the payphone opposite a rank of hotels owned by Luke Eckhart. The hotels employed cleaners and kitchen staff ferried in by a van owned by Vince Waverly, whose son, Max, had a tattoo that matched Bex's.

In a week of coincidences, this was one too far.

Max had emerged from the barn, even though Jessica had peered through the window and not seen anyone. He might have been working behind the hay bales, or high in the rafters, but wouldn't he have spotted her? And what was going on with the van? Was it used as some sort of taxi service to bus staff to and from the centre? If so, it wasn't much of a business.

At the end of the road, the rows of overgrown trees and hedges gave way to sandy verges and a slightly wider track. In the distance, Jessica could see the silhouettes of Blackpool Tower and roller coasters scraping at the murky sky. If nothing else, she knew which way to go. Soon, the bare track became a small row of houses before Jessica found herself on the main road. She thought about catching a bus, but the walk was doing her good, allowing everything she'd seen and heard to blend into one another. Not that she was coming up with any answers, other than the conclusion that somebody was trying to fit her up.

Jessica continued following the road as the buildings started to be more densely packed. She reached a small row of shops with a minimart, pizza takeaway and hairdresser, as well as more houses. She'd just passed a brown sign pointing her towards the Tower and Attractions when Jessica felt her pocket buzzing. She fumbled around, answering the wrong phone before she realised her old one was ringing.

She answered the unknown number in time and was met by a familiar voice: 'I didn't think you were going to pick up.'

'Chief Inspector Fordham,' Jessica replied.

'You around?'

'I'm out and about. Lots to see and do in Blackpool. Why?'

'How long will it take you to get back to your hotel?'

There were too many houses around for Jessica to see the tower on the horizon but she'd been walking for long enough. 'I'm not sure – forty-five minutes.'

'I can send a car for you?'

'Why?'

'I need a word. We can meet at the station if you want?'

'No!' Jessica snapped her reply before catching herself and lowering her tone. 'I'll see you at the hotel. Okay?'

'Suit yourself. Be quick.'

It wasn't long before Jessica found herself in familiar territory. The houses and small shops became bed and breakfasts, then hotels. Before she knew it, Blackpool Tower reappeared, soaring high above the other buildings as if it had materialised from nowhere. It was the same as in any built-up place – the tallest buildings hid in plain sight until they were directly above and then it was impossible to see how they could have been missed.

Jessica walked along the promenade, passing dwindling numbers of people, until she was close to Luke Eckhart's row of hotels. She was about to head into the car park when she spied DCI Fordham sitting with his back to her on the wall next to the payphone. His coat was draped over the bricks alongside him and he was talking on his mobile.

After crossing the road, Jessica sidled up behind him, but not in time to overhear the end of his conversation as he snapped the phone onto a clip on his belt. His psychic powers were in full swing as he twisted to see her. Either that or Jessica had the ninja skills of a particularly clumsy elephant.

Fordham nodded towards the spot on the other side of his coat and Jessica took a seat, peering down at the beach below. It was warmer than previous days but not exactly summer holiday weather. Despite that, a man was lying on the sand wearing nothing but a pair of stripy below-the-knee shorts and sunglasses. He was pasty and lean with muscled arms, a gym bunny desperate for a bit of colour on his skin. There was nobody else in sight, not even a dog-walker.

'Will you look at the state of that,' Fordham said.

'The sunglasses are a bit overkill.'

Fordham peered up at the dim skies. Out at sea, there was a gap in the clouds and a slim barely-there shaft of sunlight. It was nowhere near the beach.

'This type of thing only happens in Britain,' Jessica said. 'I can't imagine Spaniards and Italians are out on the beach in this weather.'

'How's your morning been?' he asked.

'All right. You?'

'Been seeing the sights?'

'Something like that.'

Fordham reached out and touched the metal casing of the payphone. 'So, this is where your friend called you from?' he said.

'Do you want me to tell you the same thing again? You have my phone number, check the records.'

'We have – but it only tells us which phone called you, not who was calling.'

'What do you want me to say? I tell you the same thing every time we meet. I've told you it in person, on tape, with a solicitor in the room. What more do you want?'

It took Fordham a few moments to reply. He was swinging his legs, probably unknowingly. 'We got the blood work back from your car.'

'Oh.'

'It doesn't belong to Peter Salisbury.'

'Oh.' It was the same word but inflected upwards this time. Jessica sat up straighter, turning to face him. She was convinced it would come back as a match, another way of pinning his killing on her.

She didn't know what to say.

'It comes from Rebecca Kellock.'

Jessica's moment of elation was replaced by a sinking in

her stomach that was so loud, she felt sure Fordham must have heard it. She felt sick, gulping back a mouthful of saliva. 'Bex...?'

'If Rebecca Kellock is "Bex", then yes.'

'How was her blood on my car?'

He twisted to face her, loosening his tie even further as he stifled a yawn with his other hand. He seemed exhausted. She knew that feeling.

'That's what I'm asking you,' he said.

Jessica's mouth was open and she had no idea how to reply. Of everything she might have expected him to say, this was perhaps the last.

'I... it's Bex's blood?' A pause. 'But she's been missing for three months – *I* reported her missing. I found hairs in her room to pass on to the DNA lot in case an unidentified body was found – without that, you wouldn't know it was her blood. I came here to find her... If her blood had been on the back of my car all this time, don't you think I'd have noticed?'

He shrugged. 'Who said it's been on there for three months?'

'What? You think I reported her missing and kept her locked up somewhere, only to kill her now and dump her in my car boot? Then I came here to get rid of the body? After that, I—'

Jessica stopped herself, realising how bad it sounded out loud. She'd been trying to get inside Fordham's head and read his suspicions. It was a step too far. He stared at her, not needing to say anything, because Jessica already knew. If she'd been in an interview room and said this on tape, she'd have really been in the shite. It was so specific that it was close to a confession.

'I *want* to find her,' she whispered. 'She's my friend.'

'"*Friend...*"' Fordham repeated the word as if there was something dirty about it.

Jessica gripped his arm. 'What do you want me to say?'

She was holding tight, but he didn't snatch his arm away, waiting for her to realise their roles. She released him and turned away, biting her bottom lip with a sigh.

'What do you want me to say?' she repeated.

'Lots of places in Blackpool if you did want to get rid of a body,' Fordham said.

She'd had that exact thought herself and now it was coming true. He nodded behind them towards the swathe of sand dunes that coated the road back to Lytham and eventually Poulton-le-Fylde. Jessica wondered if he'd known where she'd been that morning.

'You must be able to see what's going on?' Jessica said.

'What's going on?'

'It's all so convenient. How many cases do you get where everything's on a plate? Bodies left in the open, an easy trail to the last person to see them alive, blood on a car... it's never like this. Never.'

He nodded crisply. 'Perhaps that's why I'm talking to you on a wall as opposed to at the station...?'

The man on the beach rolled onto his front, seemingly oblivious to the fact that he was sorely lacking the one thing required for sunbathing, namely the sun.

'Thank you,' Jessica said.

Fordham was quiet for a moment, still swinging his legs. She wondered if it was nerves. 'I don't know you and you don't me,' he said, 'but we both know how this looks. Whatever you might think, I'm not an idiot—'

'I don't—'

He talked over her: '—but answer me this: If Sophie Johns' body shows up somewhere and there's nothing else to go on, what would you do if the roles were reversed?'

Jessica didn't need to think: 'I'd bring you in, police officer or not.'

'Precisely. It doesn't matter if *I* think you're responsible. We've got blood on your car from one missing person; one dead body where you were the last person to see him alive. If a second body shows up, that's it.'

'What's happening with the blood on the car?'

'You know what it's like with these things. At the moment, it's unofficially official. I got a tip from the labs, but they have T's to cross; I's to dot. It'll be confirmed later today or tomorrow. For now, nothing's changed.' Fordham swung his legs around and pushed himself up, standing tall on the path over Jessica. She shivered slightly as his shadow fell across her. 'Consider this a courtesy – but the same thing stands. No holidays, no disappearing. If you're staying in town, then fine. If you're going home, then at least let your solicitor know. You've got bail to answer next week, too. Keep your phone on.'

He offered her his hand to help her up, but Jessica shook her head. 'I think I'll stay here a while.' Fordham slipped into his long coat and flapped the tails backwards. 'When will you be back?' Jessica asked.

He shrugged. 'Who knows? Tomorrow? The day after?' He checked his watch. 'It could be an hour.' He offered a thin smile. 'You're lucky,' he added.

'I don't feel it.'

He stared at her, lips pressed together. 'No, I guess not.'

With that he was gone, striding back towards the centre, hands in pockets as ever.

Jessica sat watching the lone sunbather. He was on his belly, phone at his side with headphones pressed into his ears. In many ways, she admired him. He was out in the open, defying the elements and not caring who saw.

She felt alone, too, but there was hope. Bex's blood was 'fresh-ish' – she'd been in the area at some point in the past week. She might've been forced to call Jessica as part of a trap to bring her here, but at least that meant she *was* in the area.

Hurt, bleeding and used – but *here*.

Jessica wiped the grit from her palms and stood, turning to face the car park. Somehow, everything was linked to the hotels – all she had to do was figure out how.

TWENTY-SIX

Jessica knew DCI Fordham would be back before her bail ran out in five days. He would either have a long list of questions about why Bex's blood was on her car, or they'd have found Sophie Johns' body – and then anything could happen. Jessica had seen suspects banged up in prison on remand for less. It'd be the end of her career, the end of it all. The time for sitting back and waiting for things to happen was gone.

Brandon was behind the reception desk as Jessica entered the Prince Hotel. She threw him a pinball ding-ding smile and headed up to her room. She unlocked the door and then waited next to it, watching the clock on her new phone. The seconds flipped by agonisingly slowly, but, when two minutes were up, she headed back downstairs and waited close to the stairs until Brandon noticed her. His T-shirt was a lot tighter than the clothes she'd seen him in before. He was in good shape and he knew it.

'What's up?' he asked with a smile that he definitely wouldn't have wasted on an elderly couple who were checking in.

Jessica was more than prepared to play that game. She

flipped her hair over her shoulder, half turning towards the stairs. 'You're gonna think I'm a real wimp.'

'Why?'

'I'm like a complete walking cliché.'

'How come?'

'I was upstairs in my room, about to get undressed to have a shower...' she tugged on her sleeve to make sure he got the message, 'but there was a spider in the sink.'

He broke into a grin. 'Old buildings like these attract spiders, I'm afraid.'

'It was huge, all legs and... *teeth.*'

Brandon snorted at her. 'You could see its teeth?'

'Well, maybe not, but it was bloody big. I left the door unlocked. Can you...?'

This time he actually winked, flexing his arm muscles as he rounded the counter. 'I'll see what I can do.'

'Please make sure you get it. I'm not sure I can go back up there otherwise.'

Brandon brushed past, treading slightly closer than he needed to. They both felt the simmering buzz between them as he continued up the stairs, turning back to look at Jessica over his shoulder. Well, that or the electrics were on the blink, which was perfectly plausible.

'Be right back,' he said.

Jessica waited where she was, listening to his disappearing footsteps. As soon as Brandon was out of sight and sound on the floor above, she dashed for the counter, sidestepping around it in one smooth movement and entering the office. The desk next to the door was a mass of clutter, with pens scattered across the surface alongside a fearsome spike that had been used to spear hundreds of invoices. There were rubber bands, a ball of string and a click-clack office toy. Jessica was careful not to nudge anything as she slipped around it and moved to the back of the room. There were two safes, neither hidden from view. One was a small box, half a metre square at most, which was pinned high on the wall. The other was three times the size and more, underneath the counter with an old-fashioned dial on the front. Considering that guests were seemingly all offered a cash discount, Jessica guessed the larger, more secure safe was where the money ended up. There could be thousands in there if it was undeclared. Tens of thousands.

Jessica eyed the dial before blinking back into the room – she was wasting time. She turned to the smaller safe, typing 1-2-3-4 into the push panel on the front. There was a small beep and then the door swung open. The inside was thankfully well ordered, with rows of hooks that had numbered stickers above, each containing a key. At the far end were two spaces marked with an 'X'. One hook was empty, presumably the maid's skeleton key. Jessica pocketed the other key and then relocked the safe before darting back to reception.

She sat on the bottom stair, surprisingly out of breath considering she'd not done much. Her heart was racing, chest tight. It took her a couple of minutes to compose herself. She was used to tiptoeing the line of acceptable and not – but this was hurdling it, barrelling down the other side and disappearing over the horizon. She might not have been guilty of anything to do with Peter Salisbury, Sophie Johns or Bex – but she was now a definite thief, which could technically be called 'breaking'. The 'entering' was just around the corner.

After a few more minutes, she heard a door closing upstairs and then footsteps. Brandon rounded the banister and then sat himself next to Jessica on the bottom step.

'Got it,' he said.

He'd done bloody well considering there had been no spider.

'My hero,' Jessica replied, nudging his shoulder with hers.

'Are you going to be all right up there...?'

Jessica wasn't sure if it was a genuine question because he thought she was creeped out, or if he was asking for an invitation. It didn't matter either way. She hauled herself up using the banister and moved up a couple of stairs as Brandon stood. 'I'll be fine,' she said. 'Thanks for helping.'

'My pleasure.'

She continued up to the first floor and waited on the landing, listening in case there were any guests nearby, or if Brandon was going to follow her for whatever reason. She could hear movement a few floors above – probably the maid hefting the vacuum cleaner around – but it was otherwise quiet.

Something was going on in the hotel and Jessica was determined to find out what. She headed along the corridor, looking for anything not quite right. There were the expected rows of numbered doors, some more faded than others, all looking a little tatty. Jessica hadn't seen any guests on the same floor as her in the few days she'd been staying – though, in fairness, it was hardly a hotel in which to spend lots of time.

Jessica reached the end of the corridor having seen nothing other than the lifts and closed bedroom doors. She checked both ways and then tapped on door number thirty. There was no answer, so she tapped slightly louder, wincing as she called 'maid' as quietly as she could while still wanting to be heard.

Still no reply.

After another check behind her, Jessica slipped her stolen key into the lock and turned it. There was a satisfying click and then she was inside. She wasn't particularly bothered about what was inside, more in testing the key. As it was, the interior of room thirty was much like the one in which she was staying, with dated furniture and a musty, ancient smell. There was a thin layer of dust on the mirror and other surfaces, meaning it had likely not been cleaned since the end of the summer. The hotel probably used only a handful of rooms off-season, perhaps spread across the floors to ensure everyone had a sea view, even if being able to see the ocean from one of the rooms was like polishing the contents of a skip.

Jessica locked the door to room thirty and headed back the way she'd come, padding quickly across the carpeted floor and doing her best not to make any noise. She passed more numbered doors until she reached one close to the far end that was marked 'private'. It had been open when the maid was dragging the vacuum cleaner around that morning. It took a wiggle and some silent swearing, but the key eventually fitted, with the door opening into a store cupboard. Jessica wasn't sure what she was looking for, but it wasn't a selection of buckets, tubs of soap and cleaning fluid, plus boxes of the small toiletries that were left in every room. There were mops, brushes and dustpans, as well as a large space for the cleaning cart. Nothing of any particular interest.

After relocking the cleaning cupboard, Jessica continued along the corridor to the wall at the end. There was a black and white framed photograph of Blackpool in its glory days, heaving with tourists, glittering and new. Jessica stared at it for a few moments, surprised at how little had changed on the seafront. The shops might have different names, with chain restaurants, hotels and pubs elbowing their way in, but all of the main attractions remained.

She passed the fire exit and started back the way she'd come, counting down the rooms as she passed them, ready to head up to the second floor. It was only as she passed it that Jessica realised room thirteen wasn't room thirteen at all. It was opposite the store cupboard but there was no number on the front. Twelve and fourteen were on either side but there were no markings on the door in between. Jessica slipped in the key and it turned easily. She peeped into the dark space, fumbling along the wall for a light switch. There was a fizzing from above and then a white strip bulb dazzled, leaving Jessica blinking as she stepped through the door and pulled it behind her, not quite clicking it closed.

The mysterious room thirteen was smaller than the room in which she was staying – but three or four times the size of the cleaning cupboard opposite. It might have been a hybrid half-room but was being put to good use. There were dozens more boxes of toiletries, plus piles of napkins, plates, cups, cutlery, notepads, pens and a seemingly infinite number of disposables that would keep the hotel up and running for years. There were even half a dozen boxes containing small packets of biscuits in the corner. In the event of a nuclear strike, assuming the hotel guests liked sugar and showering, they'd be set for a very long time.

Jessica picked around the shelves looking for anything interesting, but it felt like browsing at a cash and carry as opposed to doing anything useful. She was about to leave when she spotted a large plastic tub stashed at the back of the space, half covered with a blanket. The top was obscured, but the bottom read 'PROPERTY' in black felt-tip.

Underneath the blanket, there was a soft monkey at the top of the lost-property bin, his brown button eyes staring accusingly at Jessica as she picked him up and squished his middle. His soft fur was matted through years of love and he had a soggy bottom from years of sleepy squeezes. Someone loved and lost him. There was a baby's dummy and various items of clothing, none of which looked that appealing. Anything valuable would likely be held for a day or two and then mysteriously disappear. This was the box of crap that guests had left behind on purpose that none of the staff could be bothered to repatriate for themselves.

Underneath a horrific Christmas jumper with actual baubles on the front, Jessica found a soft rhino with a tusk missing. There was a small tear on its back, with fluffy white foam spilling out. Of the items in the box, it was the thing that looked most loved. There'd be a heartbroken kid somewhere, wondering where he or she had left the toy. Jessica smoothed the fur absent-mindedly with one hand as she started to repack the box. It was only as she tried to return a red top to the box when it unfurled itself, a single word staring out at her so brazenly that it might as well have said 'look at me'.

'BABYLON'.

It was the same word from Henka's top. With everything that had happened since she'd spoken to Maryla in the Polish deli, Jessica had almost forgotten about the fates of Henka and Jacek. The Polish couple had disappeared together and Henka's photo had been used on the poster that had enticed Jessica to call Peter Salisbury in the first place.

Maryla had told Jessica that Henka and Jacek were always looking for time together, a place where they could hide away from their disapproving parents and get up to the type of things that young couples in love did when they were by themselves. Five-star luxury was one thing when it came to romance, but for kids with little money, it made perfect sense that they'd find a ropey hotel away from the centre that gave discounts for cash.

Jessica put down the rhino and held the vest top in her hands. The cotton was bobbled, well-worn, much-loved. Henka had been wearing it in many of the photographs pinned to the wall in her bedroom. She had been here, probably with Jacek. But it wasn't the type of thing she'd leave behind on purpose.

If Henka had gone missing from this place, did that mean Bex could have done as well? If so, why – and where on earth were they?

Jessica believed Brandon when he told her he hadn't seen Bex – but he'd only worked at the hotel for a fortnight. There was every chance he'd not seen her. Either that or he was a bloody good liar.

After returning the rhino to the box, Jessica re-covered it with the blanket and slipped it back into position. She kept hold of Henka's top, folding it down as snugly as she could and tucking it into her waistband. Jessica stood and switched the light off, opening the door and stepping back into the corridor – where she was in such a hurry to leave that she walked straight into the maid's cart. She stepped backwards, wincing from the pain in her toe, as the woman stared at her in confusion.

TWENTY-SEVEN

The door to the cleaning room opposite was open and there was no way for Jessica to pretend she hadn't just been in the storeroom. She clicked the door closed, trying her best not to look guilty. The skeleton key was in her pocket, the door unlocked.

'I, er... got a bit lost,' Jessica said.

The maid peered from Jessica to the door and back again, eyes narrow. Her lips were curved into an O, as if she was going to say something, but she swiftly turned back to the cleaning cart and tried to drag it into the cupboard.

'Are you okay?' Jessica asked.

'No English.'

'It's just that... you looked like you understood me before.'

'No. No English.'

'It looked like you recognised my friend. Was she a guest here?'

The maid ignored her, grabbing the cart and yanking it hard, bumping it over the small ridge into the cupboard. Jessica glanced quickly along the corridor, half expecting Luke

Eckhart to be there, as he had been before. This time it was clear.

'Was she a guest here?' Jessica repeated.

The maid shook her head quickly. 'No English.'

'There's nobody to be scared of. If you've not seen her, that's fine – but you have, haven't you?'

The maid stepped out of the cupboard and peered along the empty corridor, fussing with the pockets in her uniform.

'I've seen you being dropped off by that white van every day. Vince's van.'

No reaction.

'Mr Waverly's van,' Jessica added, this time getting a response. The maid shrank back towards the doorway, arms wrapped around her stomach. Her eyebrows had joined in the centre of her forehead and she took a large gulp.

'Meester Waverly...?'

There was a hint of European accent, but nowhere near as strong as Jessica might have suspected. She was terrified.

'Who is he?' Jessica pressed. The maid tried to push past but Jessica took her arm, trying not to squeeze too hard. 'Is he your boss?'

'No English.'

'Do you know Henka Blaski? Or her boyfriend, Jacek? They stayed here. They're Polish. I don't know if you are, or—'

Jessica was interrupted by the dinging of the bell on the counter below in the foyer. The maid pulled her arm clear and hurried for the stairs, not looking back but not descending either. She waited at the top, turning from Jessica to the stairs. Even though she couldn't see what was happening below, Jessica knew.

Ding-ding-ding.

She moved to the top of the stairs, edging around the maid and peering through the banisters to see DCI Fordham standing at the counter. Brandon was emerging from the door that led to the café, removing his earphones.

'Can I help you?' he asked the officer.

'I'm looking for one of your guests,' Fordham said. 'Ms Daniel. Do you know if she's here?'

'She was a minute ago – she's probably in her room.'

That was enough for Jessica. She darted back to the landing and into room seven, heading for the window. There was a pair of marked police cars outside, with uniformed officers standing nearby.

Shite.

Fordham had told her he'd be back, but she'd expected a little longer than the hour or so she'd had. The response wouldn't have been like this for the confirmed results of the blood test on her car, which meant they must have found Sophie Johns' body. She needed more time.

Jessica skirted out of the room, clicking the door closed behind her and locking it. The maid stared at her open-mouthed as the voices below started to get louder and then the staircase creaked. Jessica dashed to the end of the corridor and the photo of Blackpool as it used to be. She rammed down the horizontal bar for the fire exit and burst through the door onto a cold set of concrete steps. She was about to set off downstairs when she felt a hand on her arm. The maid had followed and was standing in the doorway shaking her head.

'What?' Jessica hissed.

The maid pointed down, shaking her head. 'Men,' she said.

Jessica squeezed herself against the freezing metal rail, peeping down to see that the stairs twisted and turned – but eventually ended up emerging at the front of the hotel. Precisely where the officers were waiting for her. She jumped at the noise from beyond the fire exit as Fordham knocked on the door of room seven.

'Where?' Jessica asked, trying not to panic.

The maid gripped Jessica's arm and started to head up to the next floor. Figuring she had little to lose, Jessica allowed herself to be dragged along. The maid moved quickly but quietly, making little noise, even though the steps were solid concrete. They rushed past the entrance to floors two and three and then opened the door to floor four. Without a word, the maid hurried along the deserted corridor, pausing momentarily at the top of the stairs. The sound of fist banging on a door echoed from three floors below. It wouldn't be long before Fordham got Brandon to unlock the door. When he realised she wasn't there – and Brandon told him he'd not seen Jessica leave the hotel – the uniformed officers would start their search. Skeleton key or not, there'd be no hiding place in the end.

'Is there a way out?' Jessica realised she'd put all her hopes on a complete stranger who'd shown little indication that she understood English.

The maid continued along the hall, waving an arm for Jessica to follow. From below, the banging had stopped. Brandon would be opening the door to her hotel room any moment.

The maid paused in front of a green metal hatch in the wall. There was one on the first floor that Jessica had assumed was a fire hose. She pointed to Jessica and then the square.

'What's in there?' Jessica asked.

The maid frowned, probably annoyed at Jessica's stupidity. She lifted the catch, holding the flap in place, and then creaked it open. There wasn't a fire hose inside. Jessica felt her heart rate increase again as she saw the cube of a dumb-waiter hatch. There were sheets and towels folded across the bottom but more than enough space for Jessica to fit inside. She didn't need to be told twice: spinning and lifting herself until she was sitting inside the mini elevator. She folded her legs underneath herself and ducked her head into the confined space.

'Under,' the maid said, pointing downwards.

'Basement?' Jessica asked.

The maid nodded and then pressed one of the buttons on the wall. Jessica hugged her knees tight as it felt like an earthquake was rocking through her. The lift moved slowly but quietly – especially considering how much the cable was vibrating. Jessica was grateful she'd not gone too crazy with her meals – a few more pounds here and there and she could be hurtling downwards at a far greater speed.

The hatch clanged closed above and Jessica held her breath as the dumb waiter continued to move down. It was almost entirely dark, but there were a few shafts of light coming from somewhere above, allowing her to see the bricks. A few times, the lift bumped forward and back, colliding with the tunnel and sending a thin shower of cement tumbling. Jessica clamped her eyes closed, holding her breath, waiting... waiting... waiting. Sod the Big One roller coaster – this ride was far more terrifying.

It took Jessica a few moments to realise the lift had stopped descending. There was no ding, no electronic doors sliding open, just a halt to the bone-quaking tremors. She opened her eyes and realised she was still shaking, could still feel the vibrations. She took a couple of breaths and then reached through the darkness, pawing at the metal panel. There was a slit along the centre where the doors snapped together, but, as she fingered around the edges, Jessica started to panic that the hatch could only be opened from the outside. She tried to adjust the way she was sitting but only succeeded in banging her head.

'Breathe,' she whispered to herself. 'Come on.'

When she tried again, Jessica found the catch instantly. There was a lever concealed on the inner wall, rough to touch and riddled with rust. She pulled it down carefully and was instantly flooded by light as the doors popped open. It took her a couple of seconds to get her bearings, but she was in a dimly lit room lined with washing machines, tumble dryers and a large steam press.

Jessica's legs creaked as she unfurled herself from the lift and tried to stand. She'd only been inside the dumb waiter for a minute at most, but it was so cramped that she was left feeling like someone twice her age. She cricked her neck and cracked her knuckles as she stepped into the empty room. There were pipes running across the ceiling and around the walls, plus a large pile of clean, pressed sheets. This room did go some way to explain what the maids did all day. In the summer, they'd be busy cleaning. There were far fewer guests as winter approached, yet they were still arriving early in the morning and leaving late in the afternoon. Presumably, the rest of their time was spent in this hothouse. Heat poured from the pipes, creating an improvised sauna, with sweat beginning to bead on Jessica's forehead.

She wiped her face dry and then quietly closed the doors to the dumb waiter. The ceiling was only a few inches taller than she was and when she stretched up, she could actually touch the roof, something she wasn't sure she'd ever been able to do before. It was incredibly disorientating, confusing even, as if she'd crossed into some sort of hobbity underworld.

Her senses felt sluggish, but Jessica soon realised the light was coming from a window above a pair of the washers. It was wide but not very tall and would definitely be a squeeze. It was a *really* good job she hadn't overindulged at mealtimes.

The window had been painted with gloopy white gloss at some point in years gone by, welding the frames closed – or at least they were until Jessica climbed on top of the washing machine, ducked under the low ceiling, lifted the catch and then rammed her shoulder into the wood. It took three attempts, but the window flew outwards, popping like a tin can in a microwave as flecks of paint and wood exploded free.

There was no time for messing around. Jessica squeezed herself through the gap, feeling concrete underneath her hands. She scrabbled on the gritty ground, heaving her legs through the window, which clanged closed behind her. Dust, sand and shingle scraped at her skin, but Jessica was out. She was flat on her front, lying on a patch of wasteland at the back of the hotel next to the bins. She pushed herself up, trying to brush away the dirt, but it was far too late for that. There were rat droppings close to the nearby drains and a partially chewed pizza box within touching distance, not to mention a fly-tipped sofa.

There was nobody in sight, so Jessica ran for the wall at the back. She jumped, clasping the top and ignoring the shooting pains as she wrenched her arm muscles and heaved herself over the top. Without pausing, she dropped down to the other side, landing on all fours with the grace of a drunken, elderly cat. Jessica turned, trying to get her bearings, and then headed for a weed-ridden ginnel as fast as her legs would take her.

She was out of breath, covered in dirt – and possibly worse – but she was free... for now at least.

TWENTY-EIGHT

Jessica ran for all she was worth, bolting along the lane until she lifted herself over a locked metal gate and emerged at the back of a row of shops. There was a bank of wheelie bins, a skip and some disintegrating wooden pallets pressed against a wall. With her hands, arms, clothes and probably face covered in dirt, it was likely she'd get a few sideways glances if she were to venture onto the main streets of Blackpool. Jessica winced, held her breath and opened the lid of a large wheelie bin. Inside was the filth and horror she expected, but she skimmed around the edges until she found a flattened cardboard box that was as clean as she was going to get. She pulled it out and then wiped as much of the filth from herself as possible. It wasn't quite dressed, primped and ready for dinner at the Ritz, but it would do until she could come up with something better.

She'd brought very little to the hotel anyway, but her pockets were packed with posters of Bex, her police warrant card, far more cash than she'd ever usually carry and her two phones. The moment she pulled out her old one – the good one – it started to ring with an unknown number that would likely be DCI Fordham. If not him, then her solicitor asking where she was. Jessica turned the device over and jabbed the tip of her fingernail into the hole that made the SIM card pop out. The phone instantly stopped ringing.

The card was tiny and solid. It had served her well, but all relationships came to an end: this one in particularly brutal fashion as Jessica dropped the SIM card down the drain. Now *that* was how to instigate a break-up.

After a bit of back and forward with the phone companies, the force could track a person by their phone signal if they *really* needed to find somebody. Her phone had been an even more loyal sidekick than the SIM card, but it was no time for sentimentality. Jessica switched the device off and then dropped it in the wheelie bin, covering it with a few items before closing the lid. She couldn't remember if it was insured. The salesperson would have definitely offered it, but Jessica had little heart for shopping, especially technology shopping, and there was every chance she'd have bought what she needed and scooted for home. Ah, well...

One of the few things in Jessica's favour was that the police didn't know for sure that she'd deliberately escaped. Brandon had been in the café when Fordham had shown up, meaning there would've been a window in which Jessica *could* have left the hotel without him noticing. Couple that with the fact that her phone *could* have run out of battery – and she'd done nothing wrong. They'd try calling her and contacting her solicitor. After that, they might go to Manchester and try her house. They had her car, so they'd be looking at the transport hubs to see if she'd caught a bus or train, then checking her credit and debit cards. That'd all take time, which at least left Jessica with a glimmer of hope that they wouldn't stick her on the most-wanted list any time soon. When they found out she'd withdrawn the maximum amount of cash on successive days, they'd start worrying that she'd planned everything – but that was a little while off.

'I've done nothing wrong,' she said out loud to no one but herself.

Jessica checked that her remaining phone was switched on and then headed along the path until she found the main street. There was a fancy-dress shop across the road with rows of garish masks in the front window that she recognised from her walks around the town. Apart from the mini supermarket next door, the area was still largely residential, with rows of terraces stretching away from her. The shop helped Jessica get her bearings and she hurried along the road in the general direction of the town centre until the houses gave way to bed and breakfasts and, eventually, shops.

By keeping half a dozen streets away from the promenade, Jessica was able to move relatively unnoticed. It was late afternoon and the sky had gone from a bluey-grey to very purple. Within an hour or so, it'd be dark and the temperature would plummet. The daytimes might be just about warm enough for sunbathing lunatics, but it was nudging freezing after dark and Jessica didn't have the clothing for that.

The smell of salt and vinegar was hanging on the breeze, drifting from the myriad of local chippies hoping to entice visitors. Jessica turned the corner just as half a dozen women in matching bright pink T-shirts half staggered, half fell down the stairs at the side of a casino. They were pissed, cackling as they clasped onto one another in order to stop themselves tumbling onto the pavement. Each of the shirts had different slogans – 'Big Momma' (who was *definitely* big), 'Bridezilla' (who was vomiting into the gutter), 'Maid of Dishonour' (who was swigging from a bottle of Blue VK, while smoking and chatting on her mobile phone), and 'Superbitch' (who was holding back

Bridezilla's hair). Jessica couldn't see the names on the back of the final pair, but they were busy squaring up to one another, arguing over an electronic cigarette.

She crossed the road, not making eye contact, only to walk into a second cloud of cigarette smoke from a bunch of suit-clad workers standing outside an office. She caught the phrase, 'yeah, but Julie's such a whore', before slipping into an alley.

As she emerged onto another shopping street, Jessica stopped, frozen, like a cat caught with a dead bird in its mouth. A police community support officer was striding through the centre, his dark stab-proof vest making him look like he'd gone swimming and forgotten to get rid of the buoyancy aid. The PCSOs weren't official police officers but were routinely sent out on patrol to act as the force's eyes and ears. They were unpaid volunteers, meaning the job attracted certain types of people. Some were genuinely community-minded, hoping to help out. Good men and women who put themselves in danger for the greater good. A minority were desperate for the tiniest amount of power to hold over people. This PCSO was definitely the latter. He was walking upright as if he had a board strapped to his back, hands clasping onto the lapels of his stab vest, peering from side to side in case there was someone he could throw an icy glare at. Given his limited powers, there was little more he could do than that, but most people wouldn't know that – especially the tourists.

It was too late for Jessica: she had already stepped out of the alley when his gaze slipped across her. For a moment, she thought he'd stop and come over, before calling for backup. As soon as he looked at her, he turned away again, distracted by some kids up the road kicking around a squished can of Vimto. His head snapped around towards them as if he'd set eyes on the Great Train Robbers riding Shergar and then he was off, bounding along the street with an ever-lengthening stride.

Jessica spotted one of her flyers about Bex stuck to a lamp-post across the road. They were useless now that she'd ditched her phone, but it did give her an indication of where she was. She continued along the road away from the PCSO for a short distance and then slipped into another narrower alley, continuing until she found herself at the Help the Homeless centre. From there, she surprised herself by retracing the route she'd taken when she met Fran. She lost the trail a few times, but it wasn't long before she found herself close to the chain-link fence by the train tracks.

It was easy from there. Jessica emerged onto the cul-de-sac and hunched through a gap in a fence until she was in the familiar overrun garden. The grass was wetter than the previous time she'd been, seeping through her socks – again – as she followed the crunching stones to the back door of the house.

Jessica knocked four times, waited, and then patted the door twice more. Nothing happened for a few seconds, leaving her to stew over the possibility of spending a night outdoors in the wet and the cold. Perhaps it would rain and she'd need to find somewhere undercover where the police wouldn't think of looking for her? Was this worth it? Then there was a clunk and a click, and the door of the Shanty swung inwards.

Melissa was there, the woman whom Fran had called the 'mum' of the house. She was wearing the same earphones as the last time Jessica had seen her, the sprawling grey-black hair recently washed, still wet and more of a shambles than before as it tried to strangle her. She blinked a few times, one hand on the door handle.

'Oh, it's you,' she said.

'Can I come in?' Jessica asked.

'Um... hang on.'

Before Jessica could say anything, the door was closed in

her face with the quietest of clicks. She hugged her arms across her front, beginning to feel the bite of the cold as the doubts scratched at her again. She'd come here because, well, she had nowhere else. There was no easy way to get back to Manchester and she didn't want to involve her friends in what was going on. It was either give herself up to Fordham and hope for the best, or try to take control of her own fate. She still needed somewhere to sleep, though.

Time passed, she wasn't sure how long. It was probably only a minute or so, but Jessica's teeth were chattering. She didn't think it was the cold, more that the adrenalin of her escape had worn off, leaving her with the weight of what she'd done.

This was as bad as it got. There would be no winners from here.

With another clunk-click, the door opened again and this time it was a concerned Fran standing there. She was wearing her deerstalker but it was looser, slightly askew in a way that shouldn't work but did. Her skin didn't seem as pale as the previous time they'd met and the moment she saw Jessica, her arms were outstretched, welcoming her in.

'I didn't expect you to come knocking,' she said. 'You want a cup of tea?'

There were times in life when everything had gone wrong, when every decision seemed wrong. Where hope was tough to come by and friends even harder. *Those* were the times for which tea was invented.

'I'm so glad you have a kettle,' Jessica said, blowing into her hands and stepping inside.

Jessica and Fran sat in a corner drinking tea as Jessica explained everything that had happened since they last met. It had only been a day but felt like a lot longer than that. By the end, Fran's loud puff of breath said it all.

'How much trouble are you actually in?' Fran asked.

Jessica was on a beanbag, cradling a chipped Mr Strong mug for warmth, even though she'd long finished the drink.

'Potentially, a lot.'

'You reckon they've found the body of that girl?'

'Sophie? They must have done. With that, the body of Peter and Bex's blood on my car, I'll be lucky to get out on bail.'

'Don't they usually bail everyone?'

'For the most part. If you're considered a danger to yourself or others, you might go on remand. With me, I'd be considered a flight risk because this could end my career.'

Fran opened her mouth and then closed it. For a moment Jessica thought she was going to ask the key question – 'did you do it?' – but she didn't. Her gaze darted towards the main door, betraying her thoughts.

Jessica gave her the answer before the question had been asked. 'They won't be coming for me – not yet,' she said.

'How do you know?'

'Because the main guy, Fordham, knows something's not right. If I can realistically claim I didn't know the police were looking for me, then I've done nothing wrong. I'll say my phone died, and it's not as if anyone could claim otherwise. I'm bailed to appear at Blackpool Police Station in five days. I wasn't bound to stay at a certain address, so I'm free until then. If they put out a public appeal to say they're looking for me, that doesn't mean I've seen it – but if an officer tries to stop me, then I can't run. I'll have to give myself up.'

'So you have five days?'

'Four really – and tonight. But they might put my face on the front of tomorrow's paper and that'd make it harder to stay anonymous.'

'But you've got four and a bit days to either figure out what's going on – or hope the police do?'

'I guess.'

Fran was on a beanbag of her own. She squished herself lower and leaned forward, voice barely a whisper. 'What if time runs out?'

Jessica knew her mug was empty but lifted it to her lips anyway, chewing on the rim. She wasn't sure what to say but Fran was staring at her. Given that she and her girls were now a part of this, she deserved an answer.

'I'm not sure,' Jessica replied. 'I'll have to go to the station to answer bail. I'll be arrested, interviewed. I can only tell them what I've said over and over – that I don't know anything – but everyone says that.'

'Your career?'

Jessica shook her head. For a police officer, being arrested – let alone charged – for a double or triple killing was the end.

Fran didn't press any further, standing and offering Jessica a hand. 'What can we do for you?'

Jessica stood and held up her phone, the cheap one that didn't do much. 'Have you got a charger for this?'

With a flick of her eyes, Fran had Jessica peering towards the corner of the room, where four chargers were plugged into an extension lead. 'Probably. Ellie set the electricity up. I don't know what she did but it doesn't go through the meter, if you know what I mean. What else do you need? We can't really help with money.'

Money wasn't a concern, not yet. 'A shower?' she asked.

'Our water supply works. The pressure's awful, but we can do that. There are some spare clothes in a box upstairs, too. Something will probably fit.'

'Somewhere to sleep?'

'We can do that, too. There are spare beds upstairs. You won't have a room to yourself, but—'

'Thank you.'

Fran placed a hand around Jessica's shoulders and led her towards the stairs. 'What are friends for if not to shelter you from the police?' She laughed but Jessica didn't. She was too busy trying to figure out how her life had fallen apart so quickly.

TWENTY-NINE

After her shower, Jessica's first few hours at the Shanty were a strange affair. The back door was knocked on and opened at regular intervals, and there were around a dozen women who seemed to live there. They were a mix of ages and races, with no apparent house prejudice, other than the fact that men weren't allowed.

Some were friendly, some not so much, preferring to find their own corner to read, use their phones, eat, or do whatever else they wanted. Some sat by themselves, saying nothing until Fran offered a motherly 'hello' and then left them be. Jessica expected that the women would be arriving because they wanted a bed for the night – but some of the residents left after eating and headed back into the cold. All of that was seemingly normal, with no questions being asked and little more than a smile and 'stay safe' from whomever was closest to the door.

The thing that both amazed and slightly disconcerted her was how quiet everything was. At home, Jessica often left on the radio or the television as background noise. Ever since Bex had disappeared, it had become almost a ritual to turn something on first thing in the morning and the moment she returned home from work. She used to find solace in the peace, but that silence had become a deafening reminder of how alone she was. At the Shanty, some of the women used headphones to listen to music and the radio, but there was no obvious noise aside from the quiet whispers to one another. Fran said there were three rules – no drugs, men or noise – and everyone was adhering. With the windows boarded and the light hidden, the residents of the street likely had no idea who was living under their noses. To organise all of this was smart – but to maintain discipline was incredible. Fran really had something special about her.

She had left Jessica in the company of Ruth, the woman whose husband had disappeared off to Spain with their company's money. Ruth was wearing the same large Green Bay sweatshirt from the day before and cradling the well-thumbed paperback like an infant with a teddy. She clutched it as if it were her solitary possession... which it might have been.

Ruth showed Jessica the ropes in the kitchen, barely letting go of the book as they boiled a can of soup on the stove. They shared it between them, drinking from mugs, and then Ruth opened one of the cupboards and took out a sealed plastic triangle of sandwiches.

'They went out of date yesterday,' she said, holding up the pack.

'Are they okay?'

Ruth couldn't quite allow herself a smile, but she pressed her lips together. 'They're always fine. One of the girls, Tina, knows this lad who works in a supermarket. They're supposed to throw away out-of-date food for health and safety reasons – they'd get sued for poisoning people if they gave it away, I guess. Anyway, he leaves a load of food in a bin bag at the back of the shop each night and it feeds us for a day or so. It's usually sandwiches, but there are the odd cakes.' She ripped the seal of the front and offered the pack to Jessica. 'Beef and mustard,' Ruth added.

Jessica took one, sniffed it and then took a large bite. It tasted perfectly fine – *better* than fine, in fact. There was something deliciously enticing about eating forbidden food.

Ruth had the other sandwich herself and they moved into the living room, finding a spot underneath the lamp in the corner where it was just them. Ruth held the book on her lap, fingers stroking the curled corners of the cover.

'How long are you going to be here?' Ruth asked, peering at the floor.

'I'm not sure. Maybe a few days? Not long.'

'Fran doesn't show many people where we live. She must've liked you.'

'I guess.'

'What's your story?'

Jessica put the final piece of sandwich in her mouth to buy herself time. She must have failed to hide how uncomfortable she was, because Ruth added: 'It's okay, you don't have to say.'

Jessica took a deep breath through her nose, still delaying. 'Things have just gone a bit... *wrong* recently.'

'They say you're police...' Ruth tailed off and started picking at a loose thread hanging from her sock.

There were four other people in the room, each in their own space. Jessica glanced around, suddenly feeling watched, even though none of them were paying her any attention. 'That's right,' she replied.

'Are you here to...?'

'I'm not a threat to anyone. I only wanted to find my friend and then things spiralled out of control. I'm here because I needed help.'

Ruth nodded slowly, lowering her voice further, even though there was no chance of being overheard. 'Everybody trusts Fran and if she says you're all right, then people will take her at that.'

Jessica nodded appreciatively but knew that worked both ways. If Fran turned on her for any reason, she could cause an awful lot of trouble.

After retrieving her phone from the bank of chargers, Jessica returned to the corner, sitting next to Ruth, who had opened her book. She fiddled with the basic Internet on her phone, managing to get onto the Blackpool Police website, and the *Gazette*'s. Luckily there was no mention of her, although that would only be a matter of time. Jessica thought about calling Izzy, if only for someone to talk to. It would have been nice to hear a familiar voice that believed everything she was saying – but it wasn't fair. Jessica would be doing that for her own reasons, dragging Izzy into something that could get her in trouble.

She thought of her mother, too, who lived in a residential home on the outskirts of Manchester. She was always complaining – justifiably – that Jessica didn't call her enough, but this was too big a burden. Jessica's mum wasn't exactly frail, not even particularly old in the grand scheme, but she would worry herself half to death if Jessica were to explain what had happened. She had unwavering faith in the emergency services, too, and would urge Jessica to give herself up. That was the problem, though. Jessica knew how things looked, how easy it would be for a Criminal Prosecution Service lawyer to talk about her being a flight risk. If her name came out in the media, she might think about dealing with her mother then.

Jessica was about to start looking for Fran in order to ask which bed was hers when Fran burst into the living room, accidentally kicking over a teacup. It went spinning across the room and clattered into a wall, though didn't shatter. It was the loudest noise Jessica had heard since arriving at the house.

Fran peered around the room until she settled on Jessica. She was out of breath: 'You free?'

Jessica's instinct was to joke – she was hardly about to head out for a night on the town – but Fran's wide eyes made it clear something serious was happening. 'Yes.'

Fran turned her hand around to show her phone. 'Alison's just called in – that guy I told you about, the one who drives around the streets and tries to get girls to go with him – he's back.' She reached around the corner, grabbing a thick jacket and slipping her arms inside, then picking up another and holding it out towards Jessica. 'If we go now, he might still be there. He normally does a couple of loops.'

Jessica felt drawn into doing as she'd been asked. Before she knew it, she was next to the back door and putting on the heavy winter coat. Fran opened the door but Jessica touched her arm. 'I'm not sure if I'm police any longer,' she said, checking behind to make sure nobody was listening. They weren't – it wasn't the way of the house. 'There's not a lot I can do, even if he is there.'

Fran broke into a small grin. There were wisps of her nearly grey hair poking out from her deerstalker. 'You might not be police, honey, but you're one of us.' She winked. 'Now put your hood up. Don't want those nosy police bastards seeing your pretty face, do we?'

Fran and Jessica barely spoke during the walk, with Jessica shrinking into the coat as much as she could, hoping they didn't run into any officers who might be looking for her. As it was, she needn't have worried. Fran knew the side streets and back alleys as if she'd designed the town herself. She hurried from one to another without slowing until they were close to the centre. Jessica was beginning to get a feel for the area herself, spotting shops and buildings that she recognised, but

Fran moved so quickly that there was no time to stop and figure out how one place linked to another.

Before Jessica knew it, they were on a crumbling street, standing underneath an archway of a bed and breakfast that had gone out of business. The windows were boarded up with cheap chipboard that was doused with poorly spelled graffiti. There was a faded sign pinned above the door advertising vacancies that were very unlikely to be honoured.

Fran sat on the step underneath the overhang and patted the spot next to her. Jessica sat, keeping her hands in the pockets of the jacket, where it was warm. The B&B was a little set back from the road and flanked on either side by takeaways. It was a few minutes after nine, not quite time for the theatres to kick out. A few people passed by, chatting and going about their business. No one paid them any attention. They were invisible.

'This is one of our pillars,' Fran said.

'Sorry?'

'There are a few places around town where the girls know to head for if there's a problem. This is The Fell. It went out of business years ago. Because of the way it's set back from the street, nobody notices you. You could sit here all night and not be bothered, as long as you keep the noise down. If one of the girls has a problem but they're too far from the Shanty, they head for one of the pillars.'

'Why do you call them that?'

'They're pillars of the community – *our* community. I can't remember whose idea it was now.'

Jessica was becoming unnerved by the constant referrals to 'the girls'. It wasn't so much the idea of them sticking together, more that it came with an implication that women were good, men bad. Whenever Fran talked about things, the edge was clear in her voice. Jessica wanted to say something, but she needed Fran more than Fran needed her.

As silence hung between them, Jessica took in what she could of the street. There was a betting shop directly opposite, with a bakery on one side and a newsagent-cum-seaside tat shop on the other. The windows of the betting shop were plastered with posters advertising special offers, with only a narrow shaft of light spilling through the door. Once inside, its punters had no view of the outside world. The newsagent and bakery were both closed, with thick steel shutters clamped onto the pavement. Jessica was watching a couple walk hand in hand on the other side of the road when a figure darted around the entrance to the B&B and plopped herself next to Fran. It had happened so quickly that Jessica had almost missed it. The figure was a waif of a girl who Jessica hadn't seen around the Shanty. She was wearing a leather jacket over leggings that hung loosely because she was so slim. Her blonde hair was bright, even in the dimness in which they were sitting, and she had hooped earrings that were so big, Jessica was surprised she could keep her head lifted.

'You okay, Ally?' Fran whispered.

The girl burrowed her head on Fran's shoulder in much the same way that Ruth had done at the Shanty. She was probably still a teenager, but the sunken nature of her eyes and jutting cheekbones made it hard to tell.

'He's still around,' she replied.

Fran put an arm around her and gestured towards Jessica. 'Jess, this is Alison; Ally, Jess.'

They whispered 'hi' to one another and then Fran continued: 'What was he doing?'

'Driving around like usual,' Alison replied. 'It's the first time I've seen him in about a week.'

'Did any girls go with him?'

'No – he was over by that bingo place near the multistorey. He pulled in and talked to this girl I didn't recognise. I think she'd just popped out for a fag because she didn't say much and then he drove off. I hid in this alley opposite and that's when I called you. When I was coming here, I saw him again, driving past that blue hotel near the school.'

Fran patted Alison on the back, subliminally encouraging her to stop resting on her shoulder. Alison sat up and started to suck her thumb. 'Good girl,' Fran said, climbing to her feet. Jessica found herself doing the same without being asked.

'Is that far away?' she asked.

'Five minutes,' Fran replied. 'You coming?'

'What do you want me to do?'

'Get a look at the guy and his car, see what you think. You must have instincts. Is he someone we should worry about, or a bit of a loser?'

Jessica wasn't convinced she could offer any help, but there was little point in refusing. Besides, the reason she'd come to Blackpool in the first place was to look for Bex. If this man was enticing young women into his car and driving off, there could be something there.

The three of them crossed the road and followed the line of a wall until they were at the back of a pub. There were people inside, lights, music and chatter leaking onto the patio. Fran barely seemed to notice, keeping her head down and passing through a gate at the back into a deserted lane that ran along the rear of the shops and businesses. Without pausing, she hurried towards the end, quickly crossing the street in the darkest part between the street lights, and then headed down a ramp onto the lower level of a multistorey car park. She hugged the wall, sticking to the shadows until they reached the far side, where she ducked underneath a half-drawn metal shutter and led them into a delivery yard with four vans parked along the side.

Everything she did was designed to stay out of sight, to remain ignored and get from one place to another in the shortest time possible. Fran knew the streets with such perfect instinct that they were almost an extension of herself. She didn't even need to think about what she was doing.

Via a boost over a low wall, they eventually reached a yard at the back of a mini supermarket. The delivery door shutter was down, with a CCTV camera pointing in their general direction. There was a pile of folded-down cardboard boxes wedged between two wheelie bins, plus a small circle of cigarette ends drowning next to a drain.

Fran glanced towards the camera and said: 'It doesn't work,' before Jessica could query it. She headed for the bins, lifting one of the lids and reaching inside to remove a carrier bag that had the handles tied together. She undid them and peered inside, grinning as she passed a bag of bakery cookies to Alison.

'Hungry?'

Alison's eyes lit up. She tore the seal at the top and took out a chocolate chip cookie, taking a large bite before passing the bag to Jessica. It felt impolite to say no, but Jessica wasn't hungry and handed them to Fran, who retied the carrier bag and returned it – carefully – to the bin.

'One for later,' she told Jessica.

They moved into the alley that ran along the side of the shop, remaining in single file and sticking to the shade. Fran was at the front, Jessica in the middle, with soft appreciative munches coming from Alison at the back.

The mini supermarket faced a wide road that Jessica didn't recognise. There were shops on either side, but not the types found closer to the town centre. These were more orientated towards local residents – a hairdresser, florist and hardware store, with a pub at the far end. It was similar to the rank that was within walking distance of Jessica's house in Manchester, probably within walking distance of most people's houses.

Other than the faint sound of music coming from the pub,

the area was quiet. The shops were closed, but there were no shutters.

'He's been spotted cruising around here before,' Fran said after a minute or so of waiting in position. She didn't look over her shoulder.

A few cars did pass, but none of them slowed. If anything, they sped up, trying to beat the traffic lights next to the pub. Fran shuffled closer to the wall, allowing Jessica to move alongside her as she nodded towards a bus stop that had been out of view. A bright white street light blazed above, with one lone woman sitting on the bench below. She was wearing a short purple dress with a dark jacket over the top, heels tapping on the pavement as she jabbed at her phone.

'Do you know her?' Jessica asked.

'No. She probably works at one of the casinos if she's dressed like that.'

They continued watching in silence. A couple of times, the woman peered up, glancing from side to side, perhaps sensing she was being observed. Each time, she returned to her phone.

'Ally,' Fran said, nudging Jessica's arm and nodding towards the lights. A dark blue BMW had crossed the junction and was heading towards them on the other side of the road.

Alison squidged in between Jessica and Fran, barely taking up any space. Her thumb had been in her mouth again but she removed it with a soft plop and whispered a solemn: 'That's him.'

Jessica found herself holding her breath as the car slowed. It passed them but the driver was looking the other way. As it reached the bus stop, the driver stopped directly under the street light. They couldn't hear the individual words, but the passenger side window was down and the driver said something to the woman in the purple dress. Jessica stepped out of the shadow to get a closer look at the driver. Fran was tugging her backwards but Jessica was undeterred, shrugging herself free and edging a few paces along the street. She stared at the car, the overhead street light giving her a near perfect view of the driver.

The woman at the bus stop peered up from her phone, pulling her jacket tighter as she shook her head. The driver said something else and she replied with a frown and something Jessica couldn't hear. Instantly, the car's engine growled and the BMW zoomed away, disappearing around the bend, out of sight.

'Hey.' Jessica felt a hand on her shoulder, turning to see Fran's face screwed up with concern. She'd drifted far further along the pavement than she'd realised, twenty or thirty metres from the safety of the shadows. 'What's going on?' Fran added.

'It's the driver.'

'What about him?'

'He's the man I apparently killed,' Jessica replied. 'He told me his name was Peter Salisbury.'

THIRTY

Fran stared at Jessica for a few moments, lips tight. 'Come on,' she said, pulling Jessica's arm and leading her back towards the alley that ran along the side of the mini supermarket. Alison was still there, pressed into the shadows, eyeing Jessica carefully.

'Are you sure you got a proper look at the driver?' Fran asked.

'It's him. We walked along the prom and he told me about a missing sister. He said his name was Peter, but it was all a bit weird. When the police showed me a photograph of the dead guy and said it was Peter Salisbury, I assumed it was the same person. They *looked* similar – stubble and dark hair – but I'd only met him once. I didn't think I'd know him – but it's the shape of his face. Perhaps the way the light catches it, I don't know. He was definitely the driver.'

Fran seemed lost for words, which was something of a first. Alison had no idea what was going on. She stood close by, listening but adding nothing.

'So who's Peter Salisbury?' Fran asked. 'Is he the dead guy or the driver?'

Jessica shook her head slowly, trying to remember everything she'd been told. 'Peter's father identified the body.'

'So Peter *is* the dead guy – and this bloke, the driver, gave you Peter's name to confuse you?'

That was the easy explanation, that some stranger – the man driving the car – had used Peter's identity when Jessica phoned the number on the poster. At some point after they'd gone their separate ways, he'd killed the *actual* Peter and then dumped the body. Jessica's number was still the most recent on Peter's phone, which is why DCI Fordham had knocked on her hotel room door. It made sense in a warped not-making-sense kind of way, largely because Jessica had no idea who the driver was. He must be someone with a grudge, or a reason to target her, but she'd never met him before that evening on the promenade.

Except that the easy explanation felt wrong.

It took Jessica a second or two to clock why, but then she knew. 'That driver *is* Peter Salisbury,' she said. 'The body must be someone else who looks similar. There was a wallet on the body with Peter's name, so they had no reason to assume it was anyone else. His dad then identified the body, so that was that. Things like blood work and DNA tests are expensive. It'd only be done if there were doubt over an identity. There would have been a post-mortem, but unless there was anything out of the ordinary, there's no reason it would have been picked up on.'

'Out of the ordinary how?' Fran asked.

'Say Peter had his appendix removed when he was a kid, but the dead body still had his; or if Peter was six foot and the body was five eight. That sort of thing. From what Fordham said, the cause of death was clear and they had a positive ID. If they were both men of a similar age, height, build and so on, it could easily happen. They wouldn't even have to be exact, just similar. I'm not saying these things are rushed...' she tailed off and then added, 'well, maybe I am. This is a busy town. There's no point in messing around with lengthy investigations when it's all on a plate. We're always so conscious of the budget.' Jessica stopped herself again, mind buzzing. 'Everyone thinks Peter's dead but he must have been keeping his head down.'

Fran didn't seem convinced: 'How do you know that's him?'

Jessica was about to answer when a bus passed, its engine grumbling noisily. It pulled up at the bus stop on the other side of the road and the woman in the purple dress climbed aboard before the bus growled its way towards the traffic lights and disappeared.

Jessica watched it go, assuring herself she was right. 'Peter's dad,' she said. 'He's called Greg. They have the same eyes. If you saw them, you'd know.'

'Why would his father identify someone else's body as his son's?'

'Insurance?' Alison jumped in for the first time, peering from Fran to Jessica. As soon as she'd spoken, she seemed embarrassed by it and lowered her tone as she added: 'I mean some people have life insurance, don't they? Maybe he'll get a load of money?'

Fran touched her upper arm, smiling and whispering: 'Good thinking, honey.' She turned back to Jessica and shrugged, asking silently what Jessica thought.

Jessica didn't want to say 'no' but she doubted it. 'Perhaps insurance and something else?' she said. It wouldn't be the first time someone had faked their own death to cash in, and then lived out their days as someone else until they were either caught or kicked the bucket for real. This didn't feel like that, because, if it was, why bring Jessica into it? The poster had been left on the phone booth on purpose. Faking death wasn't exactly simple – but it was easier than what had happened.

Fran sensed the confusion, remaining quiet until she couldn't stand it any longer. 'If that was Peter driving the car, then who's the dead body?'

Jessica shook her head. 'I have no idea.'

That wasn't the only question to which she had no answer, though one thing was perhaps explaining itself. Peter was a regular at the Honky Tonk diner and Sophie Johns had a thing for him. If *he* was alive, perhaps he'd convinced – or forced Sophie – to call Jessica on the night she vanished. After all, there was no way he'd ever be a suspect in her disappearance, given that he was supposed to be dead.

Jessica's head was throbbing from trying to figure everything out.

'Are you going to tell... y'know... your lot?' Fran said. She sounded concerned, though it was hard to know whether that was for Jessica's welfare, or the fate of her girls.

Things were moving too quickly, Jessica's thoughts colliding with her principles. She was scared. She could lose everything and she would be putting her faith and fate in the hands of other people.

'If I tip off Fordham and co., I'll have to hand myself in. Maybe they'll believe me, maybe not – but unless they find Peter himself, it won't make much difference.'

Fran started to say something but then stopped herself. She gasped, peering past Jessica to the lights. On the far side of the junction, the BMW had reappeared. It had stopped, ready to head back their way, this time on their side of the road. It was the only vehicle in sight, illuminated a murky purple because of the glowing red traffic light.

'What do you want to do?' Fran hissed.

Jessica was usually so calm, if not outwardly then inwardly. She brimmed with ideas and generally thought a step or two ahead of those around her. As the traffic light colour changed to red with amber, she felt frozen. All she thought was to get the number plate, though she knew it would likely do little. If Peter was driving around, trying to encourage girls into his car, someone would eventually notice and call the police. They would probably be fake plates, or a stolen car. If not that, then the car would be hidden somewhere it was unlikely to be found. It might be a lead, but it wouldn't help her in the small time frame she had.

As she flailed, there was a glance between Fran and Alison and then it was too late. Jessica said 'no', but Alison had already dashed past her, almost skipping onto the kerbside underneath a nearby street light. Fran yanked Jessica's arm, pulling her into the darkest shadows, well out of sight of the road. Part of Jessica wanted to fight, to say this wasn't what she wanted, but the decision had already been made for her.

The BMW was barely twenty metres away when it rumbled to a halt underneath the street light. The passenger window hummed down and Alison crouched, resting on the paintwork.

'What you up to?' a man's voice asked. Jessica's view of the driver was blocked by Alison's slender frame.

'Not much. You?' Alison sounded so young, so vulnerable. Jessica wanted to pull her away to safety.

Fran sensed the movement and gripped Jessica's hand, whispering: 'She's fine.'

In front of them, the driver laughed quietly: 'I'm not up to much, either. You want a ride?'

'What for?'

'Y'know... see the sights. You local?'

'Sort of.'

The engine snarled as the man revved it. 'You getting in then?'

Alison opened the door and stepped backwards to swing it open. It was only a fraction of a second, but Jessica had a clear view of the driver. He had the same stubble, the same short hair. He smiled, leering towards Alison as she shuffled into the passenger seat and then Jessica knew with complete certainty that he was the man she'd met on the promenade.

Peter Salisbury was alive – and he'd just picked up a young girl from the street and driven off with her in his car.

THIRTY-ONE

It wasn't until the car was around the bend and out of sight that Jessica finally breathed out. Fran let go of her hand and then started walking towards the yard at the back of the mini supermarket. Jessica could do nothing other than follow as Fran retrieved the carrier bag of out-of-date food from the large bin. She headed to the wall, waiting for Jessica and the boost-up needed to get over.

'Where are we going?' Jessica asked. She felt as if she had just woken up, not quite able to understand what was going on.

'Where do you think?' Fran replied. 'Back to the Shanty.' She put the bag on the floor and cupped her hands, ready to push Jessica up and over the wall.

'What about Alison?' Jessica asked.

'She can look after herself. There's not much we can do – it's not like we can follow her. She's smart, resourceful. Don't be fooled because she sucks her thumb.'

'I wasn't...' Jessica had made assumptions, but that wasn't the point. She didn't know how to express herself without making it sound patronising. 'How do you know she'll be all right?'

'Because she's not the first girl who's got into a car with a man. She knew what she was doing.'

Jessica batted away Fran's hands and cupped her own, ready to hoist the other woman up first. 'But *why* did she go?'

'Because you're one of us and we look out for each other. Ally will try to find out who he is, where he's staying, that sort of thing. Trust her.'

She stepped into Jessica's palms and, as she was hoisted up, Fran grabbed the top of the wall and pulled until she was sitting astride it. She took the carrier bag of food and then helped Jessica up before they started the walk back to the Shanty.

The house was even quieter than usual when Jessica and Fran arrived. Fran headed straight through to the kitchen and clicked the kettle on. She made them both cups of tea and then showed Jessica into the living room. There was no sign of Ruth or her book, but Ellie was cross-legged on the beanbags, using a pair of pliers to poke at the wiring sticking out of a blanket. Her black hair was held in place by a brown bandana. She had been alone in the room but smiled up at Fran, who sat next to her. Jessica took a spot close by, still uncomfortable at what had happened that evening.

Fran handed Ellie one of the cookies they'd rescued from the bin. 'Present,' she said.

Ellie's eyes sparkled as she put the pliers down and took the biscuit. She bit into it with a grin and then turned to Jessica. 'Have you had any luck finding your friend?' she asked.

'No.'

'I'm sure she'll show up.'

Jessica returned her smile but struggled to find much enthusiasm. Until she knew Alison was safe – *if* she was safe – she'd be unable to rest.

'Whatcha up to, sweetie?' Fran asked.

Ellie had quickly devoured more than half the cookie. She whirled her hand in front of her mouth as she chewed. 'I found an electric blanket in a skip on North Shore. They're cleaning out a block of flats and there's all sorts out there. I might ask if someone wants to come with me tomorrow to see if there's anything else. I'm trying to get it to work.' Ellie picked up the blanket and pointed to a rigid spot around the edge. 'The wiring's gone. I had some spare in my toolbox, so hopefully it'll be okay now.' She handed it to Fran. 'Want to try it?'

'Is it going to blow up on me?'

They grinned at one another and then Ellie winked. 'Darn! You figured out my grand plan.' She finished the cookie and then picked the blanket up and crossed to the bank of sockets on the other side of the room. She unplugged one of the phone chargers and then pushed in the plug from the blanket. 'Ready?' she asked.

'Go on,' Fran replied.

Ellie flicked the switch on the cable and then reared back as if it had exploded. She giggled and then waited a few moments before pressing her hand to the area closest to the cabling.

'It's warm,' she said, smile spreading.

'Warm as in "this might set the house on fire", or warm as in "nice and toasty"?'

Ellie pressed the switch to turn it off. 'Toasty.'

Fran applauded quietly. 'Brilliant. What are you going to do with it?'

'Mel was saying she felt cold last night. I'll see if she wants it.'

Fran pushed herself up and held her arm out. Ellie

wedged herself in for a cuddle and then stifled a yawn. 'I'm going to bed,' she said.

'We'll be up in a bit, hon. Night.'

Ellie nodded towards Jessica and then folded the blanket under her arm before heading for the stairs. There were a couple of creaks and then the house was silent – eerily so considering there were anything up to a dozen people sleeping on the floor above.

Fran lowered herself back onto the beanbag next to Jessica. 'Quite a lot of the girls either go to bed early, or they stay out,' she said. 'One or two like a drink, but they don't bring it back here. We don't exactly have a curfew, but nobody wants to be the person who wakes everyone else up. You tired?'

'Not yet.'

Fran offered the same knowing smile that she had done many times before: 'Ally will be fine.'

'I'd still rather wait.'

'Do you read? We've got a small library in the cupboard under the stairs – things we've found around and about.'

Jessica yawned, not bothering to hide it, and then shook her head. 'I think my mind needs some time to figure everything out.'

There was one cookie left in the packet and Fran snapped it in half, passing one part to Jessica. 'Eat,' she said.

She hadn't been hungry, but the moment Jessica took a bite, her stomach growled. She always lost track of mealtimes when she was stressed – and this was as serious as it got.

It wasn't until she brushed her pocket that she remembered how much cash she had on her. The women of the Shanty were busy digging around in skips and bins for food and warmth – and she could have kitted out the house.

'You can ask me,' Fran said out of the blue. She was finally taking off her deerstalker, allowing her hair to hang freely. It really was white, but not the type that might be seen on someone who had aged. It glowed healthily, astoundingly. It was no wonder she covered her head when they were outside – she'd be easily remembered otherwise.

'Ask you what?' Jessica replied.

'You know – you've wanted to ask it since we first met.'

Jessica finished her half of the cookie and brushed the crumbs from her lap, eating those too. 'How old are you?' she asked.

'Twenty-two.'

She was so surprised that Jessica forgot she was in the middle of swallowing, breathing in and sending the flecks of biscuit into her lungs. She coughed and choked, patting herself on the chest until they were free and she could more or less breathe again.

'I didn't expect that reaction,' Fran said with a soft smile. For perhaps the first time, she seemed vulnerable, arms holding her knees to her chest.

'Cookie,' Jessica coughed.

'I gathered that.'

Jessica continued patting her chest until she could inhale without wheezing. 'It's just... *twenty-two*?! I figured you were younger than you looked but twenty-two? When I was twenty-two, I was still dossing about trying to figure out what to do with my life. I was out on the lash most weekends, eating pizza or curry all the time.'

'I *am* homeless, y'know. It's not like I've got a grand career plan.'

Jessica held her hands up, indicating the house. 'I know, but... all this.'

'It's not mine. We're squatting, living under someone else's roof. It's nothing special. Your lot could come any day and turf us out. Arrest us, even. Theft of electricity, of water. Technically, taking that leftover food is stealing. Can you believe that?

They'd rather have it thrown out and eaten by rats than feed another human?'

'But the girls, the way you keep them safe... how everyone manages to eat and look after one another. How they're all warm, healthy... happy even. It really is something special. There are people out there with ten times the resources you have – more – who'd get nowhere near achieving this. You should see our lot trying to organise a Christmas party.'

Fran peered away, gazing towards the stairs. She shrugged modestly. 'It's not just me. Look at Ellie. Without her, there'd be no electricity. Tina tipped us off about the food at the supermarket. Everyone chips in.'

'But they wouldn't be here – wouldn't be *able* to chip in – if it wasn't for you.'

'People would get by.' Fran scrunched up the bag the cookies had been in and then started to crinkle the beanbag, wanting something to do with her hands.

'What happened to you?' Jessica asked, realising she might be crossing a line.

Fran didn't reply at first, though her hands stopped grinding the bag. A gentle breeze tickled the windows, but the house was impossibly silent otherwise.

'I had a husband,' Fran said. '*Have* a husband, I suppose. My parents were into religion big time. No sex before marriage and all that. They wouldn't let me out, wouldn't ever leave me alone with a boy, that sort of thing. I was home-schooled until I was fourteen and then they let me go to this academy with a syllabus that focused more on the Bible than science. My mum was one of the governors and helped set it up. When I was seventeen, I met this man through a friend of a friend. I was a kid and he was nearly forty. Mum and Dad sort of approved of him because he was related to someone they knew at the church. I thought it was normal. You do, don't you? Normal is what's in front of you.'

She turned to Jessica, wanting confirmation. Jessica nodded – she'd seen it so many times. Kids that spent their childhoods cleaning up after alcoholic and drug-addled parents thinking it was the same for everyone. Others who were pregnant at thirteen because their mother had conceived them at the same age. Nurture was a wonderful blessing but a ferocious curse.

'We had these escorted date things. It must have looked so weird – me, my mum and dad, plus this bloke closer to their age than mine. We'd all be dressed smartly, sitting in this posh restaurant and chatting about, well, nothing. Then, at the end, me and him would be left alone for a couple of minutes. We'd not even kiss or anything because I was too embarrassed.' She shivered. 'It's so *fucking* creepy.'

'You got married?'

Fran closed her eyes, wiggling deeper onto the beanbag. 'I thought I was in love and it was the only way they'd let me spend more time with him. It was all done within about three or four months of us meeting. I was pregnant a few weeks later.'

Jessica couldn't hide the surprise in her voice: 'You have a child?'

Fran gulped and took a breath. She rolled onto her side so that she was facing away from Jessica, though she continued to speak. 'He liked kids.'

'He wanted children, not you?'

'No... he *liked* kids.'

A pause. It felt like the air had been sucked from the room. 'Oh...'

'It was one Sunday. I was living in his house and he had some family over for dinner. He's got a huge family – brothers, sisters, aunts, uncles, cousins. They're all friendly in that mad scary way, where they all pretend to be friends and have big get-togethers once a month. My parents were there, too. It was a big barbecue in the garden: sun out, cloudy lemonade, cups of tea, jam and scones. Really nice in some ways. I'd gone upstairs to get changed and he was there with his twelve-year-old niece on our bed. She was scared shitless. When I opened the door, she squealed and ran for it. She told her mum what had happened, what he'd been trying to do, but he said it was a big misunderstanding. They all turned to me – his parents, my parents, his family – all of them. They asked what I'd seen and, well...'

There was silence for a long time. Minutes. Jessica said nothing, knowing what was coming.

Fran eventually pushed herself back into a sitting position, head slumped onto her knees. 'I told them I wasn't sure.'

More silence.

'I *was* sure, but it was too late. They all wanted to believe him anyway. I went to the police, but they treated it like a domestic, kept asking if he'd hit or abused me. He hadn't, not really. He didn't like me going out or wearing tops with short sleeves, or skirts that weren't down to my ankles. That was normal for me, though. Nothing happened in the end, but I was stuck there with him, pregnant. I was naive, but deep down we all know what's right and wrong, don't we? We might not care, but we know. I knew I couldn't have a kid and let him anywhere near it.'

'What did you do?'

'Ran. One day when he was at work, I packed up what I could and left. No note, no anything. He used to leave a bit of cash for me to buy groceries, so I took that and bought a train ticket. I kept going way past my stop until they kicked me off. I had to put my daughter up for adoption – there was no way I could look after both of us, not then.' She held up her hands, indicating the house. 'All of this came about in the last year. You grow up quickly when you have to. I moved around at first, but then made some friends and figured things out. One thing led to another and here we are.'

She caught Jessica's eye, but there were no tears, perhaps not even regret. Fran was steely and determined.

'Have you ever been back in contact with your parents?' Jessica asked.

'No chance.'

'You're extraordinary.'

Fran shrugged. 'If you say so.'

They were interrupted by a gentle patting on the door: four taps, a pause, and then two more. Fran leapt up, bounding across the room to the back door and unlocking the bolts. Alison pressed underneath Fran's arm as the icy breeze jetted through behind her. She was windswept, her hair a mess, rosy-cheeked but seemingly unharmed.

Jessica stood but was unsure what to do. A part of her wanted to hug the younger woman, but they barely knew one another.

'You all right?' Jessica asked, knowing it sounded pathetic.

Alison nodded as Fran clicked the door closed behind her and re-bolted it. 'That bloke is a right nutter,' she said, wriggling her arms free from her leather jacket and unclipping her hooped earrings. She flopped onto the beanbags, curling her legs under herself, Fran at her side.

'You want a cup of tea, honey?' Fran asked.

Alison shook her head. 'He drove us around for a bit and was acting like we're boyfriend-girlfriend. He kept asking what I'd been up to during the day. When I mentioned I'd been on the street, he coughed, like he didn't want to hear that. I ended up telling him I was a receptionist by day, pole dancer by night. That got him excited. He was asking what I wore in the office and all that. Total creep-o.'

'What did he say his name was?' Fran asked, glancing towards Jessica.

'He didn't. When I asked what to call him, he said he liked being known as "Daddy".'

'Eew.' Jessica and Fran made the same noise at the same time.

'Yeah, like I said, total creep-o.'

'Did he take you anywhere specific?' Fran asked.

'We drove around for a bit and then he started going down these dark roads without street lights. He kept saying, "Nearly home, baby," and then he pulled up next to these really dark trees. He said we were home and I was like, "Where are we?". He kept saying "home". He asked if I was going to go inside with him – but there was no way I was doing that. He said he'd pay and took this big wodge of notes out of his jacket. There was hundreds there. He gave me fifty "for being a sweetheart".' Alison winced as she took two twenties and a ten-pound note from her jacket, pressing them flat on the floor with her hands. 'Then he kept asking how much I wanted to go inside. I said I wanted to go back to the town centre and he was getting annoyed. Eventually I told him my friends knew I'd gone in his car, that they had the number plate and description. He got even weirder then, called me the usual – "slut", "slag", "whore", "bitch" – y'know. He screamed at me to get out. I ended up walking. Good job I could see the lights in the distance.'

Fran rubbed her shoulder protectively. 'You did really well, honey.'

'Can you remember anything else about where he took you?' Jessica asked.

Alison stuck out her bottom lip. 'Not really. It was sort of... farm-like, down this dirt track in the middle of nowhere. There were these gates that had a red semicircle thing, but that was it.'

Both Alison and Fran saw the shock in Jessica's face.

'You know the place?' Fran asked.

'I think I was there earlier today...'

She tailed off. It seemed like such a long time ago. So much had happened, but it was true – she'd been at the farm at lunchtime.

'It belongs to this guy named Vince,' Jessica stumbled. 'He has this van that picks up and drops off the maids at the hotel where I was staying. I thought one of the maids recognised my photo of Bex.'

Fran was scratching her head, watching Jessica with puzzled bewilderment. 'But this guy, Peter, wasn't there?'

'No, it was Vince and his son, Max.'

'But they know Peter?'

'I... suppose...'

'Does that mean these are the men who tried to set you up?' Fran asked. Jessica shook her head, though she had no idea. She didn't know any of them. 'Sleep on it?' Fran added.

Jessica could do little but yawn. Perhaps her subconscious would have more luck in figuring it out.

THIRTY-TWO

Jessica woke to find herself in an empty room. There were four other beds around her, some makeshift on the floor, some more traditional. All had been made perfectly, their inhabitants nowhere in sight. Jessica had a spot on the floor with a comfy air mattress and a warm, bouncy quilt. She had tiptoed in the previous night and curled up under the covers and now she was still here, apparently unmoved after a night from which she remembered none of her dreams. It had been one of the best sleeps she could remember.

At the bottom of her bed was a folded pile of clothes. They weren't hers but had clearly been left for her – and were clean. There was a pair of jeans that were a little too big but fitted well enough, plus a long-sleeve top with a fleecy lining. Jessica's other possessions were still under her pillow. Jessica put on the new clothes and headed downstairs. Alison was on the beanbags near Ruth, but there was nobody else around, other than Fran in the kitchen.

'Sleep well?' Fran asked as Jessica entered. She was wearing her deerstalker again, hiding her distinctive hair underneath.

'*Really* well,' Jessica replied. 'No snorers.'

Fran smiled. 'Mel can be a bit loud when she gets going, but she was in a different room. I've got a present for you.'

'Huh?'

'Don't expect much.' Fran peered around the kitchen until she found what she was looking for, folded up and wedged behind the toaster. She passed Jessica a copy of that morning's *Gazette*. 'That your girl?' she asked.

Jessica scanned the front page – Sophie Johns had been found dead among a copse of rocks on the far North Shore. No cause of death was mentioned, but that was two bodies in a matter of days in a similar area – and panic stations wouldn't be far off. If business wasn't bad enough, the last thing the tourism board needed was a serial killer on the loose. The police would be feeling the squeeze to arrest someone – and Jessica was top of their list.

Details were sketchy, other than what Jessica already knew. Sophie had left the diner where she worked and not arrived home. The police were appealing for witnesses, asking for calm, the usual.

Mercifully, Jessica's name was nowhere near the coverage. Her potential involvement wasn't even alluded to, meaning the Blackpool Police press office either hadn't been told about her, or had kept it back. Jessica sensed Fordham's hand, perhaps giving her a little special treatment because he knew what it would mean for her if news were to leak. He wouldn't be able to keep something like that back for long before they had to put out a public appeal asking for her to come forward.

'This is the girl who phoned me,' Jessica replied, peering up to Fran. 'I've got to get back to the farm with the red circle on the gates. It's out Poulton way. I know more or less where.'

'Do you really think there's something going on there?'

'I don't know – but that's all the more reason to have a poke around. It was daytime when I was last there.'

'So you want to go back tonight?'

'I suppose. Last time, I looked around the outside yard, the fields and the barn – but I want to get into the farmhouse itself.'

'How are you going to manage that?'

Jessica leaned back against the countertop and tugged her hair back into a ponytail. 'Well... I was hoping for a bit of a hand.'

As much as Jessica knew she had little time, there wasn't a lot she could do during the day. For one, the more time she spent outside, the more chance there was of her being discovered by a police officer. She spent the day in the Shanty, making work for herself. The women had done plenty for her and she'd done nothing in return, so Jessica scrubbed the microwave and kitchen, even though everything was far cleaner than her house anyway. Women dropped in and out through the day, but there was never any fuss. Most said 'hello', but a few kept to themselves. There was never any trouble, with everyone being respectful of one another. Some returned with food, others picked at what was left in the kitchen. Some read, some used their phones to play games or use the Internet. Jessica had short conversations with both Ruth and Ellie, but there wasn't that much to say.

Jessica's phone rang once during the day with a number she didn't recognise. If she'd discovered what was going on, it might have been Izzy, who had the new number. Jessica didn't answer in any case.

As it began to get dark, Jessica started to feel nervous. It was something she wasn't used to, an emotion she had largely taught herself not to feel, but it was hard to get past the fact that she was running out of time to exonerate herself.

From around half past eight that evening, most of the

women had already started to settle, either heading out for the night, or taking a book or battered magazine to bed. A couple were still sitting around the living room, but none were talking. Fran had been on her evening food run, retrieving a pair of carrier bags filled with sandwiches and leftover pastries, and then she waited with Jessica in the living room.

'You ready?' she asked.

Jessica checked the time on her phone for what felt like – and possibly was – the hundredth time that evening. It was a few minutes after ten o'clock. 'Let's go.'

Fran picked up a backpack, unbolted the door and led the way. They didn't touch the illuminated areas of the centre and, within minutes, were hurrying through a council estate. The houses and businesses soon stretched further apart, street lights fading, until they were on the outskirts of the town. Fran slowed her pace as the pavement disappeared, leaving them walking along the verge of a dusty, deserted road. The sky was cloudy, dousing everything in a misty grey glow. Jessica could see where she was going, but not more than fifty or so metres ahead. It wasn't freezing, but she could see her breath and was grateful for the thick coat borrowed from the Shanty.

On the rare occasion a vehicle passed, Jessica and Fran shrank into the bushes, waiting until the path was clear and then continuing. Fran knew the general direction, with Jessica taking over the further they travelled. She'd already walked the route once in reverse and, with the sparse landscape, it wasn't too difficult to retrace her steps, even in the dark.

It was a few minutes before midnight when they arrived at the overhanging trees Jessica had seen the day before. The gate with the red semicircle was bolted across the path and there were tyre tracks in the nearby mud.

'You sure you want to do this?' Fran asked, resting against the gate.

Jessica ducked underneath the barrier and narrowly avoided the same puddle she'd stepped in the previous day.

'I'm not sure I have any better ideas. Thanks for coming. I don't know what I can do to thank you.'

Fran tilted her head, but her expression was lost in the darkness. 'There'll be something.'

'Are *you* sure about this?' Jessica asked. 'None of this is worth it if you're not safe.'

This time Jessica could see the grin. 'I had a good-girl upbringing, remember? I might be a little late to the party, but it's about time I caused some carnage.'

Fran hoicked herself over the gate and trudged through the overhanging trees, not worrying about the mud. Within a few seconds, she was swallowed by the darkness as she followed the hedgerow, leaving Jessica alone at the gate.

Jessica waited for a couple of minutes and then continued through herself. She kept low, remaining tight to the hedges until she found a spot with a good view of the farmhouse. She was within thirty or so metres, on a patch that was starting to dampen but was not too wet. There was an upstairs light in the farmhouse and another in what looked to be the kitchen. Other than that, the rest of the house, the yard and the barn were all in the same miasma of darkness through which they'd spent the evening walking.

She didn't dare take out her phone to check the time, so Jessica continued to wait in the bushes. Every now and then, there would be a scratch or a scrape from nearby. Jessica wasn't scared of the dark, not really, but her heart jumped every time, her mind racing with illogical conclusions about what lay out of sight.

Eventually, it happened.

Max had told Jessica that his father was paranoid about being robbed – and it was time for a show. There was a fizzing clatter of metal and then a loud pop. Fran was at the far end of the field and had lit a firework and sealed it in a rusty old pot. She'd promised Jessica it would be noisy, but this went beyond that. The noise was so loud that Jessica jumped. Within seconds, more lights were coming to life within the house. The front door banged open and the massive silhouette of Vince Waverly emerged onto the yard. He had one leg cocked as he tied his laces, calling over his shoulder for Max. The younger Waverly dashed through the door, turning in a circle.

'What was that?' he asked.

'Shush!'

The two men stood in silence for a few moments – and then Fran struck again. There was a bang-bang-bang and then the sound of glass being smashed on the far reaches of the farm. Jessica had asked Fran for a diversion, but had said nothing about causing actual damage.

Bit late now.

Jessica thought they'd go haring off in search of the potential poacher or vandal, but Vince's next line sent shivers through her. 'Go get my gun.'

She thought about using her phone to warn Fran, but there was no way Jessica could do that without revealing her own location. All she could do was hope that Fran was in the middle of running for it.

There was another pop in the distance – a second firework thundering into something metallic – followed by a fizz of sparks.

'Max!'

Vince turned back towards the house just as his son emerged with a pair of shotguns. At his side was another figure Jessica recognised, though someone she hadn't expected.

Greg Salisbury was wearing a T-shirt despite the cold, his gut and chest filling it comfortably. A little behind them was a fourth man – a distinctly alive and well Peter Salisbury. Unless bodies really were rising from the grave and *The Walking Dead* was coming true, *he* was the man responsible for so much of what had happened to her.

For a few moments, the four of them stood at the front of the house.

'Can you shoot?'

Vince was talking to Greg, who mumbled something Jessica didn't hear. Either way, Max handed him a pistol. Only Peter was unarmed. Vince had taken control, his growly northern accent crisp through the night.

'You three take the barn, I'll go for the fields. If anyone's running, shoot.'

There were no further discussions as the four of them shuffled quickly across the yard; Max, Peter and Greg heading towards the barn, Vince separating away and hurrying towards the bushes on the far side. None of them were running and Jessica suspected Greg and Vince were too old to get much speed up in any case. A bullet would still travel pretty quickly, though...

As soon as they were out of sight, Jessica ran for the front of the house. Aside from the phone in her pocket, which was *definitely* on silent, she was carrying nothing and feeling uncharacteristically athletic. She flew through the open door, giving up a few seconds to wipe her feet on the welcome mat and make sure her entrance wouldn't be spotted. She didn't know what she was looking for but knew there'd be something – there had to be.

The kitchen was generally clear of clutter, other than a chunk of cheese on a block of wood on the dining table. Jessica's mouth watered but she ignored it, dashing through into what turned out to be the first of three living rooms. There was a television and sofa in each, plus assorted nothingness: magazines, shoes, some coats, bottles of whisky. She checked a filing cabinet, but the papers at the front were ancient: invoices from a decade previously. A nearby bureau was also packed with paperwork that she didn't have time to sort through. Nothing out of the ordinary.

There was another bang from the distance, but it didn't sound like a gunshot. There was little Jessica could do other than hope Fran hadn't hung around.

As she continued upstairs, Jessica struggled to mask the sound of her footsteps. The floors were wooden, ceilings high. Every movement she made seemed to creak and echo, but there was no going back now.

The first room had an unmade double bed in the centre, clothes flung on the floor, laptop open on the bed and a vague whiff of deodorant. Jessica lifted the lid, but the computer asked for a password and she didn't have time to even guess. Nicking it was out of the question, too.

The next room had bare floorboards and was empty except for a single metal-framed bed pushed against a wall. It seemed so out of place compared to the rest of the house that Jessica stepped inside and peered around the corner, looking for any sign that it was lived in. One of the windows had a wooden board fixed where the glass should be, but there was nothing else. The lack of a carpet was making her footsteps echo too loudly and Jessica backed away.

She continued opening doors until she found herself in a games room at the front of the house. The lights were off but there was enough light from outside for her to see that the room was lined with leather armchairs. There was a pool table in the centre, a dartboard on the wall. She rushed to the window, covering her eyes and squinting into the murk. In the far distance, somewhere close to what she guessed was the boundary, she could see a light from a torch or phone. That was where Vince had headed, shotgun under his arm. It was hard to tell, but it looked like he was checking the hedges. Jessica pressed herself against the glass, feeling the coolness on her forehead, saying a silent prayer to a god in whom she didn't believe, hoping Fran was nowhere nearby.

Jessica jumped as something slammed. Her gaze shot towards the yard, where Peter and Greg Salisbury were closing in on the house. There was another bang from directly below: Max was *in* the house. Jessica stepped away from the window, but the floorboards betrayed her, squeaking and reverberating. She froze, one foot in the air, listening for confirmation that she'd been heard.

Luckily, her noise had come at the same time that Peter and Greg re-entered. Jessica couldn't hear the exact words, but they were talking with Max in the kitchen below. She'd not had much time, but Jessica had managed to peep into every room of the house and she'd found nothing. As far as she knew, there were only two doors in and out – and there was no way she'd be able to get past the trio downstairs. She'd been so focused on watching Vince in the distance that she'd failed to spot the three men who'd rushed to the barn.

Jessica peered out the window to see that the light in the distance was now close to the house. Vince was on his way back, too, and then all four of them would be blocking her escape. She wanted to know who they were, why they were working together and how she'd been dragged into a mixed-up world of misidentified dead bodies. She'd sneaked into the house hoping for answers but had failed and now she was trapped, hoping nobody would enter this room.

Staying put would be quite a gamble – the sofas were pressed against the wall, with no space to hide behind. If she moved back onto the landing looking for another spot, the bumps and groans of the ancient building would give her away.

'Shite,' Jessica whispered to herself. This had not been part of the plan, not that the plan had been anything other than getting into the house and hoping there was some piece of obvious evidence lying around for why these four men had tried to frame her.

She thought about calling DCI Fordham, telling him she was in a building with Peter Salisbury. The dead guy was a few metres below her, definitely *not* dead. That would prove something, except that Fordham's phone number was on the device she'd dismantled and then dispatched into a bin.

This was a hole she was going to have to get herself out of.

Jessica climbed onto one of the sofas, figuring the material would mask her footsteps. She moved around the room until she was at the door, where she could hear one of the men's voices drifting up the stairs.

'... what d'yer reckon it was?' somebody asked.

'Foxes? Who bloody knows.'

'You wanna finish that game o' darts?'

Jessica swung around to spy the board, where there were three darts peppering the lower half.

'Let's wait till Dad gets back.'

Jessica returned to the window, where Vince's light was nearly level with the barn. Another minute and he'd be there. She turned in a circle, trying to swallow the rising tide of panic. It was only as she nearly tripped over one of the sofa arms that she peered up, spotting the square hatch in the ceiling. When she'd been on the farm the previous day, she'd guessed the tall sloping roof meant there was probably an attic but then forgotten about it.

A circular pulley was built into the hatch and Jessica strained upwards, only just able to loop her fingers through as she stood on the armrest. She expected the flap to pull downwards – which it did – along with a stepladder that was attached.

From below came the sound of the front door slamming.

Jessica pulled the ladder down as far as it went and then

stepped across to it from the sofa. The metal rungs screeched but nowhere near as loudly as the floorboards. She hurried up, reaching for the attic floor and pulling herself up. Jessica expected the attic to be shrouded in darkness, but the opposite was true. She was blinded by the ferocious expanse of light as she blinked away the green and pink stars, reaching down and yanking the pulley upwards. The stepladder folded in on itself, the hatch coming with it until it latched in place.

She stepped backwards, immediately colliding with something hard at hip height. Jessica winced, putting her hand down into something soft and mushy. Her vision was still clouded by how bright it was, like stepping out from a darkened room into the mid-afternoon sunshine. It took her a couple of seconds to blink away the disorientation – and then she saw precisely what Vince and Max Waverly were hiding. It was perhaps no surprise they didn't have vast swathes of crops outside the farmhouse, because they had more than their fair share *inside*.

Long lines of tables stretched the full length of the house, each topped by planters containing hundreds – *thousands* – of cannabis plants. The attic was so bright because lamps hung from the roof, flooding the plants with the heat and light they craved.

Considering the illegality of what she was looking at, it was bizarre that Jessica's first thought was that the electricity bill must be sky-high. That was the perils of owning a home and paying bills. Suddenly the mundane things in life hit before anything else.

Jessica slowly made her way along the lines of plants, taking each step carefully. The floor was wooden, but nowhere near as noisy as the one below. She was sweating from the heat but didn't dare remove her jacket, not yet anyway. Every few seconds, Jessica had to wipe the moisture from her forehead as she continued along, wondering if there was a second trapdoor anywhere. She'd paced each line twice before concluding that there wasn't. There had been one way into the attic – and there was one way out.

Once she'd settled on that, Jessica crept away from the door, heading to the furthest side of the house. She could hear voices underneath and the occasional *thunk* of dart on board. Aside from the long rows of cannabis plants, the only other thing Jessica noticed in the attic was a small metallic red lock-box. It was on its side between a pair of planters on the table furthest from the door. If she hadn't have found a spot to sit on the floor and wait for the house to go silent, she'd have never seen it.

Jessica picked it out from where it had been wedged and turned it over. There was a plasticky rattle, but the lid was closed, the lock turned. It was only a cheap box and wouldn't stand up to a lot of punishment before opening, but Jessica wasn't sure she wanted to steal it. At least for now, she'd got *into* the house unnoticed. If she waited until the early hours, she hoped she could get back out again.

She slipped it back between the planters but couldn't stop staring at it. Aside from the obvious illegality of the cannabis, it was the first thing that looked off in the house. The plants were evenly spaced across the room, potted by someone who'd done their homework about what they needed to thrive. Cannabis wasn't as big a moneymaker as some, but there was still hundreds of thousands of pounds' worth of drugs if it was prepared properly. Enough to pay that electricity bill, in any case.

Which was why it was strange that the soil surrounding one of the plants close to the lockbox was dimpled and uneven. Jessica pressed into it with her fingers, finding nothing at first and then delving deeper. A few seconds later, she was holding a small metal key. It hadn't been rocket science, and wasn't quite up there with creating the Hadron Collider, but

Jessica was still chuffed with herself. She wiped her fingers clear of the caked soil and then reclaimed the box and unlocked it.

Inside were twenty or thirty memory cards that would fit a camera or possibly a mobile phone. They were nearly identical – the same brand, same amount of storage, same green and blue label on the front. The only thing different was the tiny block capital letters that someone had written on the front of each. Every one was labelled with a different female name. Jessica flipped through them one after the other until she settled on one that left her hand trembling. The box rattled as she returned it to the table, still clutching the memory card.

Written on the front was a single name: 'Rebecca'. It might have been the full name, but Jessica knew it was referring to Bex. She slipped it into her pocket and was about to relock the box when there was a resounding creak from the far side of the attic.

Somebody had opened the hatch.

THIRTY-THREE

Jessica quickly returned the box to its spot, then flicked the key into the planter and smoothed the soil down. There was nowhere obvious to hide – none of the tables had covers to shield her from view – all she could do was squat behind the legs and hope for the best. She dropped to the floor, eyeing the opened hatch on the other side of the room, though nobody emerged. Voices were echoing upwards from the games room.

'Do you get people out here often?' Greg Salisbury asked. It could only be him given that the voice belonged to someone older.

'Nope,' came the growled reply from Vince.

Jessica slid along the floor on her backside, trying to get to the corner next to the row of tables in the centre of the room. Because it was in the widest part of the house and the roof sloped downwards, there was a small amount of shadow. If anyone peered in her direction, she'd be seen, but it was better than nothing.

'Anything in the barn?' Vince asked.

'Nothing. You reckon the police might be poking around?'

'Nah, I'd have smelt those bastards a mile off. Prob'ly just kids or summit.'

'The detective?'

Jessica was most of the way across the room but stopped where she was, holding her breath. Did he mean her?

'No chance – she's busy with the Old Bill, ain't she?'

There was a loud exhalation, possibly just a breath but maybe a laugh. 'You dint say she'd be round mine asking 'bout Peter.'

'Aye, well, I dint expect that neither. She turned up here yesterday, too. Smart girl. She's still fucked, though.'

The ladder squeaked and Jessica dropped flat to the floor, feeling the grit tickling her cheek. A hairy hand appeared next to the opening, but then Vince groaned in pain and croaked: 'My bastarding back's gone.' There was a pause and then he bellowed Max's name. The hand disappeared and there was another screech of the ladder.

Jessica crawled across the wood as quickly as she could until she was squatting underneath the darkest part of the attic. She was partially obscured by the table legs in front of her and this was as good as she could manage.

At least she now knew one thing for sure: she might not know who Vince Waverly was but he definitely knew her. Somehow, for some reason, he'd instigated everything that had happened since she'd come to Blackpool.

'You see the *Gazette* today?' It was Greg's voice.

Vince moaned again, grumbling about his back. 'Aye, took 'em long enough to find that tart on the rocks. Your lad should've left her somewhere better. Might've sped things up a bit.'

'The only reason we're here is because of *your* lad's bitch girlfriend.' Greg's tone was different, fiercer, but not entirely questioning of Vince's judgement. It was clear who was the boss.

'Aye, well... speak of the devil,' Vince replied.

'What's up?' Max asked.

Vince told him that his back was hurting, so he'd have to 'do the business' in the attic. There was the sound of foot on metal, but then Greg cut in.

'Me and the lad should be off,' he said. 'Only came round to check your wires and pick up my cut, didn't expect to be chasing shadows in the dark with a gun. How's the electric holding up anyway?'

'Good enough,' Vince replied. 'The lights are staying on and last month's bill was next to nowt. You after a reference or something?' He sniggered to himself.

'I do all right myself,' Greg said. 'I've done the business for a few people – they're happy to pay me a few hundred, then only ten per cent of their electric goes through the meter. They're happy, I'm happy, even the power companies can't be that annoyed. They're still getting something.'

'I'm in the wrong business.'

Greg laughed: 'Yeah, right. You're raking it in yourself. Anyway, I had a look at that panel earlier and it's just a bit of bad wiring. You get it in places like this. Probably the same stuff in the walls as when it was built. I've patched it and will come back later in the week.'

'You definitely taking your lad this time? He was a right nuisance last night, in and out at all hours.'

'He's gotta keep his head down, but he'll be off to Spain this time next week. I'll have a word. Anyway, I'm off.'

Jessica heard footsteps, Greg calling 'Peter' and then a door closing.

'You hear that?' Vince growled. He sounded nastier when it was just him with his son.

'The end of it,' Max replied.

'Right – so hurry up and find that fucking girl, else I'll send you back to the streets you came from.'

'I'm trying, Dad.'

'Try harder. I'm going to bed. You can do the morning run tomorrow – and don't forget what's happening tomorrow evening.'

'I won't.'

There was still a lot Jessica didn't get, but things were falling into place. Bex was likely Max's 'bitch girlfriend' to whom Greg had referred – and Max was apparently looking for her.

That made two of them.

Max and Bex had matching tattoos; though, from what Jessica knew of her friend, she couldn't believe the pair had much in common, let alone that Bex would disappear to be with him having not mentioned him at any point in the past. Vince threatened to send his son back to the streets, so they might have known each other from the time when Bex was homeless.

There were still so many unanswered questions, so much for Jessica to get her head around, but it was a start.

She still had to find Bex, though.

A door slammed somewhere below and then Max muttered the word 'twat'. There was a series of metallic squeaks and then Jessica saw his hands clasping the rim around the attic. He heaved himself upwards, forearms bulging as he showed off the spider's web tattoo that matched Bex's. He swore under his breath as he twisted and sat on the ledge.

'Prick,' he mumbled to no one in particular, before standing, turning, and staring directly at Jessica.

THIRTY-FOUR

Jessica's palms were planted on the floor, ready to spring forward. Max might be bigger and stronger than her, but all she had to do was get around him and drop through the hatch. Vince had gone to bed and she should be able to get to the back door before anyone else. She more or less knew the way back to the town centre and she'd run like she'd never run before. She'd scream and be noisy, make herself noticed. Someone might call the police, but it would stop the Waverlys coming for her.

Max's gaze flitted straight at Jessica and then past as he yawned. He was holding the end of a hose in one hand and crossed to the table that was on the far side from her, before filling up a watering can.

Jessica had no idea how he'd missed her, other than a combination of the dark and the table legs. He'd been yawning, too, and might have had watery eyes. If not that, then he could have been startled by the brightness, as she had been. Either way, Jessica didn't dare move as he pottered around the plants closest to him, doing a distinctly half-arsed job of watering them. By the time he'd emptied the can, he'd barely covered a quarter of the floor space. He put the can down and crossed to the lockbox. As Jessica had done, he delved into the nearby planter for the key and then unlocked it, picking through the memory cards. The one with Bex's name was in Jessica's pocket, but he had plenty of choice.

Max continued searching through the cards, picking a couple out and pocketing them before relocking the box and returning the key to the planter. He stood with his hands on his hips, staring from side to side at the vast expanse of plants.

'Shitting morning duty,' he said, checking his watch. 'Prick.'

He rounded the first set of tables and kicked the empty watering can into the opposite wall before heading back to the ladder. He picked up the hose and flung it through, then jumped down after it. Seconds later, the stairs clamped back into place.

Jessica didn't move. She counted to ten, then a hundred, then another hundred, before she stretched out her legs. Her hip clicked, her knee creaked, her back twinged, but she managed to stand. Jessica moved slowly across the floor, trying not to make any noise before she got to the hatch. She yawned three times in succession, each stronger than the last until there were tears rolling along her cheeks.

For the first time since arriving at the farm, Jessica slipped her phone from her pocket. It was almost one o'clock in the morning and she had one text message from Fran, sent forty-five minutes previously.

CU @ shanty. X

Jessica replied to say that she was safe – for the moment – and then sat, listening to the nothingness of the night, until her phone told her it was three o'clock. Then she lowered the attic stairs, climbed down, lifted them back up and crept out of the house and across the yard. The moment she hit the path, she started to run, not stopping until she was surrounded by street lights and houses as the encompassing glow of the town embraced her and welcomed her back to civilisation.

THIRTY-FIVE

Jessica awoke in the same spot as she had the previous morning. This time she was racked with yawns, eyelids heavy, limbs floppy and useless. She was alone, surrounded by tidily made beds and a silence that scratched and scraped at her very being. She understood why things had to be so quiet around the Shanty, but the oblivion left her alone with her mind – and that was too dark a place in which to spend any time.

She got dressed into the same clothes as the day before, ignoring that the bottoms of her jeans were tinged with damp from the bushes and grass she'd waded through on the way back from the Waverly farm. Downstairs, there were a few more women hanging around than the previous days. Jessica couldn't fail but notice the sideways glances and general air of bewilderment. They had become used to living in this place, supporting one another and keeping to Fran's rules. Then, from nowhere, Jessica had arrived and there were late-night excursions and the scent of trouble. Plus, she was a police officer – at least for now.

Jessica smiled weakly towards the women in the living room and then entered the empty kitchen.

'Hey,' a voice called. At first Jessica couldn't see where it was coming from, but then she saw that the door underneath the stairs was open. She poked her head around to see Fran sitting on the floor underneath two shelves lined with books. She had a paperback on her lap, its pages curled and brown, and was wearing glasses, which she immediately removed. 'You look tired,' Fran added.

'Whatcha doing in there?' Jessica asked, crouching.

'It's peaceful. I like it under here.'

Jessica stooped to sit in the doorway and couldn't fight back a yawn.

'I was worried about you,' Fran said.

'You weren't the only one.'

'What did you find?'

Jessica slipped the memory card from her pocket and passed it over. Fran twirled it in her hand and then looked up. 'Rebecca is your friend?'

'Maybe – that's what "Bex" is short for. Max Waverly is apparently looking for her, too. I don't know how they know each other.'

'Doesn't sound good though, does it?'

Jessica could only agree.

'Ell!'

As Fran called the name, Jessica turned to see Ellie walking past the cupboard on her way to the kitchen. She ducked and smiled, though the space was already cramped with Fran and Jessica under the stairs.

'Show her the card,' Fran said. Jessica did, but Ellie only needed a quick glance before shaking her head.

'You want to see what's on that?' she asked.

'Hopefully,' Jessica replied.

'You'd need a computer or possibly a camera. It's a bit too big for a phone. There's nothing like that here. You might be able to try the library in town, but...'

She exchanged a glance with Fran and then Jessica knew that she'd missed something.

'What?' she asked, peering between the two of them.

Fran reached behind her back and pulled out a newspaper, which she passed to Jessica. As soon as the front page unfolded itself, Jessica knew why the other residents had been eyeing her with such suspicion. She didn't blame them – her face was plastered across a third of that morning's *Gazette*.

'Sorry,' Fran said as Jessica read the story on the front, before turning inside. The more she read, the more Jessica felt the hand of DCI Fordham and possibly her own colleagues from Manchester. The wording of the story, and therefore the press release from which it had been rewritten, was very smart. It said that local police were searching for a 'fellow officer' who had gone missing and was last seen on Blackpool's South Shore. It made it sound like she might be in trouble, asking the public to be vigilant in case she was still in the area, while also appealing for Jessica to come forward. The deaths of Peter Salisbury and Sophie Johns were mentioned but not directly linked to her.

That would be the next day's story.

Jessica knew this was Fordham giving her one final chance to hand herself in. He knew she had run and this was putting the squeeze on, getting her face out for the public to see and having the locals look out for her. Her colleagues in Manchester would have seen it too and tried to contact her. Her mum would have seen it. People would be worrying, with good reason, and the police would be hoping Jessica caved and contacted one of them. If she didn't know the game, hadn't been involved in similar schemes herself, she'd give in immediately. More than anything, Jessica was horrified by the anguish her mother would be feeling as she sat by herself in the residential home reading that her daughter had gone missing. She thought about calling to say she was safe, perhaps from a phone box or a different mobile she could ditch afterwards. She *wanted* to do it – but knew she couldn't. This was precisely what Fordham was after and, besides, Jessica only had a day before the full story would break anyway. When it was announced that she was a suspect in a double murder, it'd be game over. Fordham believed her – this proved it – but she could only push him so far.

'What are you going to do?' Fran asked.

'There's someone I can call – a friend.'

'Your lot?'

Jessica shook her head and handed back the paper. 'Not after this. They know they've put me in a corner.'

Ellie was now sitting in the door frame. Fran glanced at her and lowered her voice. 'The girls are worried. This is a lot of attention.'

'I know. I'll leave – it's not fair.'

'I—' Fran touched Jessica on the shoulder, but Jessica knew this was something she had to do. Fran might convince the others, might say she could stay for another day, but Jessica was putting them all in danger.

'I'm going to go,' Jessica said.

'You don't have to.'

'I really do.' Jessica started to lift herself up and Ellie shuffled backwards to let her out. She was just about to head for the stairs to retrieve her shoes when one final thing occurred to her. 'If you could just give me half an hour with the phone charger...?'

As well as some time to charge her phone, Fran also allowed Jessica to take one of the thick jackets before they said goodbye. Jessica kept the hood up and passed through the warren of alleys past the train tracks until she was well away from the Shanty before making her phone call. She did exactly as

Andrew Hunter had told her, dialling the desk number for the private investigator and then pressing 'one' as soon as it rang. There was a plip and then it started to ring again. Andrew answered almost immediately.

'Hi, it's Jess,' she said.

'Oh...' he replied, stumbling. 'I saw the stuff this morning and wondered if you might...'

'I really need your help.'

'Where are you?'

'Still in Blackpool, but I need to get away from the centre. If you go north out of the town, Blackpool becomes Bispham and the Queen's Promenade runs along the front. It's a lot quieter there. There's a hotel shaped like a castle – you can't miss it. Can we meet on the benches opposite?'

'I'm sure I'll find it.'

'How far away are you?'

'Um, hang on...' There was a rustling and Jessica could hear him talking to someone away from the phone. 'About an hour and a half,' he said. 'Sorry. Do you need me to bring anything?'

Jessica told him and then hung up, staring at her phone screen as it dimmed. There had been two more calls that morning, both from unknown numbers that were probably Izzy calling from the station. She scrolled through the sparse list of contacts, hovering over her friend's number, but didn't call.

She kept away from anywhere busy and ambled through the back streets heading north, recrossing the railway lines but staying away from the Shanty. Jessica checked the clock on her phone regularly, but it felt like time wasn't moving. Ninety minutes was a long time to be by herself, hoping someone would ride to her rescue.

Within thirty, she was at the bench she'd mentioned to Andrew. The promenade was almost deserted, with only a dog-walker and a jogger passing by on the path. Neither paid her any attention and the beach below was empty. Even the cars passing behind her on the road had stopped.

Jessica sat with the coat wrapped tightly around herself, staring out at the choppy grey sea. She checked her phone again, but there was still an hour until Andrew said he'd be there – and that was if he was on time. There could be traffic, roadworks, or any number of other hold-ups. Jessica glanced at the phone again, but not even a minute had passed. It was going to be a long, long wait.

THIRTY-SIX

One moment the man was about to stride past her, the next he had slotted onto the bench next to Jessica in one swift movement. It happened so quickly that Jessica turned to look at him, making sure it was the person she was waiting for.

It had been a few years since she'd first met Andrew Hunter, yet he'd not changed much. He had sandy-gingery hair with a sprinkling of stubble that was the same colour and blended in with his skin. He was now in his mid- to late-thirties, with a friendly, unassuming face that worked in his favour considering his job. He was so normal, so forgettable. No scars or tattoos, no lazy eye or one nostril that bulged bigger than the other. He was far from ugly, but neither was he particularly attractive.

'Having a good morning?' Andrew asked.

'I've had better.'

'I've been keeping an eye out for your name since we last spoke. Got a bit of a shock when I saw it online this morning.'

'Am I everywhere?'

'Not really – the local *Gazette* and a small story on the BBC website. You're small-time, I'm afraid.' He smiled, but

Jessica couldn't return it. Small-time was fine – Fordham only needed local coverage for now. It'd be a hell of a lot bigger if she were linked to a pair of murders. Then she'd be dreaming of small-time.

'I'm not really missing,' she said, turning back to the ocean.

'So I can see.'

'I mean that's not why the police want me. I'm on bail and they want to arrest me. That picture of me they gave to the *Gazette* is them being nice. They want me to hand myself in before they bury me.'

'What have you done?'

Jessica didn't reply straight away. It had taken her long enough, but she'd finally figured out that the tide was going out. Some idiot in a wetsuit was trying to windsurf close to the North Pier and she willed him to fall in.

'They think I might have killed some people. It's complicated.'

'Oh.'

'I didn't.'

'It never crossed my mind.'

She turned to him, eyebrow raised. 'C'mon, if any of my friends were accused of killing someone, the first thing I'd wonder was whether they did it. I might dismiss it straight away, but I'd think about it and it would *definitely* cross my mind. I'm just honest enough to admit it.'

His half-smile was fixed. 'You've not changed,' he said.

'Maybe.'

'They think I might've been involved with killing this bloke, Peter, but he's alive. I saw him on a farm last night. I don't know where he's gone now, otherwise I'd call the police and tell them. His father identified someone else's body and then I think Peter went out and killed this girl, Sophie, who had a crush on him. I'm connected to that, too.'

'That's a nice alibi he's given himself. No one pegs a dead guy as a potential murderer.'

'That's what I thought.'

'Who's the body they identified as Peter?'

'No idea.'

Neither of them spoke for a few moments. Jessica was still watching the windsurfer, who, much to her annoyance, was expertly skimming along the tops of the waves. He was bounced into the air but landed perfectly and continued being carried by the breeze. The cocky bastard.

'Can I ask a question?' Andrew said.

'Go on.'

'Why don't you hand yourself in? You say the photo in the paper was their way of being nice, of giving you a chance, so why not take it? They must believe at least some of what you've told them, else they'd let the dogs loose.'

Jessica sighed. 'I know... that's what I've been thinking about while waiting for you, but... I know how they work. How they *have* to work. The minute you're arrested and in the interview room, that's when the paper trail starts. Everything's documented. Common sense goes out the window and everything has to be done in a certain way.'

'Is that a bad thing?'

'Not really... it safeguards everyone – but it won't help me. Maybe they will believe me, but I'll be questioned for hours and I don't have much to give them other than conjecture and theories. There's almost nothing I can prove. Everything connects to this farm a few miles away. They're cultivating loads of cannabis in the attic—'

'—so tell them about that.'

'I would but...' Jessica stopped, wondering how best to put it. 'For one, I shouldn't have been in the attic in the first place, so explaining how I know about it is a tough one. The farm is owned by this bloke named Vince Waverly. Telling the police might get him in trouble – but doesn't really help me.'

'So what do you need me for?'

Jessica reached into her pocket and took out the memory card. 'I need to find out what's on here.'

Andrew turned, nodding towards a white and green van parked on the other side of the road.

'Good job I brought a van.'

Jessica had visions of a vehicle packed with high-tech surveillance equipment in the back, with rows of complex computer gear, plus listening devices and a full-size R2D2. Something like that anyway. As it was, the van was rented – which was probably best if Andrew didn't want to be trailed to Blackpool.

They sat together on the wooden floor inside the back of the van as Andrew flipped his laptop lid and inserted the memory card into the side.

'Couldn't you have brought chairs?' Jessica moaned.

'We can nip off to B&Q if you want? I'm sure nobody there will recognise you.'

'Fine!'

Jessica wriggled uncomfortably on the hard floor as Andrew waited for the card to register through the laptop. Once the icon appeared, he clicked it and twisted the screen to face Jessica.

'Are you ready to see this?'

'What is it?'

'There are video files labelled "Rebecca 1", "Rebecca 2", and so on, up to 17.'

Jessica stopped fidgeting, having failed to distract herself. She wanted to see the videos but, at the same time, wasn't sure that she could. The blood on her car had belonged to Bex and her mind had already filled her with thought after horrifying thought about how that could have happened. If this footage was going to reveal where the blood came from, Jessica didn't know if she wanted to see it.

'I can look at a few seconds if you prefer,' Andrew said, as if he'd read her mind. 'You don't have to watch it.'

Jessica shook her head. 'I suppose this is why I came here...'

She braced herself, expecting the worst. Andrew opened the file and it started to play automatically. Jessica gasped at the sight of Bex – it was really her. She'd already known it would be, but it was still the first time she'd seen her since the day Bex had disappeared. In that time, Jessica had feared all sorts, but here the teenager was, sitting in an office chair, facing slightly off-camera, a dark sheet covering whatever was behind her.

'Do you love me?' asked a man's voice.

Bex nodded. Her face was thinner than the last time Jessica had seen her, the teenager's cheeks hollowed inwards, eye sockets darker and deeper.

'So say it,' the voice added.

'I love you,' Bex replied. Her lips were chapped and dry and her gaze didn't leave the spot at which she was staring, close to the camera.

Andrew paused the footage. 'Are you okay?' he asked.

'Yes.'

He pointed to the screen. 'She's tied up.'

Jessica hadn't noticed, but he was right. It wasn't immediately obvious as, at first glance, it looked like Bex's arms were by her side. It was only as Jessica peered closer that she could see the angle at which Bex's arms jutted behind her, looping through the arms of the chair. She was only visible from the waist up, so there was every likelihood her feet were secured.

Andrew touched Jessica's hand and she realised she was shaking. His palms were warm and she allowed him to clasp her hand in his as he pressed play again.

'Say it properly,' the man's voice said.

'What do you want me to say?'

'You know.'

Bex leaned slightly forward, straining against her bonds. 'I love you, Max,' she said. 'I really love you. You mean everything to me.' She gulped but her tormentor didn't seem to notice. Now that she'd said the name, Jessica recognised Max's voice. The venom with which he'd sworn at his absent father the night before was underlying everything he was saying in the footage. The menace and fury was barely concealed.

'Why wouldn't you tell me that earlier?' Max said. 'Why do you always make me do this?'

'I'm sorry.'

'If you loved me, really loved me, you wouldn't make me do this to you.'

Bex bit her bottom lip, holding back a sob, breaking Jessica's heart. 'I know.'

'You know that you make me like this.'

'I know.'

'You make me bring you here, tie you up. This is your fault.'

'I know it is.'

Andrew's grip tightened on Jessica's hand as she struggled to hold it together.

'*So why wouldn't you tell me that earlier?*' Max asked again.

'*I was scared.*'

Bex certainly looked it. She was trembling, elbows bumping against the armrests to which she was tied. There was a short silence where her eyes widened as she stared at the out-of-shot Max.

'*You were scared?*' *he asked, voice as calm as if he were ordering an ice cream.*

'*Yes,*' *Bex replied, voice cracking.*

'*Why?*'

'*I just was.*'

'*Look at me.*'

Bex's gaze flicked upwards slightly. '*Okay.*'

'*Are you scared of me now?*'

Bex shivered and, even in the slightly hazy images on screen, the goosebumps on her bare arms were clear.

'*You can tell me,*' *Max added.*

'*I'm scared,*' *Bex replied, her eyes shifting lower again.*

'*What would make you feel better?*'

Bex bit her bottom lip and then started to chew on it until it popped out of her mouth again. '*I—*'

'*You can say. If I don't know, then there's nothing I can do.*'

Bex's gaze shifted slightly until she was staring directly into the camera, as if talking to anyone who would be watching. '*Jessica,*' *she said.*

Jessica gulped, reaching forward and stopping the footage mid-frame, leaving Bex staring out from the computer monitor at her.

Andrew released her other hand and breathed out noisily but said nothing.

'That's how they did it,' Jessica said.

'Did what?'

'I got a call from a phone booth on South Shore. It was Bex. She only said my name and then she was gone. But it wasn't her at all. It was Max, his dad or Peter. They replayed the audio of her saying my name. That's all they needed and that's how they got me here. Everything that's happened has come from that. They knew I'd be desperate and curious and I played into their hands. I made it so easy for them.'

Andrew's finger hovered over the button to continue playing the footage.

'Do it,' Jessica said.

'Who's Jessica?' Max asked.

Bex twisted to face him again, no longer talking to the camera. 'A friend.'

'What sort of friend?'

'Just a friend.'

There was another short pause. When he ended it, Max's tone was lower, spitting with rage. 'But you love me?'

'Yes.'

'Tell me.'

Bex's reply was monotonous, deadpan: 'I love you.'

'Tell me properly.'

She leaned in again. 'I love you, Max. I really love you. I need you in my life.'

'You love only me?'

'Only you.'

The screen flickered and then returned to the desktop screen displaying the file list. There were another sixteen videos, but Jessica didn't want to watch them. She'd seen enough. Andrew understood without asking. He closed the laptop lid and ejected the card, handing it back to Jessica, who pocketed it.

'Why did they lure you here?' he asked.

'I don't know. They're looking for Bex, too, so perhaps they thought I knew where she was? Maybe they were following me, hoping I'd lead them to her?'

'But if that were true, why set you up?'

Jessica shook her head. 'I have no idea.' She was about to add something else when her phone started ringing. She took it from her pocket, expecting to see 'unknown' on the front, but it showed Fran's name instead.

'Hello...?' Jessica answered. She'd not expected to hear from Fran again.

'Jess?'

'Yeah.'

'You need to come back to the Shanty immediately.'

'Why?'

'I can't say on the phone, but it's an emergency. Be quick.'

The line went dead.

THIRTY-SEVEN

Andrew drove them south along the promenade with Jessica ducked down on the passenger side. He asked her where she needed to go, but Jessica wasn't sure. She had learned her way around the streets by following Fran's lead of sticking to back alleys and cut-throughs. She eventually told him to follow the signs for the train station, knowing the Shanty was close by. With the ocean clinging to one side of the town, the tracks could only enter and leave in the opposite direction and she should be able to find her way.

'Did your friend say what's wrong?' Andrew asked.

'No, just to be quick.'

Andrew took a corner, following the signs, just as his phone started to ring. It was in a small holder close to the handbrake.

'Can you see who it is?' he asked.

Jessica picked up the phone. 'Someone named Jen.'

'Any chance you can put her on speaker?'

Jessica pressed the button to answer and then for speaker-phone, before holding the device out for Andrew to speak into.

'Hang on, Jen,' he called, before glancing quickly away from the road towards Jessica. He put a finger to his lips and then continued: 'Okay, what's up?'

A female voice replied. She sounded like she was in her twenties, far younger than Andrew in any case. 'Should I be worried that the police have just been around?' she asked.

'Why were they there?'

'How about you tell me what you've been up to and I'll let you know if that's why they were here?'

'C'mon, Jen. I don't have time.'

'Pfft... you're such a spoilsport.'

Jessica was trying to catch Andrew's gaze as he waited at a set of traffic lights, but he was staring straight ahead. There was the merest hint of a grin on his face.

'They were asking where you were,' the voice on the phone said.

'What did you tell them?'

'That you'd gone out on a job. They asked where and how long you'd be, all that sort of stuff. I told them I didn't know, because... well, I don't.'

'Good girl.'

'So what do they want?'

Andrew risked a quick sideways glance at Jessica as the lights changed to green. He edged ahead slowly as their lane joined another that wasn't moving. 'No idea,' he said.

'You know I'll get it out of you.'

Another glance at Jessica. 'There's nothing to tell, Jen.'

'So who's Jessica Daniel?'

Jessica didn't know whether to be angry, concerned or both. Should Andrew's assistant really be quite so... well, annoying? And how had the police figured out that she and Andrew were in contact? They'd had a connection in the past but not recently. Perhaps they were trying lots of people?

'Someone I used to know,' Andrew replied calmly, eyes not leaving the road.

'They seem to think you still do. They were asking me if I'd seen her, had some picture, but I didn't know what they were on about.'

'Did you tell them anything?'

'I don't know anything!' She paused. 'So, anyway, where are you?'

Andrew turned to the phone, frowning, and then quickly back to the road. 'Liverpool,' he said.

'Liverpool?' she repeated.

'Right.'

'Will you be back later? They said they'd try to get in contact with you, but...'

'I'm on my way back now. Give me an hour or so.'

'Okey-dokey. See you soon.'

Jessica thumbed the button to hang up and then returned the phone to the holder. 'Liverpool?' she asked.

'Your lot were still in the office,' Andrew said.

'Oh...' Jessica couldn't hide her surprise. 'How d'you know?'

'You don't know Jenny. She might have asked how long I'd be, but she wouldn't ask where I was. If she needed to know, I'd have told her before I left.'

'The sneaky bastards,' Jessica huffed.

'They're *your* colleagues,' he reminded her.

'My sneaky bastard colleagues.'

Andrew followed another sign towards the train station. They were close.

'Assuming you hired the van in your name, they'll know soon enough.'

'I'll be back in Manchester by then.'

'What will you say if they come and ask where you were?'

'I've got a private investigator licence, so I'll tell them it's confidential. If they arrest me – which they won't – I'll say I was doing a job that took me from the Fylde coast to Liverpool. What are they going to do?' He broke off to indicate and pull in at the side of the road. The train station was in sight. 'I probably shouldn't help you any more, though. Just in case.'

'I know... thanks. I owe you, well, more than one.'

'In that case, you better get on and clear your name – you're no use to me if you get booted out of the force.' He laughed to himself and then realised he'd misjudged it. 'Sorry,' he added.

'You're fine.' Jessica rubbed his shoulder. 'You ever sort things out with your ex-wife?' The half-smile gave her something of an answer. 'Like that, is it?' she added.

'Like that.'

'I'll see ya around.'

Jessica clambered down from the van and closed the door. She pulled the hood up on her coat and then headed past a petrol station towards the estate through which she'd be able to get to the Shanty.

As Jessica emerged into the now-familiar cul-de-sac, she checked her phone. It had been less than twenty minutes since Fran had called. She passed underneath the trees and squeezed through the fence until she was in the garden at the back of the Shanty. She approached the door but stopped, her wrist cocked. Jessica had been to the house a few times in the previous few days, but something didn't feel right.

After their conversation that morning, Jessica had thought she wouldn't see Fran again. It was a shame because she did like her, but Jessica's presence was putting the rest of the women in potential danger. Not only that, Jessica hadn't said it, but there were a fair few people in the Shanty who knew her face and name. All it would take was a careless word – perhaps even a deliberate word – and the police would be onto her. Jessica trusted Fran, but did she trust the others?

She put her hand back to her side, staring at the door, wondering if she actually *did* trust Fran? The phone call had come out of the blue – and what could Fran possibly want that was worth bringing Jessica back here? That was worth endangering the women she'd done so much to help?

Could DCI Fordham be waiting on the other side of the door?

It was a horrifying thought, not only because of the fact that Jessica would be left in custody, fighting for her career, reputation and freedom; but also because of the betrayal. Jessica was hard-wired to be sceptical of people, to query their motives, yet she'd taken Fran at her word throughout.

She raised her hand again, ready to knock but still holding back. This was the test of who she was as a person. After everything she'd been through, not just this week but in the past year, could she *really* trust a stranger?

Jessica knocked four times, paused and then tapped twice more. She held her breath as the bolts unclicked, expecting Fordham.

It was Fran and she was smiling. 'That was quick,' she said.

'I wasn't far.'

Fran nodded over her shoulder. 'You coming in?'

The invisible creature itched at the back of Jessica's neck, whispering in her ear, telling her to turn and run.

'Of course,' Jessica replied, stepping forward.

Fran stepped around her and bolted the door in place. No way out. She offered Jessica another smile and then led her along the hall towards the living room, pausing by the door.

'Everything all right?' she asked.

'You said it was urgent…'

'Well… it sort of is.'

Fran stood to the side, blocking the living room and nodding towards the kitchen. Jessica turned and gasped. She was so surprised that she stumbled into Fran, using the other woman's shoulder for support.

Standing in the kitchen, fingers cradling a steaming mug, was Bex.

THIRTY-EIGHT

'Oh...' Jessica didn't know what to say.

Bex's head was bowed slightly and she peered over invisible glasses towards Jessica, wearing a small, weary smile. 'Hi.'

They stared at one another for a few moments and then Bex's head drooped and she burst into tears. Jessica bounded across the room, taking the mug and putting it on the side, before wrapping her arms around Bex's shoulders. The teenager bobbed up and down, sobbing uncontrollably. She was trying to speak but the words were lost to an asthmatic series of gasps. Jessica held her tight, feeling the jutting, sharp bones poking from her shoulders. She'd been slim to begin with but had lost even more weight in the months since she'd left Jessica's house.

'It's okay,' she cooed, smoothing Bex's hair as she pressed her face into Jessica's shoulder.

Bex continued to cry, although she slowly regained her breath until she eventually pulled away, using her sleeve to wipe at her nose and eyes.

'I'm sorry,' she croaked.

'It's fine,' Jessica replied.

'If the pair of you want some privacy, you can use my room,' Fran said.

Bex nodded and then picked up her tea and a ripped courier satchel, which she hooked across herself. She and Jessica followed Fran upstairs into the bedroom Jessica hadn't seen the inside of. It was a small box room with a single bed slotted into an alcove and clothes folded on the floor.

'You'll be left alone in here,' Fran said, as she eyed Jessica.

She was about to close the door when Bex gulped: 'Thank you'.

Fran smiled at her. 'You're very welcome,' she replied, before closing the door with a soft click.

Bex shuffled until she was in the corner and put her bag on the floor. She hugged her knees to her chest. Her sleeves hung long and limp, covering her hands. Now that Jessica had time to look at her properly, she could see the crescent curve of a bruise around Bex's eye, another looping around her jaw. Her hair was longer, probably uncut since she'd left Jessica's. It was unwashed and starting to matt together. The small ring was still hooped through her nose but it hadn't been cleaned any time recently and the silver had faded to a dull grey.

'It's so good to see you,' Jessica said, leaning her head against the wall.

'You too.'

'I've been looking for you since... well...'

Bex nodded, understanding. They both knew about the day Bex had gone missing. 'I didn't know you were here until this morning,' Bex said. 'I've been keeping my head down away from the centre, trying not to be noticed – but I was so hungry. I went to this Help the Homeless place, hoping to get something. First, I saw your photo on the front of the paper. They said you were missing and I didn't know what to think. Then I didn't even get inside the shelter. There was this blonde girl nearby, staring at me. Then I realised I was standing next to a poster with my face on.'

'I put those up.'

Bex nodded. 'She said her name was Alison, that someone named Jessica was looking for me. Then she brought me here.' She took a deep breath and then sipped her tea. 'It's hot,' she whispered.

'Tea generally is.'

Bex smiled sadly. 'Been a while since I had a proper brew.'

Jessica waited, hoping Bex would answer the question without her having to ask it, but the teenager leaned back further and stared at her feet.

'Where have you been?' Jessica eventually asked.

Bex shivered, still staring at her feet. 'Max,' she whispered.

'I've met Max Waverly – and his father. I was at their farm. But who is he?'

Bex frowned, drawing her knees tighter to herself and shrinking away. 'You know them?'

'Not like that. I followed a trail to them. I was looking for you.'

'Oh...' Bex's chest rose as she inhaled. She peered past Jessica towards the closed door and, for a moment, seemed like a stranger. Someone whom Jessica had never met.

'Max is crazy,' she said. 'We sort of knew each other when I lived on the streets in Manchester. It's hard to describe if you don't know it. There's a community. You don't know every-one's names but you recognise faces and sometimes share information about places to sleep or eat. I was friendly to him once or twice and he took it the wrong way. This was a couple of years ago, maybe a bit more. He got it into his head that we were boyfriend–girlfriend.' She rolled up her sleeve and showed Jessica the spider's web tattoo. 'I had this, so he got the same thing done. He thought it'd impress me, but it was just weird. I shouted at him, screamed, told him to leave me alone.

There were people around and he ran off. That was the last time I saw him – well, the last time until that morning at your house.'

'What happened?'

'I was cooking in the kitchen and the doorbell went. I thought it was a parcel or something, so opened up and he was standing there. He had his hands in his pockets, all casual, as if it was perfectly normal that he was there. Like he was my boyfriend dropping round to take me out. I must've stepped back in surprise because he's suddenly in the house, in the hallway.' Bex started blinking quickly, the rhythm of her speech speeding up. 'He was smiling, all friendly, asking how I was. Then, before I could say anything, he had this knife.' She held her hands out, indicating the length of a large blade. 'He told me to go with him. It was like I was watching someone else, like it was on TV or something. I remember walking out of the house and he was right behind me. I looked back and he was hiding the knife in his belt. There was this white van and he told me to get in the back. I thought about running, but he was so close and there was no time.' She reached out and grabbed Jessica's wrist, desperate for her to understand. 'Afterwards, you play it all back. You wonder why you didn't run, didn't scream, but it's hard to explain. All I could think was that he had the knife. I couldn't work out how he knew where I was.'

'How did he know?'

Bex shrugged. 'I still don't know. He never said and it wasn't like I was going to ask. I only found this out later on, but Max was *never* homeless, not like me. He used to run away from home a lot, then he'd get bored after a while and call his dad to pick him up. Who'd do that?'

It took Jessica a moment to realise that it was a genuine question. 'It sounds like a cry for attention,' she said.

'Someone would go *that* far to be noticed?'

'You said he was crazy.'

Bex tilted her head to agree. Jessica had no idea what Max *actually* was. She'd heard his voice in the footage on the memory card, ordering Bex to say she loved him. There were all sorts of correct medical terms, but 'crazy' was all-encompassing and would do for now.

'Anyway, his dad would pick him up and things would be okay for a month or so, then he'd run away again,' Bex continued. 'He'd end up in a city somewhere in the north. After he took me, he kept saying how he loved me so much that he'd return to Manchester over and over to look for me. He'd make me say I loved him too – but I'd only said maybe a few dozen words to him before that. He'd constructed this whole fantasy in his head.'

'What did he do?'

Bex peered away again. 'He kept me locked in the house. I think his dad let him do it because it stopped him acting up, like I was the person who kept him normal. If you can call it normal.'

'On the farm with the red semicircle on the gate?' Bex nodded slowly, eyeing Jessica sideways, confused. 'I told you I went there to look for you,' Jessica added.

Bex nodded once more. 'They put me in a bedroom upstairs. Max and his dad would work during the day and I'd be locked inside. The window was bolted in place and it was a long drop anyway.' Bex must have seen something in Jessica's expression because she stopped. 'You've been in there?'

'Last night. Fran distracted them and I sneaked inside.'

'Looking for me?'

'Looking for something. I didn't know they had you. How long ago did you get away?'

Bex shook her head, continuing from where she'd left off. 'In the evenings we all ate together – Max, his dad and me, as if we were some sort of family. Max would ask about my day, as if I'd been out to work and had a normal life. His dad would eat his food and say nothing. He knew it was mental. Max used to record me. He'd make me say I loved him, that sort of thing.'

Jessica slipped the memory card from her pocket and put it on the bed between them. Bex stared at it and then picked it up, eyes widening as she read her own name.

'There were cards with other girls' names on, too,' Jessica said.

'Oh.'

'You didn't know that?'

'No.'

'Why do you think Max's dad let it happen? Because he loved his son?'

Bex closed her eyes, her words almost lost because they were so quiet. 'He'd visit me, too.'

'Oh.'

Jessica didn't know what to say. She wanted the rage that was building within her to explode but had to stay strong for Bex. If she wanted to expose the Waverlys for what they had done, being angry wasn't the solution. She had to be smart.

The fury could come later.

'There were others, too,' Bex whispered. 'This guy, Peter, used to come over for meals and he'd sleep in one of the spare rooms. He always looked at me funny.'

'Did he—?'

'No, but he knew what they'd done. He was there with his dad. I don't know why.'

'His dad's an electrician,' Jessica said. 'He rigged their meter to keep the power output down. There's a massive cannabis factory in the attic. I think he's taking a cut.'

Bex peered up but couldn't meet Jessica's gaze. She stared at a spot somewhere around her belly button. 'I guess that's why it was so warm all the time.'

'Have you been there all this time?'

'They told me they were watching my friend.'

'Me?'

A nod. 'They said that if I tried to run or anything, that they'd come after you. They told me all these horrible things they'd do to you. They didn't know your name at first, but they kept asking who I'd been staying with and where my mum was, that sort of thing. I didn't have much choice other than to tell them.'

'It's fine.'

She shook her head. 'It's not. At first it was just Max, but then it was his dad. They'd ask what you were like, where you worked, all those sorts of things. I told them everything.'

Bex sat with her head hung limply, arms lifeless. Suddenly Jessica knew how the Waverlys had led her into such trouble. They'd had the full rundown on who she was and how she would likely act. There was a bit of luck involved, but they'd done their homework.

'Sorry,' Bex said.

'Don't be.'

'The more I told them, the more they said they'd get you if I ever left. But I couldn't take it any longer. I'd been working on it for weeks, telling Max that he was tying me up too tight, that he was hurting me. Slowly, he started to do the knots looser, then he stopped tying them at all. There was a morning when they both drove off in the van. I watched them out the window, waiting a few minutes and then I smashed the glass with my elbow.' She rolled up the sleeve covering the arm without the tattoo and showed Jessica the honeycomb of scabs.

'I thought you said it was too high to jump?' Jessica said.

Bex spun around and lifted her top, exposing a mottled mound of bruises and bumps. 'It was – but at least I didn't land on my legs.' She sniffed back a sob. 'I'm sorry they came for you, but I couldn't stay there any longer. I thought they might be bluffing.'

Jessica shuffled forward and put an arm around her. 'It's really not your fault.' Bex snuffled another sob, nestling deeper on Jessica's shoulder. 'Why didn't you call me when you got away?' Jessica asked.

'I didn't have your number, or any money. It only happened a couple of weeks ago. I've been hiding, wondering what to do.'

'You could have called the police.'

Bex pushed herself away, shaking her head. 'You don't understand. Max's dad is obsessed with the police. He hates them and was always going on about them. He said that if they ever come for him, he'll burn the barn down before they can do anything.'

'Why would that stop them arresting him?'

'It wouldn't.'

Jessica stared at her. 'Sorry, I don't get it.'

'You don't know what's in the barn?'

'No.'

'That's where he keeps the slaves.'

THIRTY-NINE

'Slaves...?'

Jessica uttered her response before she'd had a chance to think about it, but the truth was that she knew something was not right with the maids at the hotel.

'Max explained it one night,' Bex said. 'He thought I'd be impressed, like it's some really clever business plan. His dad brings these people over from Europe and keeps their passports. Poles and Albanians, I think. He forces them to work in cafés and hotels for his friends, who pay him instead of them. He drops them off and picks them up, but always keeps some of them back at the barn. He tells them that if anybody thinks about running from their work, that he'll kill the rest. When Max told me that, he was laughing. He thinks it's genius.'

'That's awful.'

'I had to play along, telling Max how smart it all is.'

'Saying it is one thing, believing it is another.'

Bex nodded, though it didn't look like she agreed.

'I'm still confused about something,' Jessica said. 'Well, a lot of things, but one in particular.'

'What?'

'I get that you escaped and that Max is off his rocker – but why did they do all of this to me? I understand that maybe they wanted to find you, perhaps even get me as vengeance, but they've killed people to try to frame me. That's more than revenge.'

Bex reached down and picked up her bag. 'That's because they don't just *want* to find me, they *need* to find me.' She opened the flap of the bag and pulled out a laptop, putting it on the bed between them. 'After I jumped out of the window, I smashed the back window and went inside to get this. It's Vince's and has all the details of his slaves. He buys them and keeps track of how much he gets paid by each business owner. He's obsessed by money and is always going on about how so-and-so owes him.' She lifted the lid and typed in a password before handing it over to Jessica.

'How do you know the password?'

'Max used to have things written on his hand all the time because he'd never remember. There were all sorts of names and words at various times. After I got the laptop, I tried a few things and it got me in.' She pointed at the screen. 'Open that file on the desktop.'

Jessica did and scrolled through the file, amazed. Vince Waverly might be many things, but he certainly liked keeping records. Stored within the spreadsheet was a list of names, with passport numbers, a price he'd paid for each person and then monthly amounts he'd been paid. He'd even tallied for things like 'food and board', plus 'upkeep', as if they were his tenants and were working willingly. The arrogance was astonishing. He was treating these poor people – real human beings – as if they were a commodity. It was evil on another level.

So much now made sense. Vince needed the laptop and his best chance of luring Bex into the open was to lure Jessica. He knew Bex wouldn't go to the police automatically because she feared for the lives of those in the barn. It was no wonder he'd raced out of the house when Fran had caused a distraction the previous night. He thought that if he could get Jessica in enough trouble, get her name and face in the papers, then Bex would come out of the shadows and reveal herself. Peter and Greg Salisbury had gone along with him because they were friends and invested in the various moneymaking schemes. It was a gamble because she was a police officer, which was why he'd tried to frame her. He needed her occupied, confused and off-the-ball because his only real target was Bex. He thought Jessica might do things like put up posters around the town and ask the right questions trying to find Bex. What he *hadn't* figured was that Jessica would run for it when Blackpool's police came knocking.

Jessica guessed that the body of 'Peter' was actually one of the slaves. Vince would have hoped that was enough to get Jessica arrested, but when that didn't work he needed a plan B – which ended up being Sophie Johns. With 'Peter' apparently dead, the real Peter was free to do the dirty work with impunity.

It was complicated, but it probably had to be. Somewhere along the line, they'd have been watching Jessica and known Bex hadn't been in contact. She had gone to ground and they needed the laptop back. They'd laid the trap and Jessica had fallen for it. They probably hadn't expected her to do something like stay in Luke Eckhart's hotel, but when she did, it made life even easier for them. Her room had been searched because someone, perhaps Luke if he was in on it, was hunting for the laptop. Eckhart was certainly compliant, in as much that he was using Vince's slaves.

For the most part, Vince's plans had worked out – except for the fact that they still hadn't found Bex.

'Did you know anyone named Sophie?' Jessica asked.

Bex shook her head. 'I was never allowed to leave the house. Sometimes Max talked about Peter having a girl in the house – I think that's why he stayed over – but I never knew about it until after. Max and Peter used to hang around a lot.' She tucked the laptop back into her bag, stretching her legs. 'What now?' she asked.

'We should take the laptop to the police. It's everything they'll need.'

Bex cradled the bag to her chest. 'We can't. Vince will set fire to that barn. There are people inside.'

'I didn't see anyone when I was there.'

Bex shrugged. 'They always mentioned the barn. They might have it rigged with explosives or something.'

'Could he mean a different barn?'

'I don't know, they only ever mentioned the slaves in the barn. That was it.'

'But—'

'I don't know!'

Bex's frustration burst out, but Jessica had to ask another question.

'Did you ever actually see them, Bex?'

'I... well, no. I suppose not.'

'I can go through my people – Iz, Archie, the guv. They'll—'

'No.' Bex glared at Jessica fiercely. 'You don't know Vince. He'll actually do it. He's not just *saying* he'll kill those people, he will. He told me he'd come after you and look what he did.'

'We should call the police, Bex. They're experts. They'll know what to do.'

'That means *you're* an expert, that *you* know what to do.'

Jessica had only ever seen Bex speak so determinedly once before – and that was on the very first night they'd met, when she was still living rough.

'I wish I did, but I don't even know where they are in the barn – if they're there at all,' Jessica said. 'There are these hay bales in the corner. I suppose there could be a hidden space behind. They could be locked up there but it didn't seem that big.' She cradled her head in her hands. 'I can't think,' she said.

'Jess...'

She looked up. 'What?'

'It's the first of the month today, isn't it?'

'I think so. Why?'

'Because that means tonight's the auction night.'

FORTY

Jessica could tell by the tyre tracks on the lane leading to the Waverly farm that something was different. When she had been there the previous night, the lane was largely clear, except for a coating of dust, and solo tyre tracks. Less than twenty-four hours later and the same spot was covered with muddy thick marks from where a cavalcade of vehicles had headed along the darkened track.

Together with Fran, Jessica kept tight to the hedgerow, away from any potential headlights. As soon as they could, they pushed through the greenery, emerging onto an over-grown area close to the lawn at the rear of the farmhouse. The whole of the area at the back was filled with darkness, but there was a yellowy glow seeping from the front and a low rumble of voices. Not just Vince, Max, Greg and Peter – but many more people.

Bex hadn't witnessed the auctions themselves, but she'd seen the vehicles and heard the basics from Max. After all her resistance to going to the police, Jessica had been insistent that it was the best thing to do with the laptop. The problem was that Bex knew Vince far better than she did. If he said he was going to burn down the barn with his slaves inside, if there was any possibility that the building was rigged with explosives to do just that, then could Jessica *really* risk that happening?

She knew that she couldn't.

None of that helped her current predicament, however. She didn't know exactly where the slaves were, let alone how to get them to safety. All she'd been able to tell both Fran and Bex was that she'd not actually been inside the barn, only getting a peek through the window.

Jessica and Fran remained close to the hedge as they edged towards the farmhouse. The yard was taken up by a dozen or so vehicles. There were cars and vans, a couple of 4x4s and a flat-bed American-style truck. As they neared the area close to the gate, there was the scratching of tyre on gravel and then a people carrier accelerated through, stopping next to one of the vans. Two men got out, not bothering to lock it as they headed directly to the barn.

When Jessica had been hiding in the attic the previous night, Vince had told Max not to forget about what was on the next day. This was clearly what he meant. As Bex had told them – the first of the month meant auction night.

'Do you know the layout?' Fran whispered.

'Not really.'

'Bex would've been useful.'

'She doesn't know the barn either and there's no way I'd have let her come back here.'

'What do you want to do?'

'There's a broken window on the other side of the barn that's close to the hedge. If we can get round there, we can at least hear what's going on.'

'After you.'

There was no point in risking being seen by heading across the yard, so Jessica continued following the hedge until she was a fair way past the barn, away from the lights. She dashed across the mushy mix of mud, grass and grit until she was out of breath but close to the parallel hedge that signalled the other boundary. Fran wasn't far behind, wearing far more appropriate clothes than Jessica had. She had boots and waterproof trousers. Jessica was in trainers and the same jeans she'd had on for two days. The bottoms were drenched and heavy with mud and, because they weren't hers to begin with, the fit was becoming increasingly uncomfortable.

She pulled them up and then started back in the direction from which she'd come until they were close to the barn. The assorted bushes and trees were as tightly packed as when she'd first visited and a flailing branch narrowly avoided smacking Fran in the face as Jessica pushed through. The narrow finger of wood bent back as Jessica shunted it to the side and then whipped viciously past her.

'Whoa,' Fran gasped instinctively as she stepped backwards.

The branch fizzed through the air and pinged back into place as Jessica and Fran froze, wondering if they'd been heard. If they had, then the low chatter from inside the barn was uninterrupted and, a few seconds later, Jessica continued edging along the barn's length. It didn't take long until she was close to the window, through which the errant branch was still growing. Jessica sat on the mix of mud, leaves and grass and shuffled until she was sitting directly underneath, Fran at her side.

'My arse is wet,' Fran whispered.

'Mine too – and there's a bloody rock digging into me.'

Jessica didn't dare move it in case she made too much noise. They sat in silence, but it was hard to overhear anything because the people inside were talking over the top of one another. That all changed with the clanking of some heavy bolts and the sound of the main barn doors being opened. Jessica risked popping her head up, but there was little danger of being seen because the inhabitants of the barn were all facing to where a large van was reversing through the double doors. The centre of the barn was drenched in bright light from above, likely connected to Greg's dodgy meter work. Despite that, the edges and corners were clouded by thick shade, giving Jessica a reasonable view of what was going on with little chance of being seen. She gazed up to the rafters, but there was no sign of any people, nor was there anyone close to the straw bales on the far side.

It dawned on her that the vertical metal bars bolted into the corner wasn't a secure storage area at all – it was more like a small prison. She wondered how she'd missed it the first time, though assured herself that most buildings on farms didn't come with built-in jails. The tractor was still parked by itself, but there was little else to see other than the crowd of people.

Jessica wondered if Vince's threat to burn down the barn and the people inside was simply that – a threat – an empty one, because those people weren't here. Bex wasn't to know that, though, and her concern for the welfare of those she'd not met was hearteningly wonderful.

The van's grumbling engine came to a halt and the driver's door was flung open. An enormous man dropped down to the ground and reached back to the cabin to retrieve a pump-action shotgun. Everyone had stopped and was staring at him as he thrust the loading mechanism up and down with a thunderous click.

'Vincent,' he said, nodding towards the farm owner, who was standing nearby. The accent was heavily European but clear enough to make out.

'Axel.'

For a moment it looked as if they were going to shake hands, but then Axel veered away, heading to the rear doors of his van. With Vince nearby, it made him look even more of a behemoth. Vince wasn't small and had thick arms with a solid chest – but Axel towered over him. He was comfortably over six feet tall, with a build that either came from steroids or some sort of pump. He looked like an Action Man doll, all muscles and square jaw, with short dark hair with a flat-top. As if the shotgun wasn't enough, he was wearing the biggest toe-capped boots Jessica had ever seen. She thought people with size ten feet or above were a bit freakish, but this went way beyond that. He'd probably be able to fill out clown shoes.

'Fugging traffic,' Axel grumbled to the assembled crowd. 'Always with the traffic.'

Vince snorted among a series of laughs from the onlookers. Jessica counted sixteen people present, the majority of whom were men. She hated the fact that this might enforce Fran's prejudice, but it wasn't the time to talk about it.

'Let's hurry,' Axel added, reaching for the handle but turning to Vince at the final moment. 'Okay?'

'Fine by me, big guy.'

Axel frowned, which was a terrifying prospect given how intimidating he looked in the first place. Vince took a small step backwards, closer to where Max was watching with his arms folded. Jessica could only see the side and backs of those present, but it didn't look as if Peter and Greg Salisbury were there.

'Christ, he's big.' Fran was next to Jessica, ducked low with her nose and mouth below the window, eyes peering over the top.

Jessica didn't reply.

Axel heaved one of the van doors open and then leaned in and growled something in a language Jessica didn't under-stand. He stepped back and then people started emerging from the van. Axel shouted at them as he levelled the shotgun, ordering them into one long line. There were men and women, all roughly early- to mid-twenties. Their arms, faces and clothes were speckled by dirt and they all blinked, disorientated, into the bright lights.

The final man out of the van was a little taller than the others, with olive skin and deep black hair. He tripped as he climbed down and then muttered something in his native language. In a flash, Axel stepped across, reeling back with the shotgun and thumping the solid metal butt into the man's temple. He crashed sideways, landing on his head and bouncing, though not unconscious. He rolled over groggily and then stumbled to his feet, holding his hands in front of himself protectively as Axel approached.

'No,' he said as a trickle of blood swam around his eyes.

Axel spat a flurry of words towards him and then the man took his place on the end of the line, struggling to stand straight. Axel walked along the back of the line and then across the front until he was back where he'd started. He held his arms into the air, pointing the gun at the ceiling in the process.

Vince took the hint, telling the crowd to hurry up. At his instruction, those who had been watching in silence surged forward. They broke off into ones and twos, moving in closely to examine the individuals along the line. It was like a market stall as they poked and prodded, squeezing arm and shoulder muscles, asking some of the men and women to remove clothing so they could look for scars or anything else that might hinder their ability to work.

'It's like they're hunting for the best piece of fruit,' Fran whispered.

Jessica didn't disagree. It was appalling: dehumanising and degrading. Once or twice, a couple of the men winced as one of the potential buyers jabbed at them, but any indication of annoyance was immediately met by Axel raising his shotgun.

Eventually it was over and the crowd returned to where they'd been standing, creating a crescent around Axel, who pointed to the first man in line. He looked terrified, jumping as the larger man clumped into position behind him. He had a thin covering of stubble and short dark hair; slim but not particularly muscled.

'This one's a cook,' Axel declared. 'Good cook. The best.'

'Two hundred,' someone shouted, but his accent wasn't local, it was Scottish.

'Three,' another voice retorted. Again he wasn't local, pronouncing the 'th' as an 'f'.

Jessica suddenly realised what was going on. People had come from all over the country for this. She'd not been able to figure out before what was in it for Vince. He was some sort of pimp who'd hire out *his* slaves, so why would he be allowing other people to buy them?

Jessica ducked down, with Fran following suit. 'Is your phone any good?' Jessica asked.

'It's all right.'

'While they're all in here, can you go and take photos of everyone's number plates?'

Fran opened her mouth to say something, but then changed her mind. 'No problem.'

'Hey,' Jessica added quickly. 'Don't get seen.'

'I won't.'

Fran squirted along on her backside and then pressed up through the bracken until she was at the edge of the barn. Within a few seconds, she was gone.

By the time Jessica popped back up, the bidding was up to four hundred and fifty.

Axel was frowning at the masses, lips tight, gun waggling ominously from side to side. 'He not going for that.'

Vince turned back to the crowd, almost pleading. 'C'mon, lads, this bloke's a top cook. You'd pay more than that in a weekly wage.'

'Five,' someone said.

Axel was still shaking his head. 'Thousand.'

Vince glanced nervously from Axel to the crowd. 'That sounds fair. C'mon, fellas, someone's gotta have a grand set aside. He's a fucking gourmet chef in his own country.'

That brought a ripple of sniggers and then someone shouted 'six'.

'Six?' Vince repeated, turning to Axel. 'Any advance on six?'

Nobody spoke, everyone watching the big man nervously.

'Six,' Axel confirmed.

The collective sigh of relief was so loud that Jessica heard it. A man stepped forward from the crowd, digging into his pockets and pulling out a folded wad of notes. He counted six hundred into Vince's hand and then patted his new purchase on the shoulder.

'What's your name?' he asked.

The man peered from his buyer to Axel, whose expression didn't change. 'Piotr,' he said.

'Gotcha. We've got a long journey, pal – and you're going in the boot, so best get going.'

He removed a dog's collar and lead from his other pocket and unclipped it. As soon as his purchase saw it, he cowered away – but only got as far as Vince, who stood firmly, gripping the man's neck between his fingers and squeezing. The man squealed, but his buyer showed no emotion, strapping the collar around the man's neck and then yanking the chain.

'C'mon, time to go.'

He led him around the van and out into the yard. Soon after there was the sound of an ignition. Jessica could only hope Fran had a picture of the number plate – it was the only way they'd trace him.

It wasn't long before Fran returned, saying she'd pictured all of the plates, but the evening was a horrifying spectacle. After the third sale, Jessica couldn't watch any more. She slumped down the wall, closing her eyes and listening as the men and women were bought in ones and twos. There were a couple of bidding wars, presumably for the bigger, stronger men, and then, one by one, the vehicles pulled away, heading home to wherever they lived, shiny new purchases in toe as if they'd gone Christmas shopping.

Jessica had lost exact count, but, in all, Axel had made around thirty thousand pounds. She had no idea what Vince's cut was, not that it mattered.

Another engine flared and then there was a short silence. Jessica propped herself up, peering through the gap in the window. Apart from Axel, Vince and Max, there was one man remaining. He was trying to stand tall but failing as he shivered. His teeth were chattering as he tried to peer sideways towards where Axel was tapping the barrel of his shotgun on the ground.

'You want him?' Axel asked Vince.

Vince shook his head. 'Wrong time of year.'

'Two hundred? That's a bargain. Good bargain. You stealing from me.'

'I'd never steal from you.'

Axel clucked his tongue. 'You funny, Vincent. Two hundred, yes? We shake on it?' He offered his hand, but Vince didn't take it.

'I have no use for him.' He prodded the man's slim shoulder.

'One hundred?'

Vince continued shaking his head. 'He's not worth it. I'll never get that back. He's not strong enough to build, he doesn't cook. I'd only use him as a cleaner and I've got plenty of those.'

They stared at one another, but this was a battle Axel wasn't going to win. 'Fine,' he snapped, whacking the side of his van with his fist. Without warning, he lunged forward, viciously backhanding the man and sending him sprawling to the floor. A spray of blood flew towards the centre of the room.

Before the man could move, Axel was on him, yanking him up by the neck, leading him towards the back of the van and throwing him inside. The doors slammed shut with an echoing bang and then Axel and Vince stared at one another.

'You coming inside?' Vince asked.

'I have ferry to catch.'

'You've got time, ain'tcha?'

Axel nodded slowly. 'You have food?'

'Aye, we've got plenty. Let's move your van, then come on in.'

Axel returned to the driver's seat and then pulled his van forward onto the yard. The red tail lights burned into the darkness and then the barn doors were slammed closed and locked in place.

Max was alone in the barn. He turned in a circle, humming softly under his breath and then went to a panel on the wall, near to the door. He pressed a button and then a fizz signalled darkness as the overhead lights blinked off. There was momentary light from the person-sized door next to where the van had exited and then Max was outside, too. His footsteps resonated into the distance and another door slammed. Then there was quiet.

Jessica felt Fran's fingers fumbling on her arm in the dark.

'What do we do now?' Fran asked.

'Now we make sure there's nobody in the barn – then we call the police.'

FORTY-ONE

Jessica went first, carefully levering herself into the barn while simultaneously trying not to snag her skin on the shards of glass that remained in the top part of the window frame. Fran followed but without the crowd and the vehicles, the space was full of squeaks and echoes.

'Should we put the lights on?' Fran asked.

'No. It'll have to be phones.'

With the vague glow of the moon, it wasn't completely dark as a murky grey light seeped through the skylights above, providing a series of spotlights around the floor.

'Did Bex say people were being kept here?' Fran asked, though she already knew.

'Somewhere.'

Jessica headed for the bales of straw, rounding them and finding herself facing even more. There was no space behind it, let alone room for people. She kept looking.

'There's no one here,' Fran said.

'Shhhhh...'

Jessica held up a hand and then lowered herself to the ground and pressed her ear against the ground. There were wooden planks lined diagonally across, but everything was covered with a crust of straw, dust and sand.

'Can you hear that?' Jessica whispered.

Fran dropped to her knees close to Jessica. 'Actually, I can.'

It was very low, almost completely lost to the sounds of the night, but there was a murmuring. Jessica had once lived in flats with her friend, Caroline, and their downstairs neighbour used to leave his television on overnight. It sounded exactly the same, a low mumble of voices as opposed to any specific words.

'There must be a hatch somewhere,' Jessica said.

Her phone was basic and had no flashlight, but the screen did have a backlight. It was feeble, but Jessica ran her hand along the grain of the wood, using the light in an attempt to find the hidden door. Fran separated away, using her better phone to do the same as they crawled along the width of the barn.

'Here,' Fran called eventually. She was sitting next to the tractor, not needing her phone as the natural spotlight created by the moon glimmered onto a spot on the floor next to the enormous back wheel. Unless a person was specifically looking for it, the hatch would have been hard to spot. It was made of wood and covered with the same gritty sand as the rest of the floor. Fran swished away a coating of dust to reveal a thick circular clamp that was bolted to the ground by a heavy padlock.

'We're never going to get through that,' she said.

'We bloody are.'

Jessica hurried to the window and leaned through, picking up the stone that had spent the best part of an hour digging into her side. It was a little bigger than her fist, with one sharp edge. She returned to the padlock and then rocked back, lunging forward and thrusting the stone against the metal, trying to do it quietly.

Nothing happened, other than that her finger joints clicked painfully.

'Shall I have a go?' Fran asked.

Jessica passed her the rock and then it was Fran's turn to fail. She smashed the stone against the join of the padlock four times in a row, each with more ferocity than the last, but it didn't give. She held her palms up to show a small cut. 'Your go?'

With a grunt of effort, Jessica smashed the rock against the arch of the padlock. Once, twice, three times. She paused, catching her breath and then hammered it once more. This time, mercifully, there was a satisfying clink of metal.

Jessica dropped the stone and pulled the shattered padlock apart, tossing it to the side. 'Thank God for that,' she whispered, showing Fran the slice across her fingers.

She looped her index and middle fingers through the hoop attached to the hatch and then pulled up. The door was far heavier than it first seemed, needing both Jessica and Fran to lift it. The reason was quickly apparent: it might have been wood on top, but there was a solid layer of metal underneath. Once they'd lifted it a certain amount, gravity took hold and the hatch flipped backwards, until it was fully open, locking into place with a clank.

The area below the barn was fully illuminated, the light blazing vertically up like a pillar to the top of the barn. A ladder stretched downwards and Jessica descended, pausing halfway down to peer over her shoulder, where there was a group of people huddling against the far wall. There were around fifteen of them, men and women, clinging close to one another, each eyeing Jessica with suspicion. The man at the front was the biggest, holding his arms wide, protecting the others as he peered past Jessica, no doubt expecting either Max or Vince to be on their way down.

Aside from the metal roof, the room seemed to be made of concrete – some sort of custom-created bunker, the type of which was usually found in Hurricane Alley, not in the north-west of England. It had been built deliberately, possibly for this purpose. There were no actual beds, though there was a line of air mattresses against one of the walls, along with threadbare blankets. A single light hung from the ceiling, but Jessica could see her breath. It was *really* cold, somehow cooler than it was in the barn.

As Jessica turned to take in the group properly, she put her finger to her lips. 'Does anyone speak English?' she whispered. Chances were at least one of them did – but nobody was risking it, not with the chance of Vince or Max following her down. 'I'm here to get you out,' Jessica added.

A woman's head poked around the side of the large man at the front, locking eyes with Jessica as they recognised one another immediately. It was the maid from the hotel, still wearing her uniform. Her eyes were wide with fear and bewil-derment.

Jessica breathed in and noticed the smell. There was a hose in the corner hanging over a grate, with a bucket at the side. She had to turn away because it was too horrendous to contemplate.

'Come on,' Jessica said, nodding towards the ladder, hoping at least one of them would follow and then the rest would take the hint.

'Hey!'

Jessica turned to see where the noise had come from. Built into the corner was a series of criss-cross metal bars that had been bolted to the wall to create a cage. Behind the bars were two people that Jessica recognised instantly. She walked across to them, eyes boggling.

'Henka?' she said. 'Jacek?'

The young couple stared back at her in confusion and then

looked to each other. 'You know us?' Henka said.

'It's complicated but... yes. Your parents and Maryla are still looking for you.' There was a noise from behind and Fran dropped down from above. She turned to take in the horror as the other group of captives backed away, still expecting one of their captors to arrive.

'Can you get us out?' Jacek asked.

Jessica looked at the large padlock clamped to the door. 'I don't know.'

There was another noise from behind and this time Jessica turned to see the larger man advancing on Fran. He wasn't being aggressive as such, but he was bigger than her and frightened.

Jacek shouted something at him in Polish and the man stopped where he was, turning to the far corner.

'Tell him to follow us upstairs,' Jessica said.

Jacek shouted something else and the man continued to stare at Fran, before dropping his arms.

'How did you end up here?' Jessica asked.

'We were at this hotel,' Henka said. She had a slight accent, but her English was perfect. 'We stayed overnight and then, in the morning, Celina was there.' She nodded across the room.

'The maid?'

'Right. We said something to her in Polish and she replied. Then the owner guy started shouting at her, telling her to go upstairs. Jacek started to say something, but the owner had this stun gun thing. The next thing we know, we're in this van – then we're here. He's using them as slaves.'

'That's why we're getting them out of here.'

'What about us?'

Jessica glanced at the padlock again. The rock might do it, but they didn't have time. 'We'll have to come back,' Jessica replied. 'Please trust me. I won't leave you.'

Henka reached out, taking Jacek's hand and squeezing. 'Just get them safe.'

Jacek called out something else in Polish and then the remaining prisoners started to move towards the stairs. Jessica stepped across to them, about to lead the way up when she noticed four small plastic boxes attached to the ceiling, next to the hatch. There were no wires, but they were aligned to face each other, each with a blinking red light.

'What's that?' Fran asked, pointing up.

Jessica was about to answer but there was no need as a man's voice sounded from above. '*That*,' he said, 'is a silent alarm.'

FORTY-TWO

Jessica shrank back as the tip of a shotgun poked through the hatch, followed by Max's face.

'I think you should come back up here,' he said, snarling with a mix of confusion and amusement.

Fran's eyes were wide with terror as she stared at Jessica, wondering what the plan was.

'*Now*,' came Max's command from above.

Jessica had no choice but to climb. She pulled herself up onto the floor of the barn, where she was met by the hulking figures of Vince, Max and Axel towering over her. The lights were on and each of them was carrying a shotgun, levelled directly at her. She held her hands up, fingers splayed wide as she shuffled towards the tractor's back wheel, giving space for Fran to haul herself out. When they were both clear, Max poked his head back through the hatch and glanced around before satisfying himself they'd done no damage to the room below. He slammed the lid with a thunderous clang and then advanced on Jessica, shotgun barrel pointed at her head.

'Where is she?!' he boomed.

Jessica knew she shouldn't but couldn't stop herself. 'Who?'

'Rebecca! You know who!' He raised his gun, ready to smash the butt into Jessica's skull, but thick fingers gripped his shoulder and pulled him back.

'Not yet, Max.' Vince nodded towards the cage that was built into the wall on the far side. Max took the hint and grabbed the scruff of Jessica's collar, hauling her partially to her feet and then dragging her across the barn. She tried to keep up, to stop her legs scraping on the ground, but he was moving too quickly. Her cheek thumped into the wall as he slung her inside, closely followed by Fran. The door was slammed closed and Vince clamped a padlock into place. He rattled the metal door back and forth to prove the point that they were trapped.

There was just enough space for Jessica and Fran to stand next to one another. Even if they'd wanted to, there was no room to sit. Jessica's back was pressed against the hard wall, cheek throbbing. There was no way out, nowhere to go.

Max levelled his gun again, focusing on Jessica. 'Where's Rebecca?'

'I don't know.'

'You're lying.'

'I'm not.'

Max stepped forward. He was so furious that the veins in his eyes were red, raw against the whites. 'I won't ask again,' he said. His arm was trembling, finger resting on the trigger. He was bare-armed and Jessica could see the spider's web tattoo that matched Bex's. There was writing on his hand, too: passwords or other information he couldn't remember otherwise. She stared back at him, trying to stand firm but worrying about Fran. She'd come here because Jessica had asked and now they were both trapped.

'Max!' Vince's tone was firm. 'Step away, Max.'

'No, Dad.'

Max wrenched his son's shoulder backwards and then shoved him sideways. 'I said *step away*.'

Father and son glared at one another, neither wanting to give way until, eventually, Max took a step backwards, lowering his weapon. Vince turned to face Jessica, moving closer to the vertical bars and stooping until he was almost eyeball to eyeball with Jessica. She could smell alcohol, see the small pocks of hair that he'd missed shaving.

'You *are* lying,' he said. 'You've seen her. Your face was everywhere this morning and I know she'd have seen it. She'd have come looking for you. I can see it in your face. I *know* you've seen her and I want to know where she is.'

Jessica held his gaze, speaking slowly and deliberately. 'I don't know.'

He nodded slowly. 'You know it's all over, don't you? You walked right into everything.'

'I've seen Peter. I know he isn't dead.'

'So?'

'So who was the body you dumped?'

Vince shrugged, confused. 'What does it matter? I dunno. One of them.' He thrust a thumb towards the hatch.

Jessica stared past him towards the tractor and the hidden basement. 'How can you do all of this?'

'All of what?'

'They're people you're keeping down there. Real, actual people. They have families. They deserve a life.'

Vince's forehead rippled with wrinkles. He stared at her as if she was speaking a different language. 'They owe me,' he said.

'How?'

'Who do you think paid for them to come over here? They could be living in some shitty little village in the middle of nowhere. I *paid* for them to be here and they owe me.'

'They're *people*.'

Axel sniggered and Jessica peered around Vince to see the hulk of a man smiling at her. He scratched his head with the shotgun. 'Just shoot her,' he said, accent a little thicker now he wasn't addressing a crowd. 'Quick.'

'I'll do it,' Max said, barging forward, only to be batted away by his father.

Vince thrust a thick finger towards him. 'You're on thin ice, boy. This is all because you wanted your little toy. *You're* the one that let her go.'

'I didn't *let* her go.'

'Same difference.'

Vince turned back to Jessica. 'Your little friend took something of mine and I want it back.'

'Tough.'

He raised an eyebrow. 'Really?'

'You're not getting what you want.'

Vince stepped away, one eye cocked, grin fixed. His teeth were crooked and yellowing, with a rickety filling obvious at the front. 'That yer final answer?'

'You might say I'm done for, and maybe I am, but as soon as that laptop finds its way into the hands of the police, you're toast as well.'

He nodded in apparent agreement. 'Hey, boy.'

Max stepped forward, peering between his father and Jessica. 'What?'

'Go open that hatch over there. She's going to tell me where my property is and, if she don't, yer gonna start shooting people one by one.'

FORTY-THREE

'No!' The shout had escaped before Jessica could stop it.

Vince grinned viciously through the bars at Jessica. 'Yer choice,' he said. 'Now, where's yer girl and where's my records?'

Jessica's mind was racing. She couldn't give up Bex and the laptop but neither could she allow those poor people enslaved under the barn to be hurt either. All she could do was stall. Try to delay and delay until...

The lights went off.

It wasn't simply a flicker. The barn went from being bathed in the artificial light from above, to cloaked with darkness. The moon was still throwing spotlights down through the ceiling, but the instant change was such a shock that even Axel growled.

'What is this?' he said. Jessica couldn't see him, couldn't see any of them, but the accent was clear.

There was a clang on the bars that made Jessica jump. She could feel Fran at her side, clinging to her arm for comfort, but Vince was somewhere ahead. She could smell him.

'What have you done?' he shouted.

Jessica backed against the wall as much as she could, but there was no real escape. She felt flecks of his spit landing on her. 'I'm in here,' she replied.

'Boy!' Vince shouted.

In the darkness there was a clatter and then Max gasping an 'oof' as he stumbled over something. 'Dad...?'

'What's going on?'

'I dunno.'

'It's that Salisbury. I *knew* he'd done a botch job on the electrics. Wait till I get my hands on him.'

Fran squeezed Jessica's hand. They knew the truth. It wasn't Greg Salisbury's dodgy wiring at all. If Ellie was smart enough to get the power working at the Shanty, then she was definitely clever enough to stop it at a rickety old farm. She'd left it a bit late, but late was *always* better than never.

From nowhere there was a bright white blazing light and a ferocious bang. Jessica clamped her eyes closed so tightly that it hurt. Fran was still holding her hand and they huddled near.

A second flashbang grenade went off, then a third. Jessica had witnessed police raids from the outside before but had never been in the middle of one. She'd heard the theory and seen the results to prove that the devices did a job, but now she could say with absolute certainty that flashbangs worked. Her ears were ringing, eyes burning. She couldn't see or hear anything.

By the time her senses started to work again, it was all over. Blue lights were spinning on the yard, spilling a ghostly glow through the door and windows. Vince, Max and Axel were all lying face-down on the floor, hands cuffed behind their backs, weapons off to the side. A tactical firearms team had stormed in, each of the members wearing night-vision goggles, weapons at the ready. One of them said something and then they hauled the trio to their feet.

There was a ping – and then the overhead lights burned

bright again. Everyone seemed surprised, especially those in night-vision goggles. Max, Vince and Axel could do little given they were cuffed, but there was a moment of confusion until the firearms team regained their senses and led the trio towards the exit and the awaiting police cars.

Jessica was still struggling to regain her own senses. There was a pink-green glow around the edges of her eyes and a low buzzing in her ears. To complete a trio, her nose was running, too.

'That was a bit tight,' Fran whispered.

'I've been in tighter.'

'Really?'

'I'll tell you one day.'

The barn was empty and, for a moment, Jessica thought she was going to have to shout to have somebody come and get them. Unsurprisingly, it was DCI Fordham who rode to the rescue, swishing his way through the doors, hands in pockets, coat-tails flapping behind him. He strode across the floor, heading directly for the cage in which Jessica and Fran were trapped. He stopped just short of the door.

'I've been looking for you,' he said to Jessica.

She nodded past him, towards the tractor. 'Can we do this in a bit? There are people down there.'

He plucked the radio from his lapel and uttered a quick set of instructions. Moments later, officers poured in. They wrenched the hatch open and then a couple descended into the gap, ready to start bringing the captives to safety.

'Happy?' Fordham asked, turning back to Jessica.

'I've been happier.'

He nodded towards the bars. 'You enjoy being behind them?'

'Not really.'

'What happened to you? You *knew* we were looking for you.'

'Were you? That's the first I've heard of it.'

His features didn't crack. 'Where have you been for the past two days?'

'I found a comfier hotel room and had a really long sleep.'

Fordham rolled his eyes, realising the answer he wanted wasn't coming anytime soon. He held up his thumb and index finger, barely a centimetre apart. 'You were *this* close.'

'To what?'

'To being buried. We had the press release ready for tomorrow and then a young woman named Rebecca walked into the station with a very interesting story to tell. Given everything that's happening here, wasn't that impeccable timing?'

'You were a little late, actually. There was an auction. People left, they—'

'We got them.'

'Oh.' Jessica hadn't expected that.

'Roadblock on the way out of here. Only one route into this place, one route out. It's going to be a busy few days processing everyone.'

'Right.'

He pointed up at the ceiling. 'One of the things I don't get – one of the *many* things – is what happened to the lights.'

Jessica deadpanned him. She could explain that he was Plan A and that Ellie with the lights was Plan B. She could even have told him about the incredible Plan C she'd come up with that would never come to fruition. Plan D was an absolute belter. None of that really mattered.

'I have no idea,' she said.

Fordham rolled his eyes again. 'You and me really need to have a chat.'

Jessica rattled the bars. 'Reckon you can get us out of here first?'

FORTY-FOUR

Two days later, Jessica was back in Blackpool, sitting on a bench a little off the promenade. The weather had taken a turn for the even colder, but at least she had her own jeans, jacket and boots to try to keep it out. The sea was blasting into the sea wall below, each crash a clap of thunder. Off to her side, a pair of seagulls were battling it out over a discarded kebab, squawking noisily at one another. Jessica reasoned that they were probably trying to palm off the grim lettuce-like stuff. Nobody liked that.

'Don't say I never buy you anything.'

DCI Fordham dropped onto the bench next to Jessica and handed her a grease-soaked white paper parcel.

'What is it?' Jessica asked.

'Fish and chips. What do you think?'

'Salt and vinegar?'

'Obviously – I'm not a maniac.'

'Gravy?'

'On a bench without cutlery?'

'Fair enough.' Jessica unpacked the paper and breathed in

the wonderfully bitter vinegar. She preferred Manchester as a place, but, bloody hell, they did good chips in Blackpool.

Fordham unwrapped his own and started to pick at the chips with his fingers. 'You've left me a hell of a lot of work to do,' he said.

'Good. The next time they're making redundancies, you can point out how busy you are. What have you got?'

'It's hard to know where to start. Murder and false imprisonment, probably. Then there's people-trafficking, possession of weapons, assault, sexual assault, money-laundering, slavery. I've never seen one person charged with so many things. Even the CPS won't be able to make a mess of this.'

'I wouldn't bet on that.'

'No, well... we'll see. I don't think either of the Waverlys are going to feel the sun on their arms for a long time.'

Jessica frowned down at Fordham's chips. 'What are you doing?'

'What?'

'Eating them one by one. You're supposed to squish them all together for maximum potatoage.'

'*That*,' he replied, 'is not even a word – and I can eat my chips however I want.'

Jessica smushed three chips together until the potato bulged, and then bit the fluffy mass in half. 'You're doing it wrong,' she said. 'One day you'll realise how much of your chip-eating life has been a waste.'

Fordham deliberately picked up a single chip, dangling it in front of her, and then ate it whole.

'I saw that the Prince Hotel was closed for business,' Jessica said.

'That was yesterday's job. We had so many places to raid that we had to bring officers in from the surrounding area. Cafés, hotels, building sites – all using people provided by

Vince. Good job he keeps records. It's no wonder the kids round here can't find work.'

'What about Henka and Jacek?'

'Reunited with their families. I wish I'd been there but...' He held a hand up in the air and yawned.

'Too lazy?' Jessica asked.

He guffawed. 'Yeah, *that*. Anyway, we've picked up *Peter* Salisbury, but we're yet to find his dad. Vince Waverly was a surprising interview. He knows we've got him nailed for all sorts and he's not the honourable type – he decided he was taking everyone down with him. We've got chapter and verse on pretty much everyone associated with this whole thing.'

'I wouldn't have expected that.'

'Me neither. He told his own solicitor to shut up twice.'

'I'd have loved to have seen that.'

Jessica set to work on her slab of fish, starting by picking off the batter and eating that by itself.

'That's how you eat fish, is it?' Fordham asked.

'Everyone knows you start with the batter first. I don't know why they bother with the fish – just sell battered batter.'

'Heart disease?'

'Nah – you've been brainwashed. What else is going on?'

Perhaps absent-mindedly, Fordham started to pick the batter from his fish. 'We've got about a dozen translators in at the moment. We've got all those people from underneath the barn staying in hotels and we retrieved their passports. We're trying to take statements, but they've been through a lot and it's fair to say they don't really trust us. For many of them, this is what Britain's like. Can't blame 'em, really. Hopefully we'll get their stories and then I guess many of them will want to go home. I don't know, really.'

'What about Sophie Johns?'

'I don't know. We've been questioning Peter Salisbury, but he's not saying much. There's so much to do, it'll all take time.

This is one of the biggest operations in our history. It was all happening under our noses and we missed it.'

'A lot of people missed it.'

'True, but... oh, I don't know.' He sighed and then ate a chip, speaking with his mouth full: 'At least we got him... *them.*'

Jessica had almost picked off all the batter, so she started on the fish. It was slimy from grease but delicious. She'd saved a few chips, too. A textbook job of eating fish and chips.

'If I ask you something, can you promise not to take it the wrong way?' she asked.

'Go on then.'

'I'm really not a complete egomaniac.'

'People who start sentences with that usually go on to say something that proves they *are* an egomaniac.'

Jessica smiled. 'Well, yes, I know. There's loads going on, obviously, but... what about me?'

She felt embarrassed for asking. She was far from the most important person in all this, but she still had to know.

'How do you mean?' Fordham asked.

'I've not heard anything officially. Am I free to go? Free to work? Everyone's acting like it's all sorted. I spoke to my mum on the phone and she was asking if I'm in trouble.'

'Was that her first question?'

'She did ask if I was all right.'

'I spoke to your super,' Fordham said. 'Some bloke named Jenkinson. I told him you were instrumental in the arrest of the Waverlys and in freeing those captives. That's all I know. Unless anyone's told you differently, nothing's changed. You were never anything other than a person we wanted to help us with our inquiries.'

'Ugh.'

'What?'

'I hate that phrase. It doesn't mean anything.'

'Quite – but the press office like it, so there we go.'

Jessica picked up a thicker piece of fish and tossed it sideways. The seagulls looked at her, looked at the fish, and then pounced on it.

'That's thirty quid,' Fordham said.

'What?'

'Littering.'

'I was feeding the seagulls.'

'There's probably some by-law about that, too.' He chuckled to himself and then screwed up his nearly empty packet, before launching it at the bin. It rolled around the rim and then dropped in.

'Why did you do it?' Jessica asked.

'Do what?'

She screwed up her own paper, suddenly not hungry. This was what it all came down to. 'You know.'

'Why didn't we tell everyone you were a suspect? Why didn't we just arrest you and keep you in? You *know* why. You're one of us, Inspector. Like you said, things didn't add up.'

'It's not right, though, is it? If I was anyone else, I'd have been in a cell. The Waverlys would still be operating. They only did all of that to try to draw Bex in – and they nearly succeeded.'

'Worked out, didn't it?'

'Is that the point? I've seen special treatment in Manchester. I've seen how it ends.'

Fordham stood and flicked his coat-tails backwards. He loosened his tie and then put his hand in his pockets. He was smiling at her, but more with bemusement than anything else. 'What would you prefer?'

Jessica thought of Chief Constable Graham Pomeroy and what he'd done to her, how he'd got away with it because of his position. How he'd done favours for his friends, knowing he was too powerful to be taken down. Was this the same?

She wiped her fingers on the paper and then crossed to the bin and put it inside. 'I've got to go.'

'Somewhere to be?'

'Something like that.'

Fordham held out his hand and Jessica shook it. 'I'm sure I'll see you again,' he said.

'You can only hope.'

He winked at her and then turned to swagger off along the promenade.

FORTY-FIVE

Jessica bounced up and down on the beanbag in the living room of the Shanty. 'I could get used to one of these,' she said.

Bex was sitting across from her on the hard floor, legs crossed. 'You definitely couldn't,' she replied. 'You like your sofa too much.'

'That is true.'

Alison, Ellie and Fran were sitting with them, each with a mug of tea. In a list of everything that made the Shanty work, tea was probably at the top.

'I've not told anyone about this place,' Jessica assured them, motioning towards Fran. 'I told them you were a friend and that's why you were at the farm.'

Fran nodded. 'I said the same – no lies there. Thank you.'

'I should really be thanking you. I'm not entirely sure how this would have played out without your help.'

'We look after our own.'

It was almost exactly what DCI Fordham had said to her, but Jessica somehow felt less sinister hearing it from Fran. She really didn't know how to feel about it all. Did the end justify the means?

Fran must have sensed the moment of insecurity because she stood, tapping Ellie on the shoulder and signalling for them to give Jessica and Bex some privacy. The other women said their goodbyes and then disappeared off into the rest of the house.

Bex shuffled across until she was on the beanbag next to Jessica and then rested her head on her shoulder.

'I'm sorry I couldn't protect you,' Jessica said, battling the lump in her throat.

'I'm a grown-up.'

'You were still living with me.'

'How could either of us have predicted this?'

'You should be proud of yourself,' Jessica said. 'Some very bad people are going to prison, and some others, who are entirely innocent, have got their lives back. You did this.'

Bex lifted her head from Jessica's shoulder and leaned against the wall, eyes closed. 'Max,' she whispered.

Jessica gripped her hand but Bex pulled away, folding her arms across herself. Jessica didn't want to ask precisely what he'd done to her. She could guess and perhaps Bex would tell her when she was ready.

'I know some people you can talk to,' Jessica said, but Bex shook her head.

Jessica still had no idea how Max knew where to find Bex. Perhaps the police would get it out of him, but, for now, it was a mystery. There was a chance he'd seen her walking around and followed her – Bex was distinctive – but Manchester was a big city.

Bex had registered for things like college in her own name with Jessica's address, but it seemed unlikely Max would have been able to view those records. But, if not those methods, then how? Bex's mother had recently come back into her life and there was a definite annoyance that Bex had chosen to stay with Jessica over her. Could she have a role? She had done horrific things to her daughter in the past but this would be taking it to another level. If Max wouldn't tell the police, then it might remain a mystery.

Jessica nodded towards the door. 'My car's a couple of streets over if you're ready to come home...?'

Bex straightened herself, unable to look at Jessica. Her body language gave the answer. 'I was thinking about staying for a little while.'

'Oh, right...'

'I don't mean—'

'It's okay, I get it.'

'It's just... I'm not sure where I call home any longer.' She nodded towards the doorway, where Fran was standing, waggling an empty mug of tea towards them and asking the silent question. 'I think it might be here,' Bex added.

Jessica gulped back her disappointment. 'I understand,' she replied, knowing that, deep down, no matter how hard she tried, she really didn't.

A LETTER FROM KERRY

Since fairly early on with writing the Jessica books, I've thought of her stories in terms of arcs. Life doesn't tie everything up into neat bows and it feels a bit weird to me if a book tidies up every loose end, leaving no questions for the reader. Sure, it might be satisfying, but it's false, too. A fairy tale. The real world isn't like that.

Littered throughout the Jessica books are ongoing stories around the individual cases. Some relate to her work; others to her personal life. The first seven books – 'season one' – told an arc of her growing up and ultimately being promoted. Books eight to thirteen are 'season two' ... and so it's here that many of Jessica's side stories are tied up.

I've been wanting to get Jessica out of Manchester for a little while. Blackpool has fascinated me since the time I first visited. It could, perhaps *should*, be a central pillar of Britain's tourist industry. A place used by the country to sell itself worldwide.

And yet... it isn't. When Jessica thinks of there being two Blackpools – the shiny, touristy front, and the neglected, gritty behind – that's me creeping into the book. As a city, it's an incredible sandbox in which to tell some stories. I hope I've done it a bit of justice here. Blackpool is in one of my other books, *Ten Birthdays*, and I'm probably a bit kinder to it there. If you've never visited, you definitely should. It's pure Britain... at least it is for me.

Either way, this is the end of Jessica's second 'season' –

which means it all begins again with book fourteen. It'll be coming soon.

Cheers for reading.

 facebook.com/KerryWilkinsonBooks

twitter.com/kerrywk

THE GIRL WHO CAME BACK

Thirteen years ago Olivia Adams went missing. Now she's back... or is she?

When six-year-old **Olivia Adams** disappeared from her back garden, the small community of Stoneridge was thrown into turmoil. How could a child vanish in the middle of a cosy English village?

Thirteen years on and Olivia is back. Her mother is convinced it's her but not everyone is sure. If this is the missing girl, then where has she been - and what happened to her on that sunny afternoon?

If she's an imposter, then who would be bold enough to try to fool a child's own mother – and why?

Then there are those who would rather Olivia stayed missing. The past is the past and some secrets *must* remain buried.

THE WIFE'S SECRET

Charley Willis was thirteen years old when her parents were killed in their family home and she was found hiding in a cupboard upstairs.

Fifteen years later, Charley is marrying Seth Chambers. It should be the happiest day of their lives, a chance for Charley to put her past behind her, but just hours after the ceremony, she is missing.

No one saw her leave. No one knows where she is.

One thing is for certain… Seth is about to discover he doesn't really know the woman he just married. And his nightmare is only just beginning.

LAST NIGHT

It's the early hours of the morning and Rose Denton wakes up behind the steering wheel of her car. She's off the road, through a hedge and in a field.

There's blood on the windscreen and bonnet – but it's not hers and there's no sign of anything or anyone she might have hit. The last thing she remembers is being in a hotel on a business trip but now she's miles away.

Back home and her daughter's boyfriend is missing. The last thing he did was argue with Rose over money. He left no note, no text, no clue as to his whereabouts.

The police have questions – and so does Rose's family. But those are little compared to the ones she has for herself.

What happened last night? And, perhaps more importantly, does she really want to know the answer?

TWO SISTERS

They told us he had been missing for nearly two days, that he probably drowned. They told us a lie.

Megan was ten years old when her older brother, **Zac**, went missing among the cliffs, caves and beaches that surround the small seaside town of Whitecliff.

A decade on and a car crash has claimed her parents' lives.

Megan and her younger sister **Chloe** return to Whitecliff one summer for the first time since their brother's disappearance. Megan says it's to get her parents' affairs in order. There are boxes to pack, junk to clear, a rundown cottage to sell. **But that's not the real reason**.

Megan received a postcard on the day of her parents' funeral. It had a photograph of Whitecliff on the front and a single letter on the back.

'Z' is all it read. Z for Zac.

THE DEATH AND LIFE OF ELEANOR PARKER

'I will never forget the night I drowned...'

Seventeen-year-old Eleanor Parker wakes up cold and alone in the river that twists through her quiet village. She remembers a hand on her chest, another on her head, water in her throat, those final gasps for air...

Her brother's girlfriend was drowned in the same river the summer before, held under the water by an unknown killer.

Determined to unlock the mystery of what really happened that night, Eleanor can't escape the feeling that something terrible links her to the previous summer's murder. But will she discover the shocking truth, before it's too late?

TEN BIRTHDAYS

There are going to be so many things I wish I could've told you in person, Poppy. I won't get the chance to do that, so perhaps this is my only way...

It's Poppy Kinsey's birthday.

She should be blowing out candles and opening presents – but hers falls on the type of heart-wrenching, agonising anniversary she would far rather forget.

The worst day of them all. The day her mother died.

But this year is special because the person she misses most in the world has left her a set of letters, one for each of her next ten birthdays.

As Poppy opens them year by year, she discovers that no matter how tough life gets, her mum will always be by her side, guiding her along the way.

Printed in Poland
by Amazon Fulfillment
Poland Sp. z o.o., Wrocław